BLEST BE THE TIES: A TRILOGY

◆◆◆

Book One

A TIME TO BE BORN,
and A TIME TO DIE

L.M. Hopson

A Time to Be Born, and A Time to Die
Copyright © 2020 L.M. Hopson

All scriptures from the
King James Version of the Bible.

Cover photo in public domain.

All rights reserved. Except for brief excerpts for review purposes, no part of this book may be reproduced or used in any form without written permission from the author.

ISBN: 9798692785589

For more about the *Blest Be the Ties* series,
go to the author's website:

theweightofstories.com
The Weight of Stories

ACKNOWLEDGMENTS

I am humbly grateful for the indulgent help and loving support of Beth and Graham Richardson, George Hopson, Ralph Davis, Carl Robbins, and other friends and family willing to provide needed feedback throughout the writing process. I also am gratefully indebted to Paul and Linda Linzey of *P&L Publishing & Literary Services* for their invaluable expertise and guidance in getting the story "out there."

Most of all, I acknowledge my total dependence on the Source of all good and perfect gifts. If there is anything in this work worthy of praise, let it be to His honor and glory. Amen.

PROLOGUE

NOVEMBER 1848
THE PRESBYTERIAN CHURCH MANSE
STAUNTON, VIRGINIA

Huddled on the cold floor outside her parents' bedroom, four-year-old Abby Graham gripped the hand of her older brother Geordie sitting beside her. After the commotion had awakened the five children in the night, they were the ones who remained in sedentary vigilance, wrapped together in the boy's bed quilt. The other three boys had wandered through the upstairs landing in restless forays of silent apprehension.

Occasionally, Annabel had scurried in and out, leaving them each time with only a few words of comfort and, unheeded, entreaties to return to their beds. The sun had risen by the time the cries and moans coming from behind the closed door had finally been silenced along with the sounds of the doctor's authoritative directives and their father's fervent prayers. Leaning her ear against the door, Abby now heard the sounds of approaching footsteps. Ignoring the doctor in the rear when the door opened and blocking the exit with her small frame, Abby demanded answers from the family's Negro housekeeper.

"Is mama better now? May I see our new baby?"

"Ya mama's gone dead, sweet baby, 'long with ya lil' baby brotha," Annabel responded, grief-stricken as she met the anxious faces of the two children.

Gone dead?

"No, baby girl… *don' go in theah yit!*" Annabel's admonition came too late.

Pushing past the two adults standing in her way, Abby rushed to the bed and climbed to the side of the silent, still figure in the place where her beautiful mother had lain the evening before when the family gathered to say their prayers and kiss her goodnight. Mama had told her to "*sleep in heavenly peace,*" and by morning she would have a new baby brother or sister.

Beside this strangely unfamiliar similitude of her mother, Abby saw a tiny, blanketed bundle with a pale blue face. There was blood on the bed linens and lower gown of the larger form, and the faintly metallic, nasty odor permeating the stuffy room prompted the scrunching of the child's delicate features into a sickened scowl.

At the foot of the bed, a red mass with what looked like a string of raw sausage filled the porcelain basin. The whole scene filled her senses with alarming shock and foreboding disaster.

"Papa," Abby whispered with a note of panic in her voice, "where are Mama and our baby?"

Jumping down and swiping the unruly locks of hair out of her face, she laid a small firm hand on her father's knee as he sat in the low nursing rocker beside the bed. His weeping countenance was almost as distressing as the disturbing, inert figures on the bed, and her apprehension grew when his only response was a slow shake of his head.

By this time, her four older brothers had silently crept into the room along with Annabel, who had swiftly directed the doctor to the front door and now threw a blanket over the evidences of birth culminating in death. The only visible trace of the disrupted cycle of life left exposed was the ashen face on the pillow.

Still shaking his head in a gesture of weary despair, her father Paul's blurred glance swept over the five young faces and he tried again to speak.

- "We… we have lost them, dear."

He choked on the words and, swallowing hard, opened his arms to the children. '*The Lord giveth and He taketh away…Blessed be the name of the Lord.*'"

His declaration faded into irrepressible sobbing and the four younger ones accepted the circle of his embrace, Ben and Geordie seeking to offer comfort as well as receive from him. Annabel stood back, weeping convulsively into the corner of her apron.

Fifteen-year-old Harry stood apart, his eyes never leaving his mother's waxen face. *It is true then*, he thought mournfully. *The God of the universe has chosen to exercise His prerogative of uncharitable providence and my mother, the only one I have ever loved, is dead.* "Blessed be the Name of the Lord," he repeated the words of Job to himself in bitter silence.

Turning his gaze on his father, weeping with his younger siblings, Harry felt detached disdain for them all. Evidently, his father's devout petitions for a safe delivery last night at their mother's bedside had fallen on deaf ears.

Harry had always struggled with believing that this Sovereign Potentate would bend His will to the prayers of those called *His people*, but with the sudden, senseless death of his mother, he now knew and must accept the truth. What God has ordained will be, and there were fixed and explicit limitations in petitioning the Omnipotent One.

Corporate recitations from *The Book of Common Prayer* in formal worship services, as well as the repetition of the *Lord's Prayer*, he could agree were *acceptable*, but certainly not those concerning private, personal matters. As a scholar and minister, his father should have known this and never have encouraged him, or anyone, to indulge, much less to believe in, such an ineffectual charade.

With a final look at his mother's inanimate features, Harry sighed and left them, again taking refuge in his father's study below where he picked up his place in the works of Calvin's *Institutes*.

"Did mama get *lost* when she went out to get our baby?" Abby asked Geordie as they watched the undertaker and his son carry a shrouded form on a litter down the stairs toward the front door. "Can we go out and find her now?"

Eight-year-old Geordie, who had reclaimed his sister's hand since Annabel shepherded them from their father's room an hour earlier, gave his older brother Ben a pleading look, prompting him to address her misperceptions.

"Mama and the baby are in heaven now, Abby. She is not *lost* like someone might be here on earth. Her body will be buried in the cemetery with our baby brother, but their *souls* are now with Jesus in heaven," Ben quietly explained.

"WHY?" Abby demanded, eyes wide with bewildered rage. "*I want my mama! Jesus cannot have her!* He can keep the baby if He wants it, but *I WANT MY MAMA!*"

Ben's efforts to pick up and soothe her were met with fierce resistance until their father, having composed himself, came downstairs and took Abby from him. She was small and light for a child her age, but could fight like a wildcat, the color of her golden-brown eyes enhancing this imagery.

The girl was still plainly agitated but, with her arms wound tightly around his neck, had begun to settle. She trusted her papa to handle all matters between heaven and earth equitably.

"Where is Davy?" Paul asked, looking around for his youngest son.

The boys gave each other a quick glance before Ben answered. "If he is not upstairs, I do not know where he is. I suppose he went outside."

"Do not worry, Papa," Geordie assured him. "We will find him and bring him back home."

Giving Abby a gentle pat on her back before going to the pegs lining the rear entry wall, Paul's middle child pulled on his coat and boots over his winter nightshirt and stockings and followed Ben outside. The two had recently tended the neglected fire in the parlor hearth, which was only just beginning to provide adequate heat to the room, and his father ruefully noted Geordie's shivers.

How was he to take care of them without her? Paul heaved a deep sigh and, opening the door to his study, found Harry who, ignoring his protests, got up immediately to leave.

"It is all right. I will go to my room," Harry mumbled without meeting his father's eyes, and made a hasty retreat. The boy's unambiguous rejection of his company compounded the weight in Paul's heart until he found himself struggling to draw breath.

The fire in the study was blazing nicely, and settling in his worn chair beside it with a weary sigh, Paul gently unwound Abby's arms from his neck and created enough distance between them to regard her troubled countenance. *What could he say when he could not bear it... could not accept it himself?*

Even now the little girl was a reflection of her beautiful mother Rosemary with her tousled mahogany brown curls, though Abby's hair was considerably shorter since Davy cut off her braids several months earlier. Abby hadn't resisted, but his mother's tears after the deed was done had devastated the budding barber. Paul's heart seized with grief as he tucked a stray curl behind her ear.

Abby's large eyes were also the same unusual color and animated quality as Rosemary's, changing in a lightening flash from bold intensity to mischievous delight. The paradoxical combination of hopefulness and escalating despair he saw now brought a large lump to his throat.

"Did you know that in the Hebrew language your name means 'father rejoices'?" he began softly and she gave a sad shrug. "Your mama called you *'Apple Abby'* not only because your cheeks were plump and rosy when you were a baby, but because you are the 'apple of your papa's eye.' Mama loved you so very much, my sweet Apple Abby, just as I do and always will. We will miss her so very much."

His voice broke, and at sight of his welling tears, her fear and indignation mounted.

"I do not *want* mama to be dead, Papa. I *hate* dead things. That lady in mama's bed *scared* me, and I could tell it was not really mama with that baby doll. She did not smell nice and clean like mama does. She smelled *awful!* Tell Jesus to *give me my real mama back!* Tell Him *right now!*"

"Though I yearn to have mama back with us, more than *anything*, I cannot. I watched her suffer terrible agonies through the night, Abby." He clasped her to his chest, tears dropping on her head. "We can only take comfort in knowing she will never suffer again."

Pushing away as his last words faded, Abby continued her protestation. "*Why*, Papa. Why did she have to be *dead? Mamas are not supposed to be dead! I want her back NOW!"*

She began to wail, and Paul suddenly felt her outrage as strongly as his pain. He was dangerously close to giving in to his own anguished, raised-fist protest to the devastating loss when Geordie rushed in with a blast of wintry wind, out of breath, his cheeks red with cold, and his eyes wide with worry.

"We found him, Papa, and cleaned it up as best we could."

Before Paul could inquire what cleanup measures were necessary, the front door slammed, and Ben dragged his six-year-old brother into the study. Davy's face was streaked with dirty tears, and his father's heart broke at the sight of him.

Laying aside his own grief and grievances, Paul focused his attention on the child who'd always engendered his greatest concerns and, though he was loving and loyal, required the most frequent administration of correction and discipline. David Alexander had emerged from the womb with indignant remonstrations and the audacity of a stray terrier. Rosemary had referred to him as her "thundercloud stuffed with sweetness."

"Are you going to tell Papa, or shall I?" Ben prompted quietly.

With his responsibility fulfilled and turned over to his father, Ben felt sympathy for the bereaved miscreant and put an arm around Davy's shoulders for support. However, when no admission came forth, he took a deep breath and rendered the report.

"He was throwing rocks at the church, Papa, and he broke one of the back windows," he finished softly, glancing down at the scowling face at his elbow.

"We stopped him before he broke more, Papa. He said he was mad at God for taking mama to heaven," Geordie offered in his younger brother's defense. "Please do not punish him. I know he is sorry now, aren't you, Davy?"

"No . . . I am not sorry about that. I could not find any more rocks big enough or I would have broken more," Davy confessed with waning defiance, wiping his tears and runny nose on the sleeve of his woolen jacket. "I am only sorry *mama is dead* and there is nothing I can do about it. I do not care about that baby though. *God* let that baby kill mama, *didn't* He, Papa?"

Paul looked into the eyes of his precious children and saw a reflection of his own sorrow and bewilderment, though theirs were mingled with a rising apprehension that he might leave them too, either by an act of God or his own selfish guilt and despair. He was well aware that nothing but divine grace, roused by pity, could keep him from sinking to that degree of despondency, and he stretched out his hand in invitation to the one needing that same merciful grace.

"Come here, Davy boy, and sit with your papa. There is room in my lap for you and always will be."

Abby obligingly shuffled to one side of Paul's lap, and after only a brief moment of hesitation, Davy climbed onto the other side. Burying his face in his father's woolen vest, he began to sob, drawing fresh tears from the rest as Ben and Geordie, needing to be close, came to lean on the sides of the chair.

Overwhelmed with tenderness for his children and his own throbbing pain, Paul lifted up a desperate prayer for them all:

"Our most merciful Father in heaven, we come to thee because, like thy servant Peter, we are asking 'Lord, to whom shall be go?' Thou hast the words of eternal life, our only source of hope. We confess our doubts, our broken hearts, but Thou promised us through your servant Isaiah that 'Thou wilt feed Thy flock like a shepherd, gather the lambs in Thy arms and carry them in Thy bosom, and shall gently lead those that are with young.' And so, in faith in Thy word, we commit our ways, our souls, and our broken hearts to Thee, our Father and our Shepherd. Amen."

CHAPTER 1

APRIL 1857

Abby had not yet reached her thirteenth birthday when her father Paul accepted the call from the Presbyterian Church in Winchester and, as she watched the budding landscape from the window of the stagecoach carrying them northward, hastily wiped the tears from her eyes. Although relieved her family was the only occupants in the cold, swaying coach, she still would not allow Papa or the boys to see her cry.

Crying was a sign of feminine weakness to which depths of humiliation she was loathed to resort in all but drastic circumstances and extreme outrage. The current situation didn't justifiably fit either category though she believed she could reasonably argue the case. Nevertheless, she felt compelled to prove once more that she was as stalwart as her brothers.

Her father's eyes were closed, and she knew he was praying. His Bible lay across his lap and his lips moved silently. He would speak to the Almighty Father about her needs, though she wondered if he was even aware of the things burdening her heart.

Her family was being uprooted and scattered to the wind and she did not approve. Abby preferred order and stability, and disruptive changes, experience had taught her, rarely improved anything, particularly those actions now in inexorable motion and even those that were beginning to occur in her own body.

The residual members of the family core were sitting together in the jostling coach although, in less than four months, Geordie and Davy would be cadets at the Virginia Military Institute in Lexington. She loved all her brothers, but Geordie was her favorite and his absence would be by far the hardest to bear.

Glancing at that best-loved sibling directly across from her, she found him watching her. Geordie also had the same coloring as their mother – porcelain skin, dark hair and eyes, while the three other boys had inherited their father's ruddier complexion, light brown hair threaded with reddish highlights, and blue-gray eyes. Abby considered all her male family members handsome, though Geordie was now as tall as their father and seemed to his sister to be as handsome as any storybook prince.

"Home will never be the same without you, Geordie," she sighed, leaning forward so he could hear her speak, the wide rim of her blue velvet spoon bonnet hiding her distress from the rest of the family.

"*My* home will always be where *you* are, Abby, no matter where that is," he assured her with a tender smile and reached for her mittened hand. "But, I confess I *am* looking forward to the military institute. I wish Papa had permitted me to go last year. Both Harry and Ben were allowed to go to college when they were sixteen."

"I know you were disappointed, but I was not. And it will be even harder to lose you now that we had to leave our home in Staunton. Winchester is *much* further from Lexington than Staunton is," she groaned. "And I feel like we are leaving mama too."

"I expect Winchester will be a great adventure for us though. Aren't you eager to find out what the Lord has in store for us there?"

Abby sighed and glanced up at her father beside her.

"I must admit a lamentable lack of enthusiasm," she answered with a hint of acerbity. "But I am glad you will be with us for the summer. According to Papa, the Lord has *preordained it all* and we dare not question it."

Without opening his eyes, Paul laid his hand over hers and gently replied.

"No, we never question what the omniscient Lord has preordained, Abby, but that does not mean I never question my own wisdom. I can only say I believe he has work for us in Winchester. We prayed together that, if it was *not* His will for us to go, He would show us by clear hindrances, and He has not. Now we are required to step out in faith."

"Yes, Papa, but surely I can be granted allowance for a little sadness in leaving our home and everyone I know." She hated the sound of petulance in her voice and hoped he didn't notice.

"Oh yes, my dear," Paul nodded, opening his eyes to look into hers. "Sadness will always be a troubling companion as long as we are pilgrims here in this life. The Lord remits our sins, but not our sorrows. Only in heaven will there be no more of either. While we are on our pilgrimage, He faithfully balances the sorrows with *blessings*. But we must look expectantly to recognize them, and it is in discovering these abundant and merciful blessings, we can at all times *rejoice*."

"I know I will be rejoicing when it is time to go to Lexington," piped in Davy. "But right now I am *hungry* and will gladly start rejoicing if there is something to eat!"

"Well, lemme heah ya *rejoicin'* Davy boy, 'cause ol' Annabel gotcha somethin' good rat heah," Annabel chuckled as she pulled a basket from under the seat. "Ya don' think I'd be sloughin' off jus' 'cause I ain't in the *kitchen*, did ya?"

Paul gave Annabel a grateful smile as he watched her cheerfully distribute sandwiches and apples to the children, again wondering what he would have done without her in the years since Rosemary passed. Annabel, who somehow seemed ageless and continued to provide warmth and comfort as well as to effortlessly meet their domestic needs, was a precious gift to them all. She had become his "property" with his marriage to Rosemary but, for his own conscience sake, was legally freed soon after. Although her role was that of a housekeeper, she was an integral member of the family and had been since the beginning.

Any reminder of his wife was enough to take Paul's breath away momentarily although the abiding work of the Spirit had eased the guilt of his role in her death. Even after the births of five children and several miscarriages, Rosemary continued to welcome him in their bed and his need for her hadn't diminished. He would have savored their physical intimacy until his last breath. After eight years, it was still inconceivable to him that he might ever love or even desire another.

Paul never ceased wondering at the benevolent providence that made Rosemary Spencer his own. Years before, after the completion of his seminary studies, he'd been accepted as a theological student under the tutelage of Rector Charles H. Grayson at Christ Episcopal Church in Charlottesville where the Jeffersons of Monticello and the Spencer family worshiped. Her family boasted their forbearers were some of the first English aristocratic settlers west of Williamsburg, and their land grant included the eight-hundred-acre plantation, Camden Hall, where Rosemary was born.

With their older daughter Garnet already established in a suitable marriage to Frank Phillips, one of Martha Jefferson's great-great nephews, John and Astoria Spencer were not pleased when their younger daughter Rosemary acquired an interest in the handsome young man with no pedigree to commend him. They could acknowledge his earnest piety and pastoral qualities, but Rosemary was their pride and joy, deserving a man who would someday reside in the governor's mansion, or even the White House. *Who was Paul Graham but the son of a Presbyterian minister of no renown whatsoever?*

The elder Spencers might have been mollified if the bright seminarian had stayed on, had given up his Presbyterian proclivities and taken his ordination vows in the Episcopal Church. Rector Grayson was nearing retirement, and, with the Spencer influence and the rector's endorsement, Graham could have owned that prestigious position. But the blood of John Knox and the martyred Scottish Covenanter's flowed through Paul Graham's veins, and, though he valued his tenure at Christ Episcopal Church, he valued the plain black robe, the unembellished administration of the sacraments, and simple preaching of the word infinitely more.

When Rosemary's purposeful attentions dawned on the smitten, socially reticent theological student, he was distrustful of his own perceptions. And by the time he was convinced of her feelings for him as well as her family's disapproval, he was sorely conflicted. If not for the advocacy of Dr. Grayson, Paul would never have encouraged her by declaring his own love nor had the courage to request John Spencer's permission to court her. But it was Rosemary herself who convinced her parents to ultimately give their disinclined blessing on the marriage.

The coach had stopped at New Market for a change of teams when Paul's thoughts returned to the present as he watched the boys and Abby sprint down the street and back again. It was warmer now and they had shed their outerwear. This was their second day of travel, and due to a problem with one of the wheels the day before, the journey would not be complete until mid-day tomorrow. He fervently wished a wealthy railroad baron would complete a line straight through the valley, but most all men fitting that description were in the North. The Shenandoah Valley was agricultural rather than industrial, requiring fewer means of transporting substantial amounts of materials or manufactured goods to market.

An hour later, with the light weight of Abby's head on his shoulder as she slept, Paul's reflections returned to their earlier conversation. It *had* been a difficult decision to accept the call to Winchester. For over twenty years his home had been in Staunton, in the manse belonging to the Presbyterian Church where he brought his bride with nothing to offer but the dwelling that was his by working tenant-ship, not by right of ownership. He'd been offered other pastorates through the intervening years but had never before felt a strong stirring within his soul that it was time to go.

The call from Winchester was different, and he could not have described it in any other way than that there was a clear sense that he was needed there. It was a smaller congregation than his church in Staunton, but size or remuneration had never been a factor in his consideration. As he'd reminded Abby, the decision had been a matter of prayer, waiting for direction, and stepping out in faith. And, though Abby as the youngest would be affected more than his sons, they had all had the advantage of stability through their formative years.

Harry would soon complete his final year at Princeton Theological Seminary in New Jersey, and he adamantly claimed this erudite community was his true home. He'd found his place in the world and intended to establish permanent residency, and Paul had reluctantly accepted the defection as well as the more subtle rejection. Harry hadn't been back to Staunton since the summer following his first year at the College of New Jersey, and his last letter, arriving before Christmas, discouraged the family from attending his upcoming graduation by referring to the great distance and inconvenience of travel.

Harry was a brilliant scholar, and Paul was impressed with his passion for theology and biblical and ecclesiastical studies in spite of his concerns that hadn't abated since the day Harry matriculated to Princeton for his undergraduate and seminary studies. The seminary had a reputation for producing scholars, not preachers, not pastors – men whose love of the word of God would be expounded in a clear and powerful way. Whether the criticism was true or false, Paul instinctively knew Harry's tendencies would lead him in that direction.

What concerned Paul more than Harry's absence from the family circle was the attitude of his heart – the absence of humility and other spiritual graces, the evidences of redemption and election in a true believer. Paul clung to the hope that his conclusions were wrong, that the evidences he longed to see were merely missed in the short missives sent, and continually prayed for him.

In contrast, thoughts of his second son brought solace. Ben wasn't the brilliant academic Harry was, but his bright mind and easy disposition was of more value in Paul's eyes. Ben wasn't extraordinary in any way, but *solid* in every way, like his father. He was the younger version of Paul and, yet untested, was blessed with a deep faith as well as an imperturbable and generous nature, valuable qualities in a man called to the ministry.

Ben would soon be completing his first year at Union Theological Seminary in Richmond, and, although Paul hoped he would be able to join them sometime during the summer months, Ben would most likely be working there to cover costs of his tuition and board. He'd been able to come home to Staunton for Christmas, but it was doubtful he would journey to Winchester where he had no ties.

The lively discussion between his two younger sons regarding which one could swim the farthest brought a smile to Paul's face. Their births were only eighteen months apart and competition had always been inherent in their relationship, although primarily instigated by the younger one's determination not to be caught deficient to any degree. Davy's proclivities were more in the active, physical realm, but his competitive spirit had also worked well as a motivator in his studies. Their relationship had invariably been tempered by Geordie's affectionate nature and Paul was thankful for the strong bond of love and trust between the brothers.

Paul remembered when, after Ben declared his intention to follow in his father's footsteps, he'd asked the ten-year-old Geordie if he too planned to be a minister. Geordie had quietly contemplated the question before answering:

"If the Lord calls me to preach, I will gladly obey, Papa. But if He does not, I want to be a soldier."

"What is it that makes you want to be a soldier, Geordie?" he'd asked in surprise.

"I want to be like David in the Bible who was brave and defeated the enemies of his God." Geordie's golden brown eyes shone, lighting up his whole countenance with earnest intent.

"I want to be a soldier too, Papa!" Davy had immediately contended.

With only a few pieces of furniture that Rosemary had brought with her from Camden Hall, Paul's books, and their personal belongings, the Grahams were soon settled into the sufficiently furnished manse on Braddock Street, recently vacated by the Reverend Andrew Boyd and his wife. But Papa was right, and Abby could count several blessings for which she could be thankful. First and foremost was Annabel.

Abby knew Papa offered Annabel the choice to stay in Staunton or come with them to Winchester, and Annabel hadn't hesitated to throw in her lot with the family. Paul also gave her the choice of one of the manse's four bedrooms upstairs or the servants' cabin all to herself. Annabel chose her own private domain in the cabin on the other side of the manse's kitchen garden behind the house and claimed to be supremely content.

With a slightly guilty conscience, Abby silently admitted she was not *only* thankful for Annabel herself but was overwhelmingly relieved. Domestic activities had never been appealing and she'd reached the age such things were expected of her. Though she'd at last resigned herself to the fact she was a member of the female sex, she did not feel like one and continued to resist the pressure to always act accordingly.

During her obligatory visit to Camden Hall in Charlottesville the summer before, her mama's sister Aunt Garnet Spencer Phillips, her cousin Lucy, and Lucy's friend Caroline had done their best to coach Abby in the fine arts of dancing, needlework, wearing a hoopskirt, managing household slaves, and even coquetry, but had found her an egregious trainee.

Abby still could feel remnants of the degradation she'd experienced when the older girls ridiculed her appearance and scanty wardrobe.

"Only Mennonites and *little* girls wear their hair in a braid," Lucy had pronounced in exasperation, lifting the dark, thick coil hanging down Abby's back.

"And wher*ever* did you get this?" Caroline had asked with feigned dismay, fingering Abby's best dress derisively.

Turning to Lucy, Caroline continued the mockery in a loud whisper. "She must have gotten it out of a *missionary barrel,* though I did not know the *heathens* in Africa were now sending *their old clothes back to poor ministers' families."*

Both girls had laughed at Caroline's sharp wit, but when they pulled the dress over Abby's head to examine her underclothes, Lucy had gasped in authentic consternation.

"You only have *one* petticoat? And *where* is your corset? When you start growing breasts you are *supposed* to wear a corset, not just a camisole! Oh, dear Lord!"

Startled, Abby had glanced down and, for further verification, felt the tiny nubs of nipple between her thumbs and first fingers. She did not know whether to be embarrassed or relieved to find she had not grown breasts overnight. As far as could be discerned, she was as flat-chested as ever and decided that was fine with her; she was barely twelve.

Later, Abby overheard the girls whispering together. "She has always been rather *backward*," Lucy had concluded in disparagement, "but now, I must say, she is positively *common*."

"Can you imagine her ever having a *beau*?" Caroline agreed with a snicker. "No decent boy from a good family would *ever* give her a second look except one of *contempt* perhaps."

Abby had suffered through that interminable visit with dwindling tolerance, silently swearing never to return. The girls' cruelty was painfully humiliating, but it was the look of disappointment growing on her aunt's face that hurt deeply, telling Abby she had utterly failed to compensate, in any small measure, for the loss of Rosemary.

As her father had encouraged, Abby accepted the advice and instruction deemed applicable as graciously as possible and ignored the rest. The only thing of genuine interest to her among these rich relations was horseback riding, though she did enjoy the physical workout required in dancing.

In Winchester, she found her inherent lack of womanly interests and proclivities was more problematic than in Staunton where she'd grown up playing with her brothers. When the other girls her age found Abby openly scornful of feminine accouterments and activities, they promptly ignored her. Consequently, aware at age thirteen that romping outside with the boys was no longer an option, Abby was often left on her own.

Solitude did not bother her greatly, though Abby could not be called an introvert. She enjoyed the company of others in general but reserved the right to be particular in the choice of companionship. She admired those with wit and intellect who shared her disdain for superficial conversation and shallowness of character, but she also possessed a deep compassion for those less gifted or culturally deprived.

CHAPTER 2

On the second Sunday that Paul filled the pulpit in Winchester, his older half-brother Seth Douglas and his family arrived on a visit from Boonsboro, Maryland. Seth, a country doctor, and his wife Corrine had no biological children but had informally adopted twin boys abandoned at age six.

Seth was well acquainted with the desperately poor and problem-ridden family. Their father Coon Logan, following in the footprints of his own abusive, alcohol-addicted Shawnee half-breed progenitor, was an even worse husband and father, and his wife Lydia, who had come from Ireland to the shores of Maryland in hopes of finding a better life, was sorely ineffectual in protecting and providing for herself and, even less so, for their sons.

The identical twins Corbin and Cullen, to whose birth Seth was belatedly called, were deaf and functionally mute though Corrine had noticed Corbin appeared to hear extremely loud noises, such as the roll of booming thunder. They were socially as well as nutritionally deprived when she found them on her doorstep, and Corrine was inspired by hitherto frustrated maternal instincts to make up for their deficiencies with abundant attention and affection. She was largely successful in this endeavor and they were the source of her great joy and satisfaction. Seth himself, though not naturally adept with children, was happy when she was happy, and the family thrived.

Abby had a vague recollection of her aunt and uncle, the earliest one when they had attended her mother's funeral. She also remembered their visit the summer Harry had completed his first year at the College of New Jersey when they accompanied him home.

They hadn't come for another visit since the adoption of the

Logan twins because, Abby learned by listening to her father discuss it with Annabel, the boys were extremely timid and had significant difficulty sleeping through the night for the first several years. Apparently, she concluded, there had at last been improvement.

Sitting in the pew beside the Douglas family, Abby observed the boy cousins with great interest. They were less than a year younger than she and over two inches taller. She met them only a few minutes before the service but quickly recognized slight differences. Though they both were slender and moved with the gawky awkwardness of fledgling cranes, Cullen was more so, and Corbin seemed to be more wary, almost vigilant in his watchfulness over his twin with identical gray eyes and sharply defined facial features.

When she was introduced by way of gestures, both boys smiled politely and bobbed their heads in identical fashion. During the service Abby watched them perform what looked to her a pantomime. They stood when everyone else stood, opened a Psalter during the singing and their Bibles during the scripture reading, but did not look at it or open their mouths. She hadn't known what to expect, and, although she had to consider their behavior consistent with what she might have reasonably imagined, they fascinated her.

Later, during dinner Abby observed her Aunt Corrine's efforts to communicate with her boys, essentially confined to facial expressions, gestures, and pointing. She also noticed that they looked to her frequently for direction and nod of approval, and adding to her mental list of differences, Abby recorded the fact that while Cullen frequently made seemingly oblivious guttural noises, Corbin did not. That struck her as rather odd but felt that remarking on it might appear rude.

"Can they read, Aunt Corrine?" she dared to ask when her curiosity could no longer be restrained.

"Certainly not, dear," her aunt responded. "You cannot expect them to learn the alphabet without hearing the sound that goes with it. But they are *very smart* and can do almost anything else," she added, sensitive to the general notion that those who were deaf and mute were also mentally deficient and should therefore be hidden out of sight as if it were a contagious disease or a reflection of the family's bad taste.

After dinner, while the adults continued to converse at the dining table, Geordie taught the twins to play shinty, a game they called stickball, in the backyard but the game ended abruptly when it started to rain.

Abby, who'd been enviously watching them from the back steps, got out her slate and chalk and, settling on the settee in the parlor, was doodling when Corbin the more inquisitive twin timidly peered over her shoulder. Abby motioned to him to sit beside her, drew a horse, and passed the slate to him with a nod.

"*Horse,*" she said with another nod.

Awkwardly Corbin took the implements and, with his dark head bent over it and his brow furrowed in concentration, copied her drawing with his left hand. Hesitantly he handed them back, a tentative look in his somber gray eyes.

"Very good!" she announced with a grin and got a shy smile in return. With a sudden stoke of inspiration Abby wrote the letters *h-o-r-s-e* and, handing it back to him, repeated "*horse.*"

Encouraged by her response Corbin eagerly took the chalk and copied the letters. His eyes now shining with triumph, he placed the utensils back into her hands and silently mouthed "*horse.*"

Now Cullen seated himself on Abby's left and the game continued until the slate had been filled and erased with drawings of dogs, cats, pigs, mice, apples, flowers, trees, and birds, as well as the name of each written beside it, their hands and faces soon wearing smears of chalk and white dust covered their clothing.

Abby was so delightfully absorbed in the game she almost missed the sounds of their laughter mixed with her own until she looked up to see the astonished faces of her aunt and uncle.

"They are *laughing!* I have never heard them laugh like this before." Tears were rolling down Corrine's cheeks as she gazed at them and then at Abby.

"Now they can read *and* write. *I taught them.*" Abby said in an awed whisper.

Her eyes shining with joy she turned to her father and announced, "Papa, I have found *my calling! I am going to be a teacher!"*

The Graham children were educated at home, their mother teaching the younger three to read using the newly published *McGuffey Reader* series and cultivating their rote memory with the *Westminster Shorter Catechism* questions and answers. She also encouraged their love of classic literature by reading aloud to them in the evening before nightly prayers.

After her death, their father took full responsibility for their education, instructing them in Latin, French, history, mathematics, science, and theology, and he found it exceedingly gratifying, for they soaked up knowledge like sponges. Abby was no exception and, after discovering her *calling,* was all the more eager to learn.

Determined to continue her success with the twin cousins, Abby concentrated on developing her teaching skills and constructed hundreds of small cards with her drawings and associated words, including simple action verbs. These were packaged and sent to Corrine with instructions to continue the lessons and her efforts were rewarded with a note of appreciation from her aunt, filled with praise for her boys' studious dedication and progress.

By August, Paul was satisfied Geordie and Davy were prepared for the academic standards of the military college and Abby and he accompanied them to Lexington. Both boys excelled on their entrance exams and Geordie scored high enough to be placed with the third classmen.

While the boys were shown by one of the older cadets to the barracks, Paul, with Abby in tow, met with Superintendent Francis Smith in his office where they were soon joined by the Professor of Natural Philosophy and Instructor of Artillery, Major Thomas Jackson.

"I understand you are a Presbyterian minister, sir," the major greeted Paul, extending his hand. "Are you a relation of the founding pastor of our church, William Graham?"

"You are correct on both accounts, Major Jackson," Paul responded with a firm handshake. "I am currently pastoring the church in Winchester and William Graham was my father's second cousin. May I introduce my daughter Abigail?"

"It is a pleasure to meet you both," Jackson bowed to Abby and turned back to Paul. "You may be assured your sons will be well looked after."

"Thank you, sir. My prayer is that Geordie and Davy will serve the Lord and Virginia honorably by their conduct and academic performance, and that the practical use of their military training will be limited to peacekeeping efforts. I am eternally grateful they shall have godly influences here as well as in the church under the preaching ministry of Dr. White, whom I know quite well. I have been told of your own thriving ministry in the Negro Sabbath-school."

"It is a Christian duty in which my wife and I are privileged to serve," he answered softly and paused before continuing.

"I am now a teacher, Reverend Graham, but as the Lord himself has said, we will continually *'hear of wars and rumors of wars,'* *'for nation will rise against nation,'* and many *more trials* before the end times. But yes, we *shall* pray for the Lord's restraint of evil against us in the hope we *will* continue to dwell in peace. If not, then I will take up my sword again as an officer in His army and lead these young men."

"Indeed, we *all* are called into the Lord's service in one capacity or another," Paul nodded solemnly. "And I am grateful that, if *de rigueur*, my sons would be led by a warrior seeking to honor his *true* 'Commander and Chief.'"

"Thank you for your kind attention today, gentlemen, but now Abby and I must say our farewells to the boys before catching a coach back to Staunton. We are blessed to have many friends there who generously provide accommodations."

Paul nodded his thanks and took Abby's arm. Pausing at the door, he turned back to the superintendent and major.

"Please feel free to contact me if a need arises."

After a tearful parting with her brothers Abby sat pensively beside her father on the crowded stage heading north through the valley. Over the mountains to the west the sun was setting, the sky brilliant with dark pinks and purples. It was beautifully peaceful though Abby's spirits remained turbulent, and she exhaled in a deep sigh.

"What is troubling you, dear? Are you missing the boys already?"

The rattling noises of the moving coach and chatter of the other occupants covered the sound of their voices, and their conversation was accomplished by talking directly into the other's ear.

"I am already missing Geordie," Abby admitted, then added, "but I am sure I will soon be missing Davy as well. I have been thinking about what you and the major were talking about. Do you think there is going to be a war, Papa?"

"No, but, as the major pointed out, there will always be '*rumors of war.*' I am aware there is growing antipathy between those who support the owning of slaves and those who oppose it, but *surely* no one would be willing to go to war over the issue," he attempted to assure her as well as himself before verbalizing his continuing contemplations.

"Although the importation of Negroes is now illegal, the damage has already been perpetrated on the multitudes who were kidnapped and brought here in chains over the last hundred and fifty years, and I have no doubt that it is still happening. Treating fellow human beings like chattel is evil, Abby, and I wonder how long it can be tolerated. The very premise our nation was built upon was the belief that *all men are equal* and should be *free*.

"I know a good many honorable men who own slaves and believe it is acceptable as long as they are provided for, treated well, and given Christian teaching. I continually pray the Holy Omniscient Lord will show them what is right in *His* eyes, not just their own, but I cannot be another man's conscience," he acknowledged with a sigh.

"Annabel says there are many free Negroes in Winchester but they are still poor folks," Abby pointed out. "Do you think they are better off than the slaves at Camden Hall?"

"I do not know, but at least the freed are not in bondage and are able to exercise greater autonomy and also have the advantage of feasible opportunities. Everyone must take responsibility for his choices, the free *and* the slave. Like the rest of us fallen mortals, some will make good choices, and some will not. Ultimately, we must all choose whom we will serve… our ideologies, ourselves, other creatures, or our Creator."

After several moments of thought Abby posed another question. "Do you think the free Negros in Winchester might have more opportunities if they could read and write well?"

Paul gazed into her earnest, young countenance and nodded. "Yes, I do. They, like all other folks, can certainly benefit from an education. Do *you* want to teach them, Abby?"

"*Yes*, Papa! Do you think I *could?*"

"Virginia Law prohibits teaching slaves to read and write but I do not think it applies to *freed* Negros. We will talk to Annabel and see what she thinks about it. Perhaps having her involved will afford an extra measure of legitimacy if it is called into question."

The first week of October, under the sway of the indispensable Annabel in the freed Negro community, Abby's "school" made an inauspicious start in the Presbyterian Church basement with seven students ranging between the ages of five and fourteen. Undeterred by the erratic attendance during the first several weeks, Abby persisted, and by the end of the calendar year there were ten young Negro children who'd successfully mastered the first *McGuffey Reader*. Paul had offered to teach the youngsters Bible lessons, but with typical tenacity, Abby wanted to take full responsibility.

There were three students who hadn't succeeded, and after weeks of restrained frustration on their account, Abby finally appealed to her father and Annabel for help. The oldest was a ten-year-old boy named James whom Paul, with Job-like forbearance, taught to whittle long-handled spoons. And thereafter James happily whittled while the other children did their lessons.

The other non-academically inclined were sisters named Ruby and Pearl, ages eight and nine, and these were informally apprenticed to Annabel who taught them to make cornbread and gravy biscuits in the manse kitchen for the consumption of all on the church premises, including the sexton.

In deference to some of the objections to the "school" voiced by several congregants, Paul stayed on the property during the four hours classes were held. One day in late November, after dismissing her students for the day, Abby sought him in the small study there at the church on Loudoun Street, two-and-a half blocks east of the manse.

"Papa, it came so easily when you taught us deductive thinking; the 'if' always seemed to lead logically to the 'therefore.' But I am having trouble teaching it to my pupils. What do you think I am doing wrong?"

Paul took off his spectacles and looked into her earnest face. "I doubt it is anything you are doing wrong, Abby, but let us work it out together. Why do you think it came easily to you?"

"I suppose it was because there was no doubt that what you taught us was *true* and could therefore be trusted, depended upon to make correct deductions. Do you think the children are questioning the validity of what I am teaching them?"

"That is certainly a possibility. If you are not in doubt of their intellectual capacity, is it also possible they may doubt *both* the validity of what you are teaching them *and* their ability to trust their own deductive reasoning?"

"It is definitely not a lack of intelligence that is the problem." Abby's brows drew together as she considered, and then she shook her head slowly. "I can definitely sympathize that I am young and not someone they have always known and trusted, which would give them reason to question my authority. But when I ask a propositional question, they look at me as if they do not even understand the question. Why would they doubt their own ability to *reason*, even enough to directly challenge the validity of the information I gave them?"

"Consider how these children's background differs significantly from your own, Abby. You have not come from slavery, and even though these are freed Negros, it has not been long since their parents or grandparents were in chains. All their self-determination was taken, and they were told they were *subhuman,* and therefore, in order to survive, they were forced to do what was expected of them. They were denied education and discouraged to think at all for themselves. If that is even partially a reason for their hesitancy to trust you or their own deductive powers, what might you do to help them?"

"I suppose I should, first of all, encourage them to assume their true status as God's highest order of creation, even above the angels . . . to whom he gave honor and authority, whom He created in his own *image*. I see what you are saying, but it will not be easy for them, will it?"

"No, it will not be easy," Paul answered with a deep sigh. "Nevertheless, it is a truth we all should consciously seek to convey in every word and deed."

Overall, the academic experiment was deemed a success, and the week before Christmas was spent making decorations for the ten-foot tree erected in the church narthex. Each child was sent home on Christmas Eve with a box of sweets, complements of Annabel and her two helper-elves, Ruby and Pearl.

The week Geordie and Davy spent at home over Christmas seemed to go far too quickly, and before Abby had time to appreciate the goodness of having them there, she was kissing them goodbye again. Only after their departure was she able to process what she'd learned about their experiences during the first months at VMI and how they were faring.

Both boys were doing well academically and enjoyed the military training immensely. Their conversations often included mention of their artillery instructor, Major Jackson, and Geordie's roommate Edmund Claiborne, who was well acquainted with the Spencer family in Charlottesville.

"Major Jackson is highly intelligent and possesses practical expertise gained during the Mexican War. Edmund and I have learned a great deal from him, and anyone can get along well in his class if they are well prepared. He does not tolerate slackers, and I do not think he should," Geordie had insisted though his younger brother protested.

"He expects too much. If we are not able to retain and repeat the lessons word-for-word, he calls us out and makes us do it again. I am not an imbecile, but there are times he makes me feel like one. Have you ever heard *one word* of encouragement or praise from him? It is bad enough to have every cadet in the classes above us calling us '*rats*'!"

"Everyone except Edmund and me," Geordie had quickly corrected. "I was called a 'rat' too, remember. All new cadets are hazed for a while, so just pretend you are a duck and let it run off your back. If you *would*, the bullies would soon lose interest in tormenting you, Davy."

The reasons Davy was able to stick it out thus far, Abby concluded from the bits of information gathered, was his brother's arbitration on his behalf and his own stubbornness and ability to "fight dirty." At the time, he was under 5-feet, 5-inches tall, and though his prudence might be questionable, he was undeniably bright and possessed a short-fused, abundant supply of adrenalin that served him well. Abby did not doubt that the older and larger bullies who harassed him learned quickly that he was a tenacious fighter who "gave as good as he got."

Two weeks later, Abby's father received a letter from Major Jackson corroborating her deductions:

Dear Reverend Graham,

I am taking the liberty to write you based on your final comment when we met in Superintendent Smith's office to contact you 'if the need arises.' Since I have had time to observe as well as to instruct both of your sons, I have concluded your concerns may have been for David in particular.

David is a good boy and a fine young soldier, but he views his temper and love of fighting as a virtue and not the sinful trait it is. I shared my observations with Major Gilham who, convinced of the need for cavalry training here at the Institute, recently acquired a horse named Dragoon donated by a local man who claimed the animal was obstinate and bad-tempered. The Major and I agreed that David should be assigned as the horse's handler and are hopeful that the object lesson will be effective in teaching him operatively what mere rebukes cannot.

Please be assured, sir, of my high regard for you and your sons. And I dare disclose the strong affinity I have for David who reminds me of young Thomas Jackson, perhaps sharing the effects of losing a beloved mother at a young age and the disproportionate need to compensate for perceived, as well as genuine, deficiencies.

I join in your prayers for David that sanctifying grace will triumph in his heart, and he will indeed honorably serve the Lord and Virginia with humility and judiciousness as well as with passion.

Your servant,
T. J. Jackson

After he'd read the letter through, an amazed Abby watched her father do something he hadn't in a great while – he threw back his head and laughed! And after reading it herself, she joined in his mirth, immensely enjoying the vision of Davy in a battle of wills with a recalcitrant horse.

CHAPTER 3

JUNE 1858

By the end of her first year in Winchester, Abby's school had grown to over twenty young Negro students, and several had completed the second *McGuffey Reader*. And, though she experienced genuine gratification in her efforts, her desire for more training as a teacher was growing.

While there were limited opportunities for higher education for women in 1858, that state of affairs presented no obstacle for Abby. In 1842 her father's close friend and fellow clergyman Rufus Bailey had founded Augusta Female Seminary in Staunton. Although she was now just fourteen, Abby was determined to go.

"*Please*, Papa," she pled at every opportunity. "William McGuffey was fourteen when he started out as a roving teacher in Ohio. I am certainly capable of studying to become a trained teacher at this age. These children in Winchester deserve to have a trained teacher, just like white children. I *know* you believe that!"

Unable to refute her arguments, Paul contacted the Reverend Bailey; Abby was accepted into the seminary and would begin her studies in August. Until then she continued to offer literacy classes to the freed slave community in Winchester.

Only the prospect of seeing her brothers could entice Abby away from her students the summer before she was to leave for Staunton, but seeing them would require another visit to Camden Hall. However much she dreaded going, Geordie and Davy had been invited by their friend Edmund Claiborne to spend the two-week leave between the end of the academic term and summer encampment at his family's plantation in Keswick, near Charlottesville.

Since his wife's death, Paul often reminisced to his children, "Among the wondrous mysteries of providence I, the son of a simple Presbyterian minister and his wife, the widow of an indentured Scottish immigrant, won young Rosemary Spencer's heart that summer." The words and the whole story of their romance and marriage he repeated were spoken with awe and misty eyes, and it was for his sake that Abby refrained from telling him how much she hated going to Camden Hall.

Upon her arrival, Abby submitted to Aunt Garnet's insistence on providing "*appropriate*" dresses and gowns for the parties and social occasions that had been planned. Lucy's wardrobe had been substantially increased three months earlier when she married Brent Forrester, and Camden Hall's two seamstresses, under Garnet's supervision, focused their full attention on making Abby presentable.

Four days after her arrival, and an unpleasant scene revolving around underclothing, Abby was dressed in a becoming day gown of fine blue linen and several crinoline petticoats (sans corset and hoopskirt), and climbed gracefully in the family's landau carriage with Lucy and Brent for an afternoon barbecue and evening ball at Vermillion, the Claiborne's plantation.

Through no lack of education in genteel decorum, Abby's undignified greeting of her brother Geordie was the first of what was to be a long list of humiliations inflicted on Lucy Phillips Forrester. ("And she *only got worse,*" Lucy lamented to her mother, who arrived later in the day for the ball.)

Abby spotted Geordie among the gathering of young people on the wide front veranda as the carriage stopped in front of the stately Georgian plantation house, and once the door was opened by the livered footman, she made a dash for him, flinging her parasol aside. Only the ribbons of her wide-brimmed garden hat prevented its flight across the lawn.

"Geordie, oh Geordie! I could barely wait to see you!"

Catching her in his arms mid-distance between them, he swung her off her feet before setting her down again. Davy was also greeted with affection, if less fervent kisses, before Geordie took

Abby's hand and found an unoccupied bench under a rose trellis.

"I am so glad Papa has agreed for you to go to the seminary in Staunton, Abby. You will become an even more wonderful teacher. And Lexington is only forty miles from there, so perhaps I can come to see you. I look forward to getting your letters, but seeing you is far more satisfying."

"I hope you will come often. I love Papa and Annabel, and I love teaching my sweet pupils, but I miss you terribly. Are you still enjoying your studies?"

"Very much. I have to study awfully hard but have found motivation to excel through friendly competition with Edmund, both in academics and martial arts. When we get back, we will be living in tents, going on long marches, and practicing what we have been learning about warfare. It should be great fun."

"Did Papa write you about the letter he received several months ago from Major Jackson? He told Papa that Davy had been assigned to a horse named Dragoon in hopes of taming both their temperaments. I cannot remember seeing Papa laugh as hard as he did when he read it!"

"Ha-ha!" Geordie roared. "No, I did not know the motive behind the assignment, and I am not surprised Papa did not tell me. But, you know, it might be working. At least Davy can get on the beast now without being thrown off and kicked. The upperclassmen were making bets on whether Davy would survive, and he *is* still in one piece as you can plainly see. He has earned respect from the majority of boys, and I think he is proud of himself. He does not seem to be as defensive and quarrelsome, so it *must* be doing some good."

Becoming conscious of expectations as a Claiborne guest, Geordie looked up to catch Edmund's eyes on them from the veranda and, taking Abby's hand again, led her up the broad front steps toward their host.

"Edmund, may I present..." he began the introduction, but before he could complete the formality, Edmund executed a deep, decorous bow and took over.

"*Miss Graham*, I am delighted to finally meet the girl Geordie admires most in the world. Welcome to Vermillion."

He was smiling broadly and lightly kissed the back of her hand she extended. He was taller and almost as handsome as Geordie, and looking up at him, she felt slightly disconcerted.

Quickly withdrawing her hand, she murmured, "I am just '*Abby*,' and thank you, sir. Geordie speaks of you with high regard."

Her brother seemed to find her uncharacteristic primness amusing and grinned. "I do not think he would mind if you called him 'Edmund,' Abby.

"Would you?" he asked playfully, turning to his friend.

"No, truly, '*just Abby*,' I would be delighted to be on first-name terms with you," Edmund assured her with another bow and a twinkle in his blue eyes. "Since I have heard so much about you, I feel as if we are old friends. The only thing Geordie neglected to tell me was just how *beautiful* you are."

"I, um... I am *not*, which is clearly the reason he never said so." Her cheeks were pink, but the golden eyes looking at him were direct and slightly defiant, challenging his repudiation.

Edmund cleared his throat and blithely accepted the challenge.

"According to Mr. Shakespeare, '*Beauty is bought by judgment of the eye*,' and *mine* judge you to be exceptionally beautiful. I hope that does not offend you because I would never want to rouse your displeasure, Miss '*Just Abby*' Graham."

He was the first young man who had ever shown an interest in her, and, though she wondered if she should be offended by his forwardness in addressing and complementing her, she liked it. *And*, she reasoned, *Geordie would never allow anyone to insult her*.

Before she could compose another objection, Edmund wrapped her arm through his own and swept her into the grand reception hall. It was a beautifully proportioned room with a graceful circular staircase to the left that widened at the bottom. An elegant chandelier hung over the center of the room above a polished Hepplewhite table and marble tile floor.

"You must meet the rest of my family," Edmund insisted as he whisked her toward an attractive blond woman directing the

Negro waiters carrying trays of glasses and delectable foods.

"Mother, may I present Miss Abby Graham, Geordie and Davy's younger sister."

"Mrs. Claiborne, how very kind...." Abby's words were barely out of her mouth before she was propelled to a distinguished white-haired gentleman and introduced to Edmund's father.

Gallantly taking her hand with a bow, Cecil Claiborne said with a slight wheeze, "Delighted, Miss Graham. As I told your brothers, I remember your father and, of course, knew your dear mother quite well."

After another polite exchange, Abby was ready to free herself from Edmund's grasp, but she was towed to the far end of the veranda and found herself face-to-face with his sister *Caroline*.

Caroline, whose face lost some of its rubicund tint at the sight of the girl on her brother's arm, had been focusing her formidable charm on Geordie and Davy, and it was clear she was now making the connection between Lucy's "unfortunate" younger cousin and the handsome cadets beside her.

Having recently returned from Paris with her mother, sixteen-year-old Caroline glowed with the confidence of her superior couture and pulchritude. She was blond and fair like her brother Edmund, but that was where the resemblance ended. Edmund had broad shoulders and a slender, long-limbed build. Caroline was short, dimpled, stylishly plump, and curvaceous. She could attract any young man she wanted and was supremely confident in her ability to dangle as many beaus along as there were eligible prospects.

"Oh, of course, you're *Abigail*," Caroline purred with an undertone of malevolence meant only for Abby's perception. "I *do* remember you now. Lucy failed to mention you were coming."

"Perhaps she wanted to give you the pleasure of *surprise*," Abby suggested, mimicking the sugary intonation. Then, taking advantage of Edmund's loosened grip, she made her escape down the steps to fetch her parasol that someone had rescued from the lawn and leaned against the hitching post.

Geordie, excusing himself with a quick, short bow to Caroline, followed her.

"What was *that?*" he asked as Abby rested the pole of her opened parasol against her shoulder to hide the view of the veranda from which she could feel the other girl's withering gaze. "I did not know you had been here before."

"I have not. Caroline came to Camden Hall the last time I was visiting there." She exhaled in a deep sigh of relief and smiled up at him. "I will stay out of her way as much as possible, and that will suit us both. I came only to see *you*, so now let us eat. Something smells delicious and I am starving."

Never before had Abby experienced the feeling of looking beautiful, and it equally embarrassed and emboldened her when she'd inspected her reflection in the full-length mirror in the guest bedroom. She thought of her mother who might have attended a ball at Vermillion when she was the age of fourteen, and it brought a wistful smile to her lips and tug at her heart. *Had she come with her mama? If only mama were here tonight.*

The seamstresses at Camden Hall and the Negro woman assigned to dress her tonight had reason for pride in the results of their labors. Abby's rose-colored silk gown, the wide skirt of which seemed enormous over the half-dozen petticoats (sans hoop), accentuated the natural flush of her cheeks. The bodice was trimmed with a band of lace that covered more of her bosom than other ladies' more stylish décolletage, whether in deference to her modesty or to obscure the shortage of womanly properties that even the (much-protested) corset could not deliver, she could not say.

But Abby had to agree that the simple rosy gold necklace and matching earrings were perfect complements to the dress and her eyes. She'd chosen to wear no ornaments on her bare, gloveless arms, just her mother's small ruby ring on her right hand that held a closed fan she didn't quite know what to do with until it grew warm enough to use. Her stockings were of thin white silk and her feet were ensconced in silk slippers of the same rose fabric as her dress.

The ringlets in her hair bounced when she turned her head and were crowned by a circlet of pink rosebuds. Her wide golden-brown eyes were shining with suppressed excitement, and she realized then she'd never noticed the long lines of her neck and the slight cleft in her small square chin, highlighting her characteristic determination.

In the reflection, Abby critically scrutinized the effect. Edmund had called her *beautiful,* and the image that looked back at her might possibly be considered so. No one had ever said such a thing about her, certainly not anyone in her family and especially Papa who, though lavish with his love, would never have encouraged vanity. For the first time in her life, Abby decided to enjoy the few advantages of belonging to the feminine gender and, with a lift of her chin, turned her back on the girl in the mirror and left the room.

The ball officially began at 8:00, but the imposing grandfather clock under the staircase was striking 8:30 when Abby made her subdued appearance. As a dutiful host, Edmund was greeting the guests as they entered the ballroom, and he smiled at the sight of her before she noticed him.

As she slowly descended the staircase, Edmund discerned the underlying discomposure beneath her erect posture and graceful glide, and he found it appealing. He was aware this was her first ball, and even that relatively minor knowledge prompted a sense of immense satisfaction in him. Abby bore the look of dignity and sensibility belying her young age and inexperience. While Edmund was admiring the vision, Geordie appeared at Abby's side, and whatever he whispered in her ear brought a grateful smile to her lips.

Stepping up to greet her, Edmund executed a deep bow. "A votra service, madame d'une beauté etonnante."

Suppressing the urge to giggle, Abby dropped a neat curtsy. "Enchanté, M. Claiborne," she replied with a becoming blush, while Geordie snorted with mirth, though he too found this entirely new version of his sister startlingly grown-up and undeniably pretty.

Many of their military textbooks were French, and Edmund and Geordie frequently practiced their skills by speaking to one another en Français, though their playfully grandiose pretentiousness may have amused a native.

Leading her to the dance floor, Geordie deftly swept her around amid the other couples while gazing at her with familial delight. Abandoning his role as host and slowly wandering in their direction, Edmund determined that the next dance with her would be his.

Later on, having danced with both brothers and Edmund several times, as well as other young admirers who lined up to take a turn, Abby had almost begun to enjoy herself. She even started to entertain benevolent thoughts toward Lucy and Caroline who'd forced lessons upon her two years earlier until, while taking a trip to the privy closet, she overheard an exchange between the two.

"You would *think* she would know she is only getting attention because they pity her, but she is acting like the *belle of the ball!*" Caroline's voice dripped with spiteful humor. "It is perfectly obvious 'you cannot make a silk purse out of a sows ear,' and you certainly cannot make a *lady* out of a *menial just by dressing her in silk!*"

"She is definitely an embarrassment to our family, and I warned mama not to invite her, though Edmund was the one who suggested it. He invited George and David and knew they wanted to see her. Now that they *have*, it is time she went back to where she came from," Lucy asserted in aggrieved vehemence.

"I think that would be best before she humiliates herself and your family further," Caroline agreed as their footsteps took them out of earshot.

Instead of returning to the ballroom, Abby furtively made her way down the back staircase and outside. She adamantly refused to be offended by their words and found solace in nursing her own disdain for them. She wasn't angry, which would indicate she cared what they thought of her, and she didn't. In fact, she insisted to herself, she had no desire to be their version of *a lady*. But she was angry with herself, though she wasn't sure why. And it was a vague sense of shame that now clung to her.

The night was lovely with a nearly full moon lighting the sky, and she'd walked a good distance from the house before she stopped and realized exactly where she was. Every room in the large house was aglow with lamps and candles, and the music of a chamber orchestra could still be heard above the muted laughter and rumble of voices, but Abby had no desire to return.

She'd taken the wide cobbled path leading to the stables and chose to continue on. Upon entering the dark cavernous structure, her eyes gradually adjusted to the dimness as she enjoyed the earthy smells and soft whinnying sounds of the horses. Cautiously approaching the first stall, she was greeted by a sizeable gelding that, after a moment of unapologetic sniffing, permitted her to stoke his nose.

"Hello there, you handsome thing," she cooed softly, finding comfort in the velvety touch. "I hope you do not mind a little company for a while. You have a very nice place out here."

When Abby hadn't reappeared, Geordie and Edmund wandered among the guests inside and out of the house seeking her. After splitting up to search more thoroughly, Edmund began questioning the servants on the grounds and was told a young woman had been seen walking alone toward the stables. Reaching the wide doorway and hearing her whispered monologue with the seemingly responsive horse, he paused with a sigh of relief.

"Abby, you had us worried about you. Why didn't you tell Geordie or me you were coming out here?"

Struggling to recover her equanimity at his sudden appearance, she offered an apology. "Oh, I *am* sorry. I did not think anyone would miss me. You have many other guests to occupy your attention."

"None whose company I enjoy more than yours," he said, coming to stand beside her. "Did you not like the ball?"

Abby was quiet for several moments before she could offer an honest answer. "It was lovely, Edmund, and I enjoyed dancing with my brothers and you. But I was just pretending to be someone I am *not*... like Cinderella dressed in a gown her fairy godmother whipped up by magic. It *is* a beautiful gown, and I felt *pretty* for the first time in my life. But all this fluff and fuss of dressing up is not *for real*, except this corset, which I will most gladly never wear again!"

The boned instrument of torture seemed to be shrinking with the moist heat of her body, and she wiggled with discomfort. Distracted by the problem of how to get out of it without disrobing, she was unable to discern whether the sound he made was one of sympathy or amusement.

Quickly concluding that her physical discomfort was currently unresolvable, Abby returned her attention to the source of her mental agitation. It was too dark to see his face, but she felt it was important that he understand why she'd left the ball, and she wanted to more clearly understand it herself.

"You have established a friendship with my brothers, but I have nothing in common with any of you, and my only connection to the Spencers is half a bloodline. I have very different ambitions. I am going to be a teacher, not a grand southern lady. My beliefs are antithetical to those of your whole social class; I am *morally opposed* to slavery. And for the past year I have been teaching Negro children to read and write!"

Her voice had risen along with her conviction, and the truth of it vanquished any lingering doubts of the source of her disquiet and injury to her pride that had driven her outside.

"Geordie read me your letters, Abby. I know the passion that drives you to become a teacher, and I truly admire you. I am sorry you did not enjoy this evening, but it does not mean we cannot be friends, does it?"

"No . . . I suppose not. But I still do not belong here. What would your parents or your friends think if they heard what I said to you? If I stay, I might offend them, or they will offend me, and I will tell them what I really think. I heard Lucy say you were the one who suggested Aunt Garnet invite me to Camden Hall, and, although I am so grateful for the chance to see Geordie." She abruptly stopped, precariously close to tears.

At that moment Geordie appeared, and she rushed into his arms and wept into his chest. Holding her close he made soothing sounds while Edmund lit an oil lantern, illuminating the stable with a soft light. Acknowledging the concerned expression on Geordie's face, Edmund gallantly attempted a diplomatic explanation.

"It seems we have had enough of balls and parties. So," he paused as an idea came to him, "I for one am ready for some *sport*. I suggest that the three of us, and Davy, take the horses for a trek into the mountains tomorrow. We can leave before the family and guests wake and, very likely, won't even be missed. Would you like that, Abby?"

Turning a tear-streaked face to him, she nodded and sniffed. "Yes, but I have no riding clothes."

"Unfortunately, Caroline has never been interested in riding, but I think I can find a pair of my outgrown riding knickers that might do if you want them. Did you know that up until the eighteenth-century women used to ride astride a horse in breeches? We have sidesaddles and standard ones, so you choose which way you prefer to ride."

Abby stared at him in amazement, then at her brother, and back again at Edmund. "You would not object if I rode *astride*… in your *knickers?*"

"Not if Geordie would not," he replied without hesitation, cocking an eyebrow at his friend.

"Who am I to object when I am a guest in your home? I would love to go, and if Abby's willing, I will not be one to protest any of the arrangements."

CHAPTER 4

Two days after her arrival at Vermillion, Abby boarded the train for home amid an amalgam of confusing and conflicting emotions. On the conflicting side was the severing of ties with her mother's family. For, despite Edmund's heroic efforts to take full responsibility for her scandalous attire and behavior the day after the ball, Abby was formally branded a *disgrace*. Her eyes burned with hot tears as she recalled the confrontation.

When they returned to the Claiborne stables, Edmund sent her on to the house while he and Geordie tended the horses. Caroline had seen Abby approaching and met her at the bottom of the back staircase when she attempted to slip inside unnoticed.

"What have you been *doing,* and *why* are you dressed in such an *outrageous manner?"* Caroline had demanded, attracting the attention of everyone within shouting distance.

"MOTHER, MRS. PHILLIPS, COME AND SEE WHAT THIS APPALLING PERSON IS WEARING! She is DRESSED like a *boy* and there is no TELLING *what she has been* DOING!"

As the crowd gathered, Abby, wishing her hair weren't a mess of untidy curls and that she wasn't covered in dusty sweat, had endeavored to provide a dignified explanation.

"I have been riding with Edmund and my brother Geordie. There was nothing shameful about it."

When Abby turned her flaming cheeks away and attempted to climb the stairs, Caroline gripped her arm and pulled her back to face the growing audience, which now included both Edmund's parents, her Aunt Garnet and Lucy, and half-a-dozen others looking agog, but not Davy or anyone else who might come to her defense.

"You went out like that?" Lucy sulkily wailed. "Mother, she has

been embarrassing our family since we arrived yesterday. *Why* did she have to come at all?"

"You had better have a good explanation for your appearance and behavior, young lady!" her aunt huffed indignantly, fanning herself at a fast speed.

"She *does*, Mrs. Phillips," came a quiet but steely voice from behind the gathered crowd, and everyone's eyes turned on Edmund while Geordie made his way through the spectators to put his arm protectively around his sister.

"*I* loaned her the knickers and invited all *three* Grahams to ride up into the mountains with me. I resent any accusation made against her, or her attire, as an indefensible insult to *me* as well as Abby."

"Well, I must say, Edmund, I do not know *where* your good judgment has gone," his mother gasped, clearly mortified.

"Perhaps, it was not quite so *advisable*, son," his father began in an effort to inject a little balm but was over-ridden by Caroline's impervious denouncement.

"You merely do not realize how *devious* she is as well as common *and* . . . contemptible," she downgraded her adjective and volume when confronted with Edmund's wrathful blue eyes peering down almost nose-to-nose with her.

As the audience of spectators slowly began to recede, Edmund approached Abby and took her hand. The welling of tears in her wide eyes and the freckles that dotted her dusty, sunburnt cheeks stirred the lump now rising in his craw and he swallowed hard.

"If no one else is willing, *I* sincerely apologize for the '*contemptible*' way you have just been *treated*, Abby. I only hope you can find enough grace to forgive them . . . and *me* for subjecting you to these unjustifiable accusations."

Now facing the remnant of witnesses, Edmund added with the steel back in his voice, "If anyone has anything else to say about this, you may speak to me *privately*."

Although no one apparently challenged Edmund after that, the damage had been done and Abby was given no choice in the matter. Aunt Garnet had immediately taken her back to Camden

Hall, packed her up, and put her on the train the following day to Staunton. She had barely enough time to thank Edmund for his gallantry on her behalf and to bid a tearful farewell to Geordie and Davy.

Since Edmund's sister was the one directing the public outrage, Abby was concerned his own family relationships would suffer permanent damage as well as hers. His distress upon his failure to expiate her disgrace was profound and he insisted on accompanying her home to apologize personally to her father, but both Geordie and Abby dissuaded him. Paul Graham had faith in his daughter without question, and, after all, Geordie also had his father's complete trust. Edmund retained a modicum of honor by writing his apologies to Paul.

The main source of Abby's regret was that, by association, her father and brothers would also be anathematized by the incident. As she had confessed to Edmund in the stables, there was no substantial familial link to the Spencers other than blood, but Rosemary's spirit was and would always be precious to them.

The truth of the matter, as well as the source of Abby's primary disquiet, was that, in spite of the fortuitous consequence, the impromptu adventure had turned out to be the happiest day of her life. Nothing, no occasion as far back as she could remember, had ever come close to that supreme delight.

Davy, whose desire to be on horseback was well sated, had declined the trek in favor of the opportunity to sleep later that morning and Edmund, Geordie, and Abby, dressed in Edmund's long-since-outgrown knickers and mounted astride a young mare named Regina, left the stables before 7:00 a.m. Edmund, with ample supplies of victuals in his saddlebag, led the way and before noon the three were atop Carter Mountain admiring the view of the valley below, and feasting on banquet remains and French wine.

Along the way Abby learned that, although Vermillion plantation cultivated crops of tobacco, the main source of operation was the breeding of thoroughbred horses for the U.S. Cavalry as well as for public sale. At Camden Hall, Abby had learned to ride two years earlier, but the restricted pleasure she'd experienced then paled in comparison to the freedom she'd relished the day before.

Under the spell of the beautiful surroundings, Regina's rhythmic gait beneath her, and the amicable companionship, all Abby's inhibitions tumbled down, and she felt as lighthearted as the breeze that blew through her unfettered hair. She hadn't known such complete ease with anyone, except Geordie, that she'd felt with Edmund.

In retrospect, this was an astonishing revelation as well as a bewildering one, considering that she'd only met him the day before. She questioned how much was related to Geordie's presence and close friendship with him and how much this sudden sense of trust and camaraderie was due to Edmund's essential self.

Nothing could change the facts of their basic differences, even though he'd already known her aversion to slavery, her school for Negro children, and her plan to matriculate to the seminary in Staunton before making her feel so welcomed. He'd read her letters to Geordie; *what else had she written in them? How much was she hoping to soon forget Edmund Jefferson Claiborne once she was back home and focused on her goals and, conversely, how badly did she want to see him again?* This was a conundrum that would only be solved in time but, at the moment, she was experiencing strong tugs in both directions.

Edmund's disappointment and displeasure with his family was not easily dismissed after Abby left Charlottesville, and, though their leave wasn't over, he returned to Lexington two days later with her brothers. Even harder to dismiss was his thoughts of Abby and remorse for his ill-considered plan and her dishonor. It was bad enough he'd compromised an innocent young lady's reputation, but he'd done it to the one and only girl who'd thoroughly captured his heart!

Graciously, Geordie carried no grudge, and, although he considered himself undeserving, Edmund was immensely grateful for the clemency offered. Geordie stated repeatedly that he himself was as much to blame, and, besides, he had absolute faith in Abby's emotional and spiritual strengths. Abby knew who she was and what she was about, and Geordie knew what was and wasn't important to her. And it *wasn't* Charlottesville society's esteem.

Edmund wondered if *he* was important to Abby. Maybe he would have been if things had turned out differently on that almost perfect day. He could close his eyes and remember every moment.

He'd been utterly and irrevocably charmed by the spunky, funny, tenaciously opinionated young woman whose femininity was not diminished by baggy riding knickers, trotting ahead of him with wind blowing through her dark brown hair as she waved Geordie's Kepi cap in mock salute, her head thrown back in uninhibited merriment. He loved that image even more than the elegantly gowned one from the night before. He'd never imagined, much less known, anyone like her, and even before they returned to the stables, had promised himself he would one day marry Abby Graham.

With a deep sigh, he now acknowledged the likelihood of success was greatly diminished. Although she'd been magnanimous enough not to blame him, he knew that, after the humiliation to which she'd been subjected, he didn't deserve her.

Paul accepted the matter with his usual quiet aplomb, assuring his daughter, since her conscience was clear, there was no need of concern. However, in response to her anxiety that knowledge of the incident might reach Staunton, he wrote to Dr. Bailey explaining the facts of the unfortunate occurrence and assuring him of his daughter's enduring virtue.

In truth Paul was not surprised by Abby's preference for Edmund's offer of adventure over ostentatious social rituals. She was her mother's daughter, and he could well imagine Rosemary doing the same. Rosemary had been vested with the same spirited independence that prompted defiance of her family's wishes and marriage to him, and he certainly had no regrets on that account. Abby not only was her mother's visual image; they had been cut from the same cloth. Paul would have expected nothing less of her characteristic boldness.

His response to Edmund's letter said much the same and offered assurance, based on both his sons' and Abby's high regard, he bore him no reproach. Paul's gracious reply did more to restore

Edmund's tormented soul than anything else could have done, and he, with great relief, invested his energies into the VMI summer encampment and curriculum with renewed enthusiasm. Nevertheless, he refrained from writing to Abby directly in fear of presenting himself too forwardly and instead depended on Geordie to send his fond regards as well as to provide him news from her.

With great anticipation, Abby began her formal education in September at the Augusta Female Seminary in Staunton. At fourteen, she was the youngest in her class but one of the brightest and most dedicated. She missed her father, Annabel, and the young Negro students, but was comforted in the knowledge she would someday return a more qualified teacher.

The academic year flew by quickly, with only a week of Christmas at home with the boys, and when she was home again for the month of July, she studied just as diligently. Most of the knowledge she'd gained her first year wasn't new, and she'd learned to satisfy herself by reading additional textbooks found in the library.

What interested her most was a critical observation of the professors' teaching styles and methods, and she entertained Paul with her descriptions and imitations of each. Overall, she was happy with the opportunity to train at the seminary but was impatient to have her studies be focused on the *hows* of teaching and the reasons behind them.

How do children best learn? Do some children learn differently than others? Are there differences in presentation based on the subject matter? There was a plethora of questions not yet addressed to her satisfaction.

Geordie had invited her to come to Lexington in May for a formal reception and dance given in honor of the visiting General Winfield Scott, and the desire to see her brothers and Edmund was very tempting. But she ultimately declined, claiming her studies were her immediate priority.

This was true to a point, but the deeper truth lay in an unwillingness to risk damaging the fragile link with Edmund in the exchange of letters between Geordie and herself – her letters read, and Geordie's responses subtly shaped by Edmund's input. She valued that link but, at the same time, it worried her to think too much of it, preferring to focus on her own chosen path rather than speculate on what might be in his mind.

Also, though it grieved her to forgo an opportunity to see Geordie, she was also skeptical of the formality and social expectations inherent in a military gala. She had learned her lesson at Vermillion, and it did not bear repeating. She did not and would not ever aspire to be a *southern belle*, harnessed by a corset and bedecked in crinolines and silk. It was an instinctive knowledge that both strengthened her sense of self and saddened her. Edmund Claiborne was someone destined by birth to expect such a match.

When word circulated through the dormitory of Abby's declination of such a prestigious event, her classmates were incredulously envious. Some of them had been sent to the seminary by fathers doubting their daughter's ability to attract husbands and would therefore need to support themselves by teaching. Others, Abby surmised, had been sent due to their excessive interest in the opposite sex. Very few came with the same passion to teach that had drawn Abby, and because she was the youngest and comeliest, she was largely resented. The attitude of her classmates generally did not bother her; it merely increased her longing for her family and determination to succeed.

When she was home for the month of July, Abby relished the deep conversations with her father and with Annabel. Discussions with Paul primarily revolved around her studies, her brothers, and the church.

Harry was now the associate professor of biblical history at the College of New Jersey and had not found a suitable young woman who measured up to both his intellectual and spiritual standards. Ben was continuing his theological studies at Union and was employed as an assistant librarian at the State Capitol to cover the costs of tuition and board.

The Winchester church was in need of a new sexton since old Walter Brady had been down with rheumatism and the Sunday school superintendent, Mr. Eugene Wells, was moving to St. Louis to live with his daughter. And, although Paul was aware of undercurrents of discord among the members who opposed the owning of slaves and those who had them, so far there had been no direct confrontations on church grounds. However, he expected the issues to boil over at some point.

Annabel obligingly enlightened Abby on the current welfare of her former students as well as the general state of the free Negro community. Delly and Jelly's mama had lost her job at the farmers' market after their daddy was caught stealing a pig, and after he had been branded, was thrown into jail. Annabel was teaching the girls and their mama to can vegetables and pickles in hopes of selling enough jars to pay his fine.

Abby's two best readers, twelve-year-old Amos Gilmore and thirteen-year-old Elize Barlow, were teaching their respective mamas to read and had been asked to teach the alphabet to the youngsters at the Negro Brethren Church. The oldest boy in the class, sixteen-year-old Jeremiah Watson, had been hired on at Shanks General Store. Abby had little doubt that Annabel had been a dynamic agent in many of the success stories.

"I been askin' 'round an' fin' out theahs a Mennonite farma thas been hepin' out the ones on the run ta git ova the riva ta the north, but I don' know any mo' 'bout it than that yit. I want to hep too 'cause I know they need it," she confided to Abby. "I ain't tol' ya Papa 'bout what I want ta do, but I will 'fore I do it. I think he's gonna lemme do what I gotta do but I, fo' sho, want his blessin' on it."

"I know Papa would not object. I believe he would help runaways in any way he can as well. While I am here, I want to help too."

Abby paused and took the older woman's hand. "And I must thank you, dear Annabel, for what you have already done for my children and me and for what you *will* do to help your people. You are truly my inspiration."

August came on the run and Abby, with persisting perplexity of emotions, left home for her second year at Augusta Female

Seminary.

CHAPTER 5

OCTOBER – DECEMBER 1859

While Paul was opposed to slavery and, when directly questioned, acknowledged such, he felt a deep responsibility to his congregational flock to cultivate a spirit of peace between the factions. But even among the elders there were those who believed slavery was a moral issue and should be handled with formal ecclesiastic discipline and others who challenged them with the argument that scriptures did not prohibit the owning of slaves, only instructed slave owners how to treat them.

As their pastor, Paul, following the example of the great apostle, took every opportunity to emphatically encourage those in the latter group in the vigilant care of their slaves *"particularly those in the same household of faith,"* even rebuking those who did not allow their slaves to attend church. Often, he felt as if he were walking a tightrope between his own conscience and pastoral compulsions.

The questionable legality and the prudence of Abby's educational activities dispensed on church premises had contributed significantly to the controversy, but Paul had stood solid on this issue. When objections were raised in a session meeting the year before, he reminded them with unwavering confidence, "It has always been a historically biblical practice to educate everyone, including 'the stranger' to read and understand the Word of God, and that is what my daughter is doing here in this sacred place. It is a Christian duty and she will not be forbidden to do so."

Protests to this interpretation declined when Abby's school officially closed the day before she left for Staunton, but the greater debate on the morality of slavery continued, gaining momentum.

Paul anticipated trouble but could not have predicted the events that would generate and proliferate the demoralizing schisms in so many churches, particularly those along the border of the Mason-Dixon Line. And he definitely could not have anticipated the active roles he and his third son would be called upon to take before the end of the year.

In mid-October news quickly spread through Winchester that the military arsenal at Harpers Ferry, thirty miles northeast, had been raided by a group of abolitionists inciting slaves to revolt, and the Virginia militia as well as the U.S. Marines under the command of Colonel Robert E. Lee had been called up by President Buchanan to effectively quell it. Three days later there was a common, momentary sigh of relief when confirmation came that those involved had been killed or arrested and order was restored.

But reactions to the incident were varied, both in positions and degrees of outrage propagated on the streets and in the press, and Winchester wasn't impervious to the ruckus. Those who opposed slavery claimed John Brown who led the raid was a hero, even if somewhat misguided in his attempt to challenge the federal government. And those who owned slaves denounced Brown as a madman and murderer who tried to deprive them of their property, but they privately lived in fear that their own slaves might be incited into insurrection. It had happened before.

Brown's trial in Charles Town was presided over by Judge Richard Parker of Winchester, and he was sentenced to execution by hanging, scheduled December 2nd. Although the cadets of VMI were not attached to the Virginia Militia at the time, Superintendent Smith offered their service to Governor Wise who, fearing the event might incite another uprising, ultimately accepted.

Smith immediately left for Harpers Ferry once he was appointed to supervise the execution and Major Jackson and Major Gilham, with the first and second classmen cadets, arrived by train on November 28th.

When Paul received the letter from Geordie with this information he determined to go in support of his son and to offer Superintendent Smith his services as chaplain to the contingent of deployed cadets. He met them there and remained until they returned to Lexington three days after the execution. Although he volunteered to pray with and for the condemned man before his hanging, John Brown declined.

On the day of execution, the cadets conducted themselves with commendable discipline and fortitude in their positions around the scaffold, many of them witnessing a violent death for the first time. One of them was Geordie Graham, standing in formation beside Edmund on the front row facing the scaffold. All was quiet when the sounds of the wagon bearing Brown and the sheriff could be heard, but Geordie remained at attention and could not see the condemned man until he was led up the steps.

It amazed Geordie that the man seemed not the least afraid to face death and even seemed cheerful as he shook his executioners' hands before his own were tied behind his back. Brown was a large man dressed in black except the red carpet slippers on his feet and it was on the slippers, at eye level, that Geordie focused his stare.

Hovering between fascination and horror, Geordie heard Superintendent Smith give the command, but it was apparently not heard on the scaffold, and required repeating before the rope was cut. With a heavy jolt the man in the red slippers dropped about two feet through the trap door of the scaffold and the red slippers disappeared below.

With extreme effort, Geordie stifled the sounds of shocked dismay as he watched the body twitch with spasms until the only movement was the lifeless mass swaying back and forth in the frigid wind. He closed his eyes but still could see the things he knew he would never forget.

Since his mother's death, Geordie's thoughts often turned to what dying would feel like. He understood that at the moment the heart stopped beating the body and soul divided and the soul would enter heaven or hell. It shook him now as never before to think that this vibrant, courageous man still swinging from the rope around his neck had walked through the mysterious veil into eternity. Geordie wondered if he would be as calm and courageous in the face of death and prayed that he would.

It seemed forever until the body was taken away and the cadets were marched back into town. When they were dismissed, Geordie ducked behind the barracks, braced his hands against the wall, and retched. Turning, he found Edmund beside him and only then did he exhale completely, supported by the bond of comradeship he knew and trusted.

Despite the private thoughts and feelings among the cadets, there was a general consensus among them that the man died "well." Also, there was profuse thankfulness for no further disturbances, though several expressed belief that, if there had been, there was no doubt about their ability to successfully deal with it.

During his time with the cadets Paul offered counsel and support as he had opportunity, and he was impressed with the spiritual maturity and leadership skills shown by both Geordie and Edmund. The latter seemed to welcome the opportunity to reconcile face-to-face with Abby's father, who appreciated the occasion to meet him as well.

Paul also took time to speak privately with Major Jackson.

"I will continue to pray these young men will suffer no lingering effects of morbid remembrances," Paul began. "They performed their duties admirably and I know you are proud of them."

"I am more grateful than proud they have been given the opportunity to test their discipline and fortitude before the day of real battle, Reverend Graham. Although there is nothing beforehand to prepare them for the *true* test of trust in the Lord and their captain, my prayer for them is that they were reminded, as witnesses to the death of one man, that we *all* must live every day prepared to stand before the Lord."

Paul quietly considered this remark. "You are right, major. My concerns were as a father for his son, not as a commander of soldiers as you are. Perhaps between our prayers for them, the Lord, in his great wisdom and goodness, will be pleased to grant them souls of trusting lambs and hearts of fearless lions."

With a smile he continued, "You are a wise man, Thomas

Jackson. Geordie tells me Davy and his fine friend *Dragoon* have had a positive effect on one another. Do you share that opinion?"

Jackson returned the smile with a slight shrug of his shoulders. "Only the Lord can see his heart, but I have noticed your Davy seems to be making peace with himself as well as the horse. Major Gilham reports he has been bitten several times, and, though I can't verify it, there are rumors *he bit* the brute back!"

"That would not surprise me," Paul's smile widened as he visualized the scene. "What is your estimation of Edmund Claiborne, if you will forgive my asking? I perceived his interest in courting my daughter, and, in this matter also, I am impelled by paternal concerns."

"Cadet Claiborne and your son George are the finest soldiers and leaders in their class. They will, no doubt, become honorable officers and gentlemen in the high tradition of Virginia Military Institute. If I had a daughter, I would not hesitate to entrust her to either one. God willing, I will live to have a son as fine as those two young men."

"Thank you, major. That validates the sentiments of my children and my own impressions as well, but I'm very grateful to have the commendation of his commanding officer. The answer to whether Edmund shall be as successful in courting as he is at the Institute rests alone with Abby who, at age fifteen, I am pleased to say, is more interested in becoming a teacher than a wife."

Paul stood and offered his hand with a smile, "And as for me, it has been a great honor to serve under your command during the last week, and if there is ever a time in the future I can be of further service to you and your young men, I will gladly come."

Finding Geordie on the station platform ready to board, Paul sensed an agitation in his countenance and probed once again. "To witness a man's death as you boys did can be very distressing, Geordie, and it is all right to admit it. In fact, there would be something amiss if one did *not* find it so."

"It *was* distressing, and I do not mind admitting that." Geordie's pause was long enough for Paul to recognize his hesitation and struggle for composure. After an anxious glance at his comrades now boarding the train to Richmond, he turned his gaze back on his father's compassionate face and gave a sigh.

"Watching Mr. Brown strangle to death was horrid, but there is something else that has occurred to me that I did not think much about before this week, and I cannot get it out of my mind. Up until now it has been a *game*, but, if I am to be a soldier, I shall not only *witness* many deaths, I shall also be an agent, a *perpetrator* of many deaths. Do you think I will be able to do it, Papa?"

Paul looked intently at his sensitive, loving son and gripped his shoulders. "If the Lord has called you to be a soldier, my dear one, He will equip you in every way. You may trust Him to do so."

With a large lump in his throat and pain in his heart, Paul waved a final farewell as the train pulled away. Those "rumors of war" Jackson had referenced a year ago had become an ominous rumble that were not abated with the death of John Brown. In fact, he'd already perceived an even louder threat of a gathering storm.

Paul knew well enough that Geordie and the other young cadets would not be exempt if war were to erupt. Only the Sovereign Father knew what would be required and exacted from them, and this earthly father could only pray for their safety and soundness of soul.

In May of 1860, Abby traveled with her father to Richmond for Ben's graduation from Union Theological Seminary and his ordination as an assistant to the Rev. Dr. Moses Hoge, at Second Presbyterian Church. It had been many years since Paul was in Richmond, and after the morning graduation ceremony concluded, Ben took them to see the church, founded and built since Paul left in 1834. Ben's ordination service was scheduled on Sabbath evening the following day.

The Gothic architecture was very impressive compared to the simplicity of the Winchester church, with four-cornered pinnacles atop the massive bell tower. Inside, they admired the magnificent stained-glass windows and the elegant beamed ceiling above.

After the brief tour Abby, thrilled with her first visit to the capital city, requested to go to the market district for some shopping. Ben declined, reminding them he was expected to perform his last duties at the library and suggested they take a tour of the Capitol instead. But Abby was more interested in the market, and after confirming they were to meet again at his boardinghouse, Ben hesitantly left them on the corner of 5th and Main Streets.

Paul, suspecting Ben's reticence had more to do with a particular commodity to be had at the market, was also reluctant to take Abby to the Shockoe Bottom District where, among other businesses, the second largest number of Negros in the continental United States were bought and sold. Abby had never been exposed to the horrendous sights, the ugly forms of depravity inherent in the human import trade. The mountains of the Blue Ridge had shielded her from the worst of its offenses, flagrantly practiced along the southeast seaboard and Deep South.

Although Abby had been around slaves and slaveholders all her life, the domestic slaves she knew lived in cabins behind a main house; the cabins were small and scantily supplied but the slaves were fed and clothed. The same applied to those that worked the farms in the valley and even on the plantations in Charlottesville. She'd seen some treated roughly and it had angered her, but she had yet to see anyone publicly abuse a slave.

Still standing on the corner beside the grandeur of the Lord's holy sanctuary, Paul explained gently but as plainly as he dared the hellish conditions of the slave market.

"I shall not refuse to take you, Abby; however, I am compelled to warn you it is *anything* but a heartening sight. Though I have not been there in many years, I cannot believe there has been an improvement in the conditions of humiliation and abuse of these poor souls. It is worse than you can ever image."

"You do not need to worry about me, Papa. I know you still think I am a child, but I am grown now, with two years of college behind me. I believe as you do that slavery is wrong and should be abolished, and if I am to teach Negro children to see themselves as made in the image of God, it is important that I know what their parents and grandparents experienced."

"If you *insist*, we will go, but we will not stay more than a few minutes. It will be crowded since it is a market day, and you must stay very close to me," he warned, his brows furrowed with concern.

Abby believed she was prepared for what she was about to see. She was wrong.

What struck her first when she entered what was known as the "slave market" was the sheer number of Negros in chains or cages, the males separated from the females. Most of them wore filthy rags and the children wore nothing at all. They sat or stood in filth, flies lighting on the ones too weak or weary to wave them away.

The second thing that commanded Abby's attention was the look in the eyes of the chained and caged "exhibits," at least those whose eyes she was given opportunity to observe. Most of them averted their gaze away from the white hordes who poked, prodded, and inspected the stock. But in those eyes that met hers, Abby saw raw pain and despair that shocked and astounded her. Never had she seen such misery in any human countenance. It was heavier than mere grief; it was palpable wretchedness.

Abby's shock and horror were so profound that over a quarter of an hour passed before she realized Paul was not behind her, and this discovery pushed her over the edge into panic. In every direction she turned, she could not see him.

Frantically, Abby pushed her way through the crowds looking for the plain black parsons hat and white collar and, in her haste, continued to collide with scenes more horrific than the last – a huge black man wearing a metal collar with spikes penetrating his neck, being led by a chain; a screaming black mother whose weeping children were being torn from her arms; two young, naked black women on the auction block being groped and fondled by several chortling white men.

But the sight that drove the panic of losing Paul from her mind and roused her to outrage and furious action was an apparent demonstration by a slave breaker flogging a young woman whose clothes had been torn from her body and whose flesh on her back and chest was stripped and bleeding. Blood spattered on the crowd as the whip flew through the air.

Pushing aside the crowd, Abby screamed, "*STOP IT RIGHT NOW! STOP HURTING HER!*"

Shielding the woman with her own body, just as the whip came down forcefully across her own shoulder, Abby gave another scream of protest and pain.

"*NO! STOP! SOMEONE HELP US!*"

Shoving Abby away with an oath, the man raised the whip again before Paul seized his arm. Surprised by the intruder's piercing glare and distinctive clerical stock and hat, the slave breaker dropped his arm with another blasphemous sentiment while Paul, without breaking eye contact, gathered Abby in an embrace and led her away.

Neither spoke until the noise and sights were well behind them. Only then did they stop and Paul, pulling out his handkerchief, wiped away her silent tears.

"I am so very sorry, my darling. I turned once and then you were gone. I should have *never* taken you there!"

Paul was himself greatly disturbed by the whole experience– the hellish market scene, the panic of losing Abby, and finally his fury at the man who harmed her. At that moment of physical contact, he could have mercilessly beat him!

Although she tried, Abby couldn't stop trembling, and was barely aware of the drive in the cabriolet back to Ben's room at the boarding house. Once inside, Abby allowed her father to dress the cut caused by the whip, and though it stung badly, she repeated several times, "This is nothing compared to that poor woman's cuts. Who is going to take care of *her? Oh, Papa, who will take care of her?*"

"I do not know, Abby. I do not know," he admitted quietly.

Still greatly shaken by the experience at the slave market when she and Paul boarded the train Monday morning on their way home, Abby remained silent until Paul persisted in his efforts to draw her out.

"Abby dear, perhaps I should have spared you. Nevertheless, though I have suffered guilt for what happened to you, I have finally arrived at peace of conscience. I do not believe it is ultimately good for children to be ignorant of the reality of evil in this world. We are never absolved by pretending it isn't there, and by so doing, evade our Christian duty to oppose it. I believe the Lord's intent in ordaining this trial is to provoke our consciences… to what action, I do not know yet, but He will show us in time."

"We *must* do something! If the Lord would give me all the gold in the national treasury, I would buy all the slaves in the country and set them free," she declared, but added with a wry twist of her lips, "I do not suppose the Lord would see fit to make that happen though."

Paul gently smiled at his daughter, her face still drawn in emotional distress and agitation.

"He is able to do whatever He pleases and that will always be what is *best,* and in his own time. He has granted you eyes to see and a willing heart in preparation for the work He has for you, so until He directs you forward, continue your education, and wait patiently."

Leaning her head on his shoulder Abby exhaled in a long, woeful sigh.

"I will try to be patient, Papa. I will *try.*"

Once more reliving the shockingly wretched sights, smells, noises, and commotions that had confronted her in the Shockoe District, Abby described it to Annabel when she returned home. Annabel listened in silence, gazing beyond temporal sight, and it was several minutes before she spoke, her deep, melodic voice soft and trembling with inexpressible sorrow.

"I rememba it. I was brought ta that place when I was jus' a small chile, as scared as a chile kin be. Ol 'Massa John Spenc'a bought my mama an' me that day. Even that long ago, I kin still rememba it.

"My mama an' me was ki'chen slaves, an' sometime it got s'hot we thought we was cookin' 'long with the puddin', but we was glad in the winta time cause we could stay wammer. But one day, I was pickin' peas in the garden an' massa's son *Will* say he wanna mess with me, an' he took me behin' the shed an' he *did*….

"They took ma baby from me an' said they foun' him a good home, but I nev'a *fo'got*. Afta that, Miz Rosemary said she wont me ta be her own gal, an' she was good ta me, an' even taught me ta *read*."

Her dark eyes refocused then and she turned them on Abby with a gentle smile.

"But ain't I thankful ta the Lawd ya sweet mama brought me with her from that house, an' ya papa gave me papers ta be *free*. The Lawd made this ol' darkie free in *this* worl' *an'* the nex'. An' when He gives us the marchin' owders, we gonna *fight* this slav'ry bidness with *everythin' we got!* That's why we heah, Abby chile… *that's why we heah ni!"*

Having grown up with a houseful of brothers, Abby was aware of the body parts and general mechanics involved in the sexual act, though the concept seemed curiously appalling to her. The male appendage was not only for pissing–it was a depository and dispenser of human *seeds*, rather like the barrel of a gun.

But she knew that what had happened to Annabel was unspeakably shameful. Tears streaked both faces, the dark and the light one, as they searched the soul of the other laid bare in the depths of their eyes, and after another moment of unbroken silence, Abby and Annabel embraced.

It shamed Abby to learn her Uncle William, whose neck had been broken when thrown from a horse, had violated Annabel, and Abby could appreciate the divine justice behind his death while still in his teens. But the knowledge her mother was compelled by love and compassion to teach Annabel to read was an epiphany. Abby had already committed her life to teaching, but the trip to Richmond and Annabel's revelations brought her to a higher level of intense purpose and resolve.

And though Congress had passed a stricter Fugitive Slave Act in 1850 mandating severe punishment for aiding and abetting runaways, Annabel, with Abby's active support and Paul's encouragement, regularly provided food and supplies from the manse pantry and cupboards to those running for freedom across the Mason-Dixon, then onboard the *Underground Railroad* to safety beyond the Canadian border.

CHAPTER 6

With the election of Abraham Lincoln in November 1860, with only 40% of the popular vote, tensions between the Northern "free states" and Southern "slave states" reached a point of no return. Many voters south of the Mason-Dixon considered the election itself a farce since Lincoln's name was not even on the ballot in nine southern states.

By the end of the year South Carolina, followed by six other states, exercised their right to secede from the United States of America. On February 4, 1861, representatives from Alabama, Florida, Georgia, Louisiana, Mississippi, South Carolina, and Texas met in Montgomery, Alabama to form a new country, the Confederate States of America.

For most Southerners, including Virginians, the issue of slavery was not the critical one but that fact did not preclude strong opinions on the subject. Since the majority of Virginians were not dependent on slaves in their daily lives and pursuits, particularly those in Appalachia and the Shenandoah Valley, the substantive issues were ones of loyalty and autonomy.

Later that same week, the monthly session meeting at the Presbyterian Church in Winchester evolved into a shouting match that paused only when Pastor Graham, who had given up trying to direct their attention back to church business, requested a formal motion to conclude, which was promptly made and seconded. It also required physical prodding on the pastor's part to remove the feuding parties out of the church building into the freezing night air, which he'd hoped would break it up, but, alas, it proved ineffectual.

The contingent upholding "states' rights" was led by Elder Pierce who, above the other voices, vehemently contended, "Of course Virginia will have to secede. Yes, we are part of the South, but, more importantly, Virginia will not stand by and concede to the opinion that the federal government in Washington can dictate on matters belonging to the prerogative of each state. That is what is at stake here, gentlemen!

"Virginia voted to join the Union with the Declaration of Independence from England, written by our own Thomas Jefferson and led to victory by our own George Washington. Neither of these brave men would ever allow Virginia to give up our right to exercise state sovereignty."

"Are you an idiot, man? Do you have any idea what secession would cost us? We do not want a civil war!" shouted Elder Sinclair. "Jefferson and Washington were willing to lay down their lives along with thousands more, representing *every* state, to establish a *united* nation and that is what we Virginians are obligated to support, a WHOLE *nation!* If Virginia refrains from joining the so-called *Confederacy*, those Southern radicals will have to back down. It is the only responsible thing to do to avoid anarchy and bloodshed!"

Their pastor could still hear them a block away as he walked home to the manse. Through articles and essays written by Charles Hodge of Princeton Theological Seminary and James Thornwell, the southern theologian from South Carolina, Paul had followed the debates within the Presbyterian denomination. He agreed with Thornwell that the church should be viewed as a "spiritual body" whose primary aim was in gathering and perfecting of saints" and should not be involved in civil matters, but disagreed with Thornwell that the institution of slavery was validated by a universal or "natural law."

Hodge believed the church had a valid role in influencing the public realm, and, though he abhorred aggressive abolitionist tactics, he advocated a gradual and lawful eradication of slavery. Hodge's views on the subject were more in line with Paul's own thinking, but he was leery of any effort to mix religion and politics. He agreed with both that politics must never threaten the solidarity of the Church but feared the direction the dissenting views were undeniably headed. His peace-loving nature couldn't shake the disquiet and clung to Christ's words that nothing in hell could destroy what He had established.

Paul's distress and sense of ineffectiveness in moderating the dispute within his own session, along with his own uneasiness, was summarily heightened when a match was struck in Charleston harbor on April 12th. After federal troops were not withdrawn from forts located in the seven Confederate states, the South Carolina Militia, commanded by General Beauregard, attacked Fort Sumter outside the city of Charleston and captured it.

The line drawn in the sand had been crossed, and on April 15th, Lincoln called for 75,000 volunteers to suppress the rebellion. His aggressive action prompted four more southern states, including Virginia, to secede and join the Confederacy. And it was on the grounds of *"coercion,"* according to the minutes of the meeting of delegates at the Secession Convention in Richmond, the vote to secede was cast on April 17th.

On the day news spread to Lexington, the cheering students of Washington College lowered the flag of the Union and raised the Confederate banner. Among them were a number of VMI cadets, including the exuberant David Graham.

Four days later Major Thomas Jackson marched the cadets to Fort Lee outside Richmond where the Confederate Army recruits were gathering for training.

The choosing of sides spread its divisive destruction not only within the country, states, and churches but also within families. In late May, Paul received a letter from his son Harry in Princeton, New Jersey.

Dear Papa,

Let me begin by expressing my apology for negligence in writing regularly. As you are well aware, my attention has always been narrowly focused, originally on my studies and now, as the youngest and newest instructor in my Department, proving my worth to my esteemed colleagues and undergraduate students. Let me assure you, dear Papa, that my negligence does not reflect lack of regard for you and the rest of the family.

I also assure you that I am well and so very thankful to have achieved what I set out to do. I find I am well suited for the life I have chosen and am also inexpressibly thankful for the preparation you gave me at home.

With the egregious actions taken by the Virginia Legislature, my concerns for you and the family have prompted me to put pen to paper. Our family has always taken a stand in opposition to slavery despite Virginia's acceptance of its practice, and, up to this time, I have been comforted in the belief that you have been able to persuade your church and community of the evils of the institution, and even the toleration of it.

As you may or may not know, at the recent General Assembly of our denomination the eminent Dr. Gardiner Spring's Resolutions were passed, and, although Princeton Theological Seminary's own Dr. Charles Hodge spoke out against it, it is up to us all to support Dr. Spring and his efforts to promote the unity of our nation under the Federal Government and the Constitution, as he so eloquently states, '… in the spirit of Christian patriotism.'

My deepest concerns are for your safety and the need for you to identify yourselves with the forces rallying to keep the Union inviolate. Therefore, I entreat you now to come to Princeton and bring my brothers and sister with you. You and Ben will find opportunities for ministry more in accord with your own righteous cause, and the younger boys' military training will be much valued in the Army of the Potomac. My young sister, I am quite sure, will be completely satisfied just to have us all together.

The Lord upholds the righteous, and the wickedness and rebellion spreading through the southern states will soon be defeated. I can see no just cause that would hold you there any longer. I hope soon to hear from you that you have taken my counsel and will presently be with me here.

Your devoted son,
Henry Paul Graham

Paul read the letter over twice before laying it aside. It grieved and troubled him in ways he initially didn't comprehend. His first clear deduction was that Harry had no deep knowledge of his family since he'd left for the College of New Jersey at Princeton at age sixteen, yet he presumed to have great insight into their hearts and minds.

And, though Paul had faithfully sent monthly letters giving him encouragement and family news, there were months with no response. The very few he'd received only concerned Harry himself with no expression of interest in the family. As far as Paul was aware, Harry had never written to his siblings.

Along with all ordained Presbyterian ministers, Paul received a copy of Dr. Spring's proposed *Resolutions* and wasn't entirely surprised it had passed. Since the North was more heavily populated, there were more Presbyterian churches than in the primarily rural South. If he had gone to the General Assembly in Philadelphia, he would have voted against it not only because he did not believe the Church should submit to any government but because he knew what the reaction would be–an inevitable rift. Paul doubted Harry had even considered these things.

In complete honesty, Paul acknowledged his first response to the missive was one of resentment and promptly prayed for forgiveness. He then chose to believe Harry wrote it with the best of intentions rather than from fear of what his colleagues would think of him with a family loyal to the South.

Regardless of his initial reaction and in good conscience, Paul was forced to seriously consider the possibility that Harry could be right. Paul had no personal convictions whether patriotic loyalties should lie with the federal government or the state, but he *did* regarding the practice of slavery. He had read William Wilberforce's *A Letter on the Abolition of the Slave Trade* and several pamphlets written by Lewis and Arthur Tappan in the 1830's, stirring up the controversy of censoring "inflammatory" literature circulated by mail.

Above the Mason-Dixon there was generally more tolerance for strong abolitionist sympathies, although Paul had heard of violent opposition against the leaders, including the Tappan brothers. And there was work, perhaps even with the clandestine activities of the Underground Railroad, that Abby, Annabel, and he could support.

Nevertheless, even if he could, Paul wouldn't dictate his children's lives. All four were mature enough to make their own decisions no matter how much he might want to protect them. He'd given them all the intellectual and spiritual training and resources available, and he must leave them under the Lord's almighty care and infallible wisdom.

In fairness, he would make them aware of Harry's request, but, knowing his children, Paul had no doubt their choice would be to stay in Virginia. Even Abby, with her fierce antislavery ethos, would never go. And he was proud of them all.

In mid-June Paul responded back to Harry, telling him the family would be staying in Virginia. *"I do not profess to understand Divine Providence, but it is my conviction that the Lord has sovereignly positioned each of us in a place of service, and in complete confidence and faith, we will remain at our stations. We covet your prayers for strength and obedience to do His good pleasure."*

It was no surprise when a reply never came.

When Harry read his father's response to his appeal, he was stung with hurt and incredulity. *Were they so enmeshed in the virulent culture of the South they were beyond redemption? Didn't they know Princeton was the Mecca of American Presbyterianism? Why would they not appreciate such inducements to avail themselves of the intellectual and cultural advantages of Princeton Theological Seminary, to sit under the teaching of Alexander McGill, William Henry Green, and the internationally respected Charles Hodge?*

Harry accepted the fact of his intellectual superiority over his father and siblings, but *how could they possibly be so pitifully obtuse and still be related to him?*

These were his first insoluble questions that left him with the admittedly feeble conclusion that he was solely his mother's child, a *Spencer* not a Graham, with highborn aptitude and expectations, though it required a disregard of the adverse implications of identifying with relations who represented every ignoble quality and practice he purported to abhor. Nonetheless, it was the only explanation he could divine and gave his wounded soul some measure of consolation. *To hell with them!*

Twenty-six-year-old Henry Paul Graham had lived the last ten years, years he considered the best in his life, in the enclave of Princeton, New Jersey. He was one of many sons of the South who matriculated to it's hallowed halls of learning; though he could not acknowledge it, he was one of the most conflicted.

He adamantly and invariably chose to align himself with critics of the South regardless of their agenda, and he had been one of the organizers behind the Society of Inquiry that became the Alexander Missionary, Theological, and Literary Society of Princeton Theological Seminary. Their inaugural discussion in October 1859 was "Ought Slavery to be Abolished?"

The topic was prompted by the current events at Harpers Ferry, and Harry had high expectations for a weighty discussion, but his hopes for a compelling debate by impassioned future moral and religious leaders of the nation were disappointed. Granted, the overwhelming consensus was an affirmative one, but the students' apathy was palpable, and feedback consisted of requests for a more interesting topic. Harry was utterly disgusted, refused to participate in subsequent meetings, and expressed only indifference when the society petered out, a victim of general insouciance.

It perplexed him no end that the community of theologians and scholars could not be drawn into what he considered THE issue of the day. He himself was driven by a need to push the matter forward whenever an opportunity presented itself, but he was seldom satisfied. His colleagues were unabashed in admitting that insurrections like the one John Brown had initiated were more dangerous to the stability of the nation than the current status of slavery and would not favor any action entailing or leading to societal disorder. Most were opposed to the owning of slaves but firmly espoused an end to the practice by the progressive, organic spread of the gospel.

Was he the only academic who understood that slavery was a blot on the soul of the nation? Couldn't they see that slavery propagated by the South was as evil as the "abomination that maketh desolate" referenced by the prophets Ezekiel and Daniel?

The demonstration by northern students the month before, raising the national flag over Nassau Hall, was somewhat encouraging to Harry before the exodus of southern students from campus, but the overall effect was ephemeral. Charles Hodges's protest of "the Gardiner Spring Resolution" at the General

Assembly felt like a betrayal that Harry took personally. In his mind, the South and slavery were synonymous, and he was intolerant of everything supportive of or smacking of sympathy toward the South. And above all, he was intent on dissociating himself from the fortuitous site of his birth.

Also in June, Paul received another letter, this one from his brother Seth with the sad news of Corrine's death.

'I do not know how you've survived all these years without your dear wife, brother. Corrine has been gone a month and my life now seems so very disorientated. If it were not for the boys and my medical practice, I should go mad. There is a free Negro woman named Naomi who comes to clean and cook, and without that help, we would likely not subsist at all.

The boys appear to feel much the same, particularly Cullen, whom Corrine seemed to carry in her hand basket, and they are finding the world without her hard to manage. Corbin has always been very solicitous of Cullen but now even more so. Sometimes I wonder if Corbin ever has a feeling entirely his own, his being so intertwined with his twin. It is as though they are but two divided parts of the same being.

The thoughts of war also plague me greatly. What can be worth tearing families apart? What is to become of us all?"

Paul immediately wrote a note of encouragement, assuring Seth that his own life was a testament to the trustworthiness of the Lord's promise to sustain His children through bereavement. He would have liked to personally offer support with a visit but was expecting Abby home from Staunton, and they had plans to return to Richmond the end of the month for the VMI graduation exercise of the Class of 1861 at Fort Lee.

Both Abby and Paul had endeavored to convince Annabel to travel with them but to no avail.

"I don' like all that train ridin.' I like to stay rat wheah the good Lawd put me an' that's rat heah! You tell those sweet boys ol' Annabel loves um and be prayin' fo' um ever' day! Tell um ta be real good boys and be careful too! They're ma own sweet babies." With a plaintive sniffle, she wiped the tears on the corner of her apron.

On July 3rd, Paul and Abby made the journey, and as the train drew nearer the Richmond depot, Paul noted Abby's anxious silence.

"Are you feeling all right, my dear?"

Under his solicitous gaze, her eyes filled with tears, which she hastily brushed away.

"I am all right, Papa," she assured him. "I am just thinking about the first time we came, and what we saw. Sometimes I dream about it, but I still do not know what I can do to help them."

Her hand moved involuntarily to the shoulder that had taken the whip's blow, and her voice faded into a whisper.

Paul, with a deep sigh, took her hand. "Nothing has changed that I am aware of. But I am glad to know, despite your distress, you still remember the terrible things you witnessed. It is something about which no one with a healthy conscience should ever be at ease or ever forget."

They were met at the depot by Ben and shared his tiny one-room domicile at the boarding house that night. There were no rooms to be had in Richmond with the influx of military and civil personnel, and without the accommodations Ben offered, the Grahams, as well as other families arriving for the graduation, would be driving in for the day.

"You know this war is the last thing any of us want, Papa, but I feel it is my duty to make a contribution," Ben announced after a light supper. "I have been assisting Dr. Hoge, who was appointed as chaplain to Camp Lee, as well as attending my duties at the church, but have been thinking of signing on as a full-time chaplain to one of the local regiments. I have been waiting until I could talk to you about it first though."

"It would not be right to discourage your sense of duty, Ben, and I will not if you believe it is what the Lord has called you to assume. Since I have never been in the military, I cannot give you first-hand advice on what you should expect, but I would imagine it would be challenging, not only the lifestyle of a soldier, which would be hard enough, but offering encouragement in the face of death, ministering to the wounded, and burying the dead. It will not be parade bands and cheering crowds like it is now. Have you thought about these things?"

"Yes, sir, though I admit it is all, as yet, theoretical. But I cannot in good conscience know that other men and their families are making sacrifices to protect Virginia and I am not willing to do so."

Ben's demeanor indicated he had something else on his mind, and Paul nodded and waited.

"The primary reason this is a difficult decision to make is… I want to marry, Papa."

Ben watched a broad smile crease his father's face and sighed with relief.

"Her name is Fiona MacLaren, and she and her family are members of our church. We love each other dearly, but I have been hesitant to ask her father for his permission before talking to you and being assured of your blessing."

Abby, who had been listening with mixed emotions regarding her brother's decision to join the army, was thoroughly enthused at the prospect of gaining a sister-in-law.

"Oh Ben, how marvelous! When may we meet Fiona and her family? Must we wait until Sunday?"

"Yes, I thought it would be better to wait until after all the graduation formalities and festivities tomorrow in hopes the boys would be able to join us for morning worship. The MacLarens have invited our whole family to share Sunday dinner with them, if you are agreeable," he added, turning to his father.

"I would be delighted to accept their kind invitation and look forward to meeting them." Paul was still smiling as his reminisces led him back to his courtship days, and he hoped Fiona's family was more receptive to Ben than Rosemary's had been to him.

All but the younger cadets left to guard the arsenal at Lexington and had come to Fort Lee in April. Jackson, promoted to the rank of colonel, was currently stationed at Harpers Ferry under General Joseph Johnston, but had returned briefly to Richmond for the graduation exercise.

The 185 cadets Jackson brought to Richmond had been given

responsibility for the training and drilling of volunteers pouring into the city, but some were also dispatched to perform this invaluable service to recruits gathering in other parts of the state. The Graham brothers and Edmund were among those who'd remained at Fort Lee.

Abby hadn't seen Edmund since leaving Vermillion two years before, and she arrived for the ceremony on her father's arm with a mixture of anticipation and apprehension. Wearing the blue linen day gown and garden hat she'd worn on the day they met, she sat between her father and Ben as seventeen cadets received a diploma and a commission as an officer in the Confederate Army. Fifteen of the graduates were commissioned as 1st lieutenants, but as the top cadets in their class, Edmund Claiborne and George Graham were awarded the rank of captain. The 2nd and 3rd classmen had been granted the rank of 2nd lieutenants in a separate enlistment ceremony the day before.

At the reception following the graduation ceremony, the two young captains jostled their way through the high-spirited crowd, and while still several yards away, Edmund caught Abby's eye and smiled. Before she could return it, Geordie engulfed her in his arms, and it was several moments before he let her go to embrace Ben and their father, who had not let go of Davy.

"I was hoping you would come, Abby. You have grown up since I last saw you," Edmund greeted her, giving her an appreciative sweep with his deep blue eyes. She didn't offer her hand and he barely could resist the temptation to reach for it.

"I am pleased to see you again, Edmund… and very proud of Geordie and you today." There was much more she wanted to ask, to say, but found herself tongue-tied.

Edmund seemed to be affected with the same reserve, and they stood smiling shyly and dumbly staring at each other, noting and admiring the changes two years had effected. At sixteen she had a more feminine figure requiring some letting out of seams in her dress and, while still slender, she'd gained almost two inches in height, peaking at five feet, three inches. Aware of his scrutiny, the color in her cheeks deepened but she held her head up and met his gaze.

She was even more beautiful than he remembered, though he preferred her mass of rich brown hair loose than neatly secured in a chignon under her hat as it was now. And having read the letter she'd written to Geordie describing her first trip to Richmond, he recognized the loss of innocence in the depths of her whiskey-colored eyes.

Abby noted the addition of muscular strength in Edmund's build, which now matched his height and frame. He was almost six-feet and carried himself well, as a soldier, an officer, engendering trust and respect. And the look he was giving her now exposed a tender side that pleased her more than she wanted to admit. It was far better to consider the other as a friend and nothing more, and she wished she could convince herself to believe it.

They were still mutely smiling at one another when Edmund's father approached, and the polite exchanges relieved the silent inhibition.

"Fetch the young lady some refreshments, son," Cecil Claiborne pointedly suggested when the formalities were complete, and Edmund gallantly complied, followed by Geordie and Davy whose appetites were aroused at the thought of food.

"Reverend Graham, I want to take the opportunity to confess my shame to you and your daughter for the way she was treated in my home. I regret not taking a vocal stand at the time to accept Edmund's assertions of her blamelessness and put the whole matter at rest. The situation was exaggerated entirely out of proportion, and I would very much appreciate your acceptance of my belated but most sincere apology."

"My daughter and I forgave and forgot long ago, sir. But your apology is acknowledged and accepted," Paul assured him, and Abby nodded in agreement. "We both have the highest regard for Edmund and are convinced you have every reason to be as proud of him as we are of Geordie."

Turning his attention to Abby, Cecil said, "Edmund tells me you are attending the female seminary in Staunton and plan to become a teacher. That is commendably ambitious, but surely a lovely young lady's priority is of *domestic* concerns. *Any* woman with average intelligence could be a teacher but only a godly gentlewoman like *you*, my dear, could be the kind of wife and mother a good man should have beside him. *especially* an officer whose duties may require his absence from hearth and home."

Edmund had returned and was standing behind his father, a cup of lemonade in one hand and a plate of sweets in the other, when he caught the look of offended embarrassment on Abby's features. Before he could ask for an explanation, Paul addressed Edmund's unwitting father.

"Forgive me, sir, but I feel obliged to offer my perspective as Abby's father. Whatever the Lord calls us to do here on earth is equally sacred. I have encouraged her, as I have my sons, to consider her calling to teach just as worthy as theirs' to become soldiers… and, in practical terms, no more exclusive of being a wife than a soldier a husband. What is *your* opinion, Edmund?"

Cecil turned to his son with a look of abashed surprise, both at his rapid reappearance and Paul's comment and question.

With his eyes fixed on Abby's, Edmund responded. "I am not certain I understand the question, sir, but if it relates to Abby's plan to teach, I believe she will be a wonderful teacher, married or not. I think *she is* wonderful!"

"I do not wish to be rude, sir," Abby said softly to the older man, averting eye contact with Edmund, "but I think this conversation is perhaps injudiciously timed. We are here to celebrate Edmund and Geordie's graduation and *nothing else* is important today. Do not you agree?"

When there was no immediate riposte, Abby took the cup from Edmund's hand and gave him a tight smile.

"Thank you for your kind remarks, Edmund. And thank you for the refreshments. I am definitely in need of a drink just this minute."

With the reappearance of Geordie and Davy the tension eased considerably and even more so when an announcement was made that photographs of the graduating class were now available. They also were informed the photographer was on hand to take family photographs and additional portraits of the graduates for their family or sweetheart.

The Grahams agreed they would very much appreciate a family photograph and moved forward to get in line. Edmund took advantage of the movement to deftly separate Abby from her family and, leading a short distance away, lay his hands lightly on her shoulders.

"Has my family subjected you to more humiliation, Abby? I encouraged Father to apologize for how you were treated before, but what did he say that offended you?"

"It does not matter, Edmund, and certainly not worthy of your concern, especially today," she answered slowly with a dismissive shake of her head.

He waited until she met his eyes before responding. "If it concerns my intentions toward you, it *does* matter."

She tried to turn away, but he held firmly to her shoulders and waited.

"You are getting ready to go to war and I am going back to college," she explained, stating the obvious as if reasoning with a slow learner. "*Those* impediments, even if there weren't other philosophical considerations, are sufficient reasons to postpone this conversation."

With a sigh Edmund dropped his hands to his sides.

"With the Lord's help the war will soon be won, and then I intend to satisfactorily address all 'philosophical considerations' and dispose of all 'impediments,' including any beliefs you may entertain that I would ever oppose your plans to teach, '*just Abby.*'"

Wrapping her hand through the crook of his arm, he gave a wry smile. "One more thing, please ignore my father's lack of perception and try to forgive him. He has never met anyone like you and is apt to make other obliviously offensive remarks before the end of the day."

His rueful warning made her laugh and they both relaxed, enabling them to enjoy the time they had together. Willfully ignoring the ubiquitous topic of war and confident boasting of military superiority around them, they reestablished the easy camaraderie they'd found in each other's company two years before.

Despite Abby's nagging ambivalence, they both knew the tenuous link between them grew stronger that day. And before they parted, Edmund carried a small tintype photo, safely guarded in a hinged case, of an impish-eyed Abby inside his shell jacket, and Abby clutched one of a dignified and unsmiling Captain Edmund Jefferson Claiborne, CSA.

When he gave it to her, Edmund explained that the exchange of photos amounted to a "promise." This unfamiliar ritual initially caused her to reconsider, but ultimately submitting to his appeal and Geordie's persuasion, Abby gave him the tintype of her likeness and a tentative promise to answer the letters he would write to her directly.

After the morning worship service, Ben introduced his family to John and Ellen MacLaren and their daughter Fiona, and an hour later all were seated in the spacious dining room. Before dinner was served, Ben had privately requested and received John's blessing to marry Fiona, and the conversation around the table was lively and amiable.

"May I say that you have been blessed with fine children, Reverend Graham," John said to Paul as dessert was served. "And we are grateful in anticipation of sharing familial ties with you, with Ben and Fiona's upcoming marriage. He has often talked lovingly about his family, and I can now appreciate his fondness for you all."

"Thank you, sir. We do not take our Lord's mercies for granted and they are truly abundant," replied Paul. "We are also grateful to you for your consideration of Ben while he has been away from home. We have greatly missed him."

Paul's eyes filled, and his smile became wistful. He reached for Abby's hand and rested his gaze on Geordie and Davy across the table. "It is a bittersweet joy to watch each one of my five children leave home to prepare for and fulfill their calling. I am learning day by day to entrust them to the Father's care, and, I must admit, it does not seem to be getting easier."

A hush fell over the gathering with the tacit reminder of the looming war.

"Have you decided if you will be volunteering, Ben?" John asked, breaking the silence.

Ben glanced at the dark-haired girl beside him before turning to his host. "I have not made a final decision yet, sir. If you and her mother will agree, Fiona and I would like to marry soon, and if so, it may have a bearing on that decision. I have no wish to leave her at all, but like Geordie and Davy, I cannot refuse to go where I am most needed. The only way I can bear the thought of leaving her is with the knowledge that she can stay here with you, that she would never be alone. She is my treasure, my future."

"Whether you go or stay, I want to be your wife," Fiona said quietly, a tear slowly winding a path down her cheek.

There was another moment of silence before John spoke. "Whether you go or stay, Ben, Ellen and I want you to be our son as you are your father's. There is no doubt a need for strong, orthodox pastors in the midst of war to preach the message of Christ. My only request is that you marry within the month and live here with her *at least* two months before you enlist. I believe she deserves that."

Ben took Fiona's hand and pressed his lips on it, his gaze never leaving her face. "She deserves more than I could *ever* give her. You are *most* gracious, sir, and I… *we* are in your debt. If you are willing to entrust her to *me*, I shall be *humbly grateful* to entrust Fiona back to *you* when it is time for me to go."

CHAPTER 7

SEPTEMBER – DECEMBER 1861

It was two months before Abby received a letter from Edmund, forwarded to her from Winchester to Staunton. The first major battle of the war had been fought near Manassas Junction less than seventy miles east of Winchester and had been, according to the newspaper accounts, a great victory for the Confederacy.

Both brothers and Edmund had been among the troops at Harpers Ferry under the command of, now, Brigadier General Thomas Jackson summoned for the engagement, and Edmund's letter abounded with respect and praise of his leadership.

Dear Abby,

May I tell you how many of my thoughts are of you? If I had the soul of Shakespeare, I would write you a sonnet describing what my heart would like to say, but beside such a master, I am woefully illiterate. I can only tell you in my boyish fashion that thoughts of you give me a sweet ache, now most essential as our days of actual combat have begun.

I cannot begin to tell you with what excitement our brigade arrived at Manassas Junction around noon and immediately was led to where the fighting was in progress. Our orders were to support the troops under the commands of Colonel Bee and Colonel Bartow, whose regiments, under heavy fire, had begun to draw back.

I wish you could have seen General Jackson, Abby. He sat on his horse rallying those troops while we got into our positions. Colonel Bee called him a 'stone wall' and that is what everyone is calling him now!

While we were firing our weapons, I did not even think about what we were doing, we just did as we had been trained. I will not describe what I saw after we stopped because I cannot. It was beyond description, more horrible than I could have ever imagined. Some of the others were crying and I wanted to, but I didn't. Nevertheless, as General Jackson said afterwards, 'we will never forget them'… the ones who died that day.

I always respected him, even when some of the other cadets called him 'Tom Fool.' He had his peculiarities and was strict but also meticulously fair, and he knew what he was talking about.

But today I saw his passion like I never saw it before. He was like some ancient warrior, like Joshua in the Bible. We all saw it and were not afraid to follow him. There was never any doubt of his belief in God, but today we witnessed his faith in action. He never forces his beliefs on anyone, but I cannot help but want that kind of faith that will keep me brave and unafraid, even with bullets flying around. Jackson says we are 'the army of the Lord,' so it must be true.

He has been given another promotion and now is Major General Jackson, in the command of the Valley of Virginia Corps. We should be heading back there soon. In answer to your prayers, Geordie, Davy, and I are safe, and we hope, God willing, to see you either in Winchester or in Staunton.

Geordie has written your papa much of what I have said to you, but it makes me happy to know I am no longer dependent on his letters to feel close to you, my dear girl.

With sincere affection,
Edmund

Before now the war seemed remote, but as Abby held the letter in her hands, she began to tremble. It was *real*, not just words on the pages of the newspaper. *Boys died* and among them could have been her *brothers* or *Edmund* who perished in such violence.

The whole thing was desperately wrong, and it needed to stop. *Wasn't there anyone with sense enough to stop it? How could life go on at the seminary as if it was nothing to worry about?* Abby could appreciate Edmund's respect for his general, but what could *possibly justify killing sons, brothers, loved ones?* It made no sense!

Rather than display the photograph and talk about her "sweetheart" like other girls in the dorm, Abby carried Edmund's likeness in the tintype photo in the pocket of her skirt during the day and hidden under her pillow at night. He was too precious to her to be cheapened by other ogling eyes or shared aloud with curious gossips.

She hadn't given him a formal promise, but she had given him her heart. It was her heart that was now radiating with pain at the thought of Edmund in mortal danger, as well as Geordie and Davy.

Abby had never had a close girlfriend, and even at the seminary among women preparing to teach, she could not achieve social assimilation. Although she considered herself on friendly terms with most classmates, there was no one whom she would consider a confidant. In her state of agitation and worry, she wanted her father who would reassure her, remind her that the sovereign Lord of heaven and earth was in control, and His presence would put her soul at rest again. Closing her eyes, she brought his image to mind.

At age fifty-one, he still was very handsome, though his light brown hair had become even lighter with gray and silver. And she'd noticed that, even with his spectacles on, he had to adjust the page in front of his eyes to read. It delighted her to make him smile; he had such a sweet smile. Papa would tell her to go to the Lord with her heavy heart when she was troubled, and He would *"cover thee with His feathers,"* like the psalmist wrote. Even as a small child she loved that imagery, which she related to the goose-down quilt in her trundle bed.

It was now suppertime at the seminary, and Abby hadn't completed her studies for the day. But exhaustion lay heavily on her, much weightier than that beloved and tattered feather quilt she'd kept for years, and crawling into her dormitory cot, she fell asleep.

Paul continued his monthly missives to Harry, carefully omitting anything controversial, and by November the letters had been reduced to only one page consisting mainly of spiritual encouragement. The only reply Harry sent in response was a short note in October reporting that he had volunteered to act as chaplain for a local New Jersey regiment, but the college had denied his request for leave because he'd had no pastoral experience.

The controversy at Paul's church escalated considerably with the eruption of war, and his efforts to assuage the rifts became less and less effective. Of the seven elders on the session, four were staunch believers in states' rights, two were Unionist with abolition sympathies, and the other seemed to take the side of whomever he was currently consulting.

Even their prayers reflected their cause as the Lord's own. Last Sabbath morning when Elder Sinclair led the congregation in corporate prayer, his passionate petition was that God would "bring judgment on the rebellion as well as an end to slavery in the land," and several worshipers had walked out of the service, including Elder Pierce and his wife Frances.

Paul, having hitherto been sustained with his private study, meditation, and prayer time, hadn't relied on the practice of journaling, but as the complexities of political and moral issues assaulted him, he began one. Writing, he found, seemed to help him think more clearly, and he daily prayed to the Spirit for wisdom he knew he did not possess.

He also sent a letter to the Presbytery of Shenandoah requesting a special meeting with fellow pastors to help one another with similar issues, but as yet he had received no reply. There were almost a dozen churches in the presbytery, the larger ones in Harrisonburg, Staunton, Lexington, and Roanoke.

Annabel continued to funnel food and supplies from and through the manse to the Mennonite farmhouse outside of Winchester, aiding fugitive slaves on their way to Ohio or Pennsylvania. Paul wrestled with his hypocrisy, encouraging her activities yet covering it under a veil of secrecy.

Aiding fugitives was considered an overt act of civil disobedience, and as the pastor living in the manse, Paul had no idea how the discovery would compromise the church and its membership. That was another issue he hoped to discuss at the presbytery meeting without initially admitting active involvement.

In spite of the controversies in his church and his own battles of conscience, Paul daily thanked God for the opportunity to be close to his two youngest sons. Jackson's Valley of Virginia's troops, known as the Stonewall Brigade, were stationed in Winchester to protect the abundant agricultural resources of the Shenandoah Valley and its strategic location north of Washington. When not on patrol the officers were billeted in town and, to Paul's supreme joy, Geordie, Davy, and Edmund were quartered in the manse.

General Jackson, himself, felt safe enough to have his wife Anna join him there and the two became very popular with the inhabitants of the whole community. The Jacksons worshiped at the Presbyterian Church and often ate Sunday dinner at the Graham's table.

Because of her illegal activities, the Jackson's presence initially caused Annabel consternation, though she immediately took a liking to their man Jim Lewis. Paul frequently heard Jim and her laughing together in the manse kitchen where they shared gossip and recipes.

"What if they fin' out wha's *goin' on heah, Pasta?"* she had whispered to Paul the first time the Jacksons came to the manse. However, after several visits, she lost her fears.

"Jim say so, an' ni I know for sho'… the Jacksons are good people. I ain't gonna worry 'bout it no mo', and they kin come ova any time they want to."

As Paul had foreseen, representatives from the Presbyteries in Virginia, Georgia, North Carolina, South Carolina, Alabama, Mississippi, Louisiana, Tennessee, Kentucky, and Texas met in Augusta, Georgia, in early December in response to the Spring Resolutions passed by the General Assembly in May. And on the 4th of December, the Presbyterian Church of the Confederate States of America was officially formed.

This action stirred up fresh controversy in the Winchester church, but the majority ruled with a vote to join the new denomination, and several families left the church in spite of Paul's efforts to maintain peaceful coexistence.

This polemical issue did not seem to affect everyone, and Abby came home from Staunton a few days before Christmas to find the manse bursting with the high spirits of the three young officers and their comrades. Those officers less motivated by the lure of worldly indulgences, but still with a need to ameliorate the homesickness, restlessness, and boredom of "wintering" there, found the manse on Braddock Street a haven of respite.

Abby welcomed the conviviality and seasonal festivities as a refreshing change from the dull routine of the seminary. After the Christmas Eve service ended, Edmund took Abby's arm and, drawing her away, offered to walk with her back to the manse. She had avoided private conversations with him but now agreed it was time.

The service tonight had provided a moment of silent contemplation and peace in which to secure her mental and emotional bearings again. Paul's text had been taken from the ninth chapter of Isaiah, *"For unto us…"* and, in particular, he spoke of the *"Prince of Peace,"* whose government and peace would never end.

Paul had concluded with a prayer written by one of the Puritan Fathers, whom he referred to as "dear old friends."

"*O Source of all good,*
What shall we render to thee for the gift of gifts, thine own dear Son, begotten, not created, my Redeemer, proxy, surety, substitute, his self-emptying incomprehensible, his infinite love beyond heart's grasp….

O God, take us in spirit to the watchful shepherds and enlarge our minds; let us hear good tidings of great joy, and hearing, believe, rejoice, praise, adore, our conscience bathed in an ocean of repose, our eyes lifted to the reconciled Father;

Place us with the ox, ass, camel, goat, to look upon our Redeemer's face, and in him account ourselves delivered from sin; Let us with Simeon, clasp the new-born child to our heart, embracing him in undying faith, exulting that he is our own and we are his.

In him thou hast given us so much that heaven can give no more."

Abby and Edmund walked in silence for several minutes before he asked the question she'd been expecting.

"Why didn't you answer my letters, Abby? I understood you to say you would."

Edmund had written again in October, this one coming directly to her in Staunton, containing fewer war references and more family news, including Caroline's engagement to Senator Mason's son, who was completing his degree at the Lexington Law School with a practicum in the State Attorney's office in Richmond.

His letter also expressed great appreciation for Paul's sermons and that he was *"learning so much more about theology. I especially enjoy the discourse following the service around the table with your papa and the General."*

Abby found the second one less distressing but hadn't recovered from the effects of his first letter.

"I honestly intended to reply, but I did not know what to say or how to say it," Abby answered softly looking up into his face, his features sharpened in the dim light and shadows of the night.

"I do not understand... *cannot* understand how anyone can think killing is *justifiable*. I was afraid for you as well as for Geordie and Davy, afraid not only that you would be killed but what killing would *do* to you."

Confounded, he stopped and considered how to answer.

"You did not answer my letters because you are offended that I am a *soldier?*" he asked, attempting to put a light note in his voice.

"*Who you are* does not offend me, Edmund. *Killing* offends me, just as slavery offends me. To me, they are both reprehensible. Can you honestly say you find *either one* of them inoffensive?"

"I am fighting to defend Virginia and the people I love, including *you*, Abby, *not* because I want to *kill* anyone any more than I want to see my own men torn to pieces. And I am *not* fighting to maintain the institution of slavery but because the bureaucrats in Washington sent their army to invade us. And *YES*, I think killing is offensive and the *Lord knows* I wish it were not necessary!"

There was no attempt at lightness now, as visual memories assaulted his senses. While he spoke, he took her cold hands and they stood linked together, their eyes searching the other's for understanding, for comfort.

It was Edmund who broke the heavy silence. "I respect you and your convictions, Abby, and if you choose not to answer my letters I will at least know *why*. But may I still write you? It would help me to know you care . . . at least just a little."

"I *do* care, Edmund . . . *very* much. And, if it helps to write me, I want you to. But I will not promise to answer them. You will have to believe my spoken words *'I care very much,'* even if they are not in writing."

In spite of her warm woolen cloak, she was trembling with cold and emotion. With just the moon as witness, he drew her into his arms and held her until the shivering stopped and he felt her body relax against his. Then he kissed her, and when she responded with equal urgency, was overwhelmed with sweet relief. The wall between them still stood, but it was breached with a large crack down the middle.

CHAPTER 8

SPRING 1862

Following Abby's return to Staunton, Jackson and his Stonewall Brigade enjoyed a relatively peaceful winter patrolling the Shenandoah Valley until March when they met General Bank's army just south of Winchester in Kernstown. After several more skirmishes, Jackson strategically moved his troops south to repulse General Fremont's forces attempting to cross over the Allegany Mountains from the west.

As they came through Staunton, Geordie sent a message urging Abby to meet them at the depot while supplies were being loaded.

"ABBY!" Geordie shouted, catching sight of her tartan cloak in the crowded station. Elbowing his way through, followed closely by Edmund and Davy, he reached her side and hugged her tightly.

"Where are you going?" she demanded, still trying to catch her breath as she returned the embrace.

"Wherever we are told to go," Davy answered, after planting a kiss on her flushed cheek. "We had to leave Bank's boys in Front Royal while we take care of another bunch of invading Yanks trying to sneak into the Valley. Do not worry though We will find them and run them off!"

Her eyes met Edmund's with a mix of anxiety and rebuke, and he gave her a wary smile.

"I . . . we are glad you came, Abby. We were not sure you would get the message in time. We won't be staying long."

"Of course I came!" she vehemently interjected. "I was concerned you might be *hurt* or something. I am relieved to find you are not."

Turning the same piercing look on Geordie, she shook her head in exasperation. "The three of you are ridiculous. I thought you said the war would not last long. It has been nearly a year since you have been playing at this and it *needs to stop!*"

The three uniformed soldiers reacted instantly to her words, but it was Davy who voiced their mutual indignation.

"What do you mean *'playing at this'*? Do you have *any idea what is going on?* We have not been *playing,* Abby! *War is damn serious, so please do not patronize or demean what we are trying to do here!*"

Geordie took her hand, though his eyes retained a look of injury. "I admit we were overly optimistic in the beginning, but we have the best generals and we *are* winning. You mustn't worry, Abby. The Lord will take care of us, and when it is all over, we will come back home to you."

A loud whistle sounded, orders were shouted, and fear choked her so that she could not speak.

"We must go now. I love you, Abby." Geordie gave the hand he held a light kiss and disappeared through the crowd, Davy following on his heels.

Without giving her time to resist, Edmund performed a swift maneuver that encircled her in his arms, and thoroughly kissed her parted lips.

"*I love you, too, Abby Graham,*" he whispered and then was gone.

Abby stood looking after him, with the feel of his mouth, the taste of him still remaining. Angry tears filled her eyes, and she whispered through clinched teeth, *"You bloody boys!* It *serve you right* if you *did get shot to pieces!"*

Three days later, Abby regretted those words. Davy was badly wounded by an exploding cannon near the small town of McDowell and transported from the field to the new hospital on Beverly Street in Staunton. Hurrying to his side, she found him wrapped in bandages, and in deep depression at the loss of his left leg above the knee.

"How do you feel, Davy?" she asked warily. "I am so very sorry this has happened to you."

"How do you THINK I am feeling?" the patient broke in with a

snarl. "It hurts like *HELL!*"

"Well, I *said* I am sorry for it. There is no need to snap at me."

"Yes there is! I know what you think of our efforts to protect the Valley. You made it perfectly clear that you have no regard for or appreciation of the danger we face trying to protect *ingrates like you!* I do not need your pity now that I cannot go back in the fight. Just go on back to your nice, *safe* little cloister while boys like me are blown to hell and spare me your *hypocrisy*," he added bitterly and turned his face away.

Swallowing hard, Abby fought back tears of sorrow and guilt. Though she lamented her remark at the depot, she did not believe she should be held responsible for her brother's crippling injury. *Hadn't she tried to warn them?* She just could not bear to see him suffer and had no idea what she could do to relieve it.

Faced with her brother's agony, the reality of the war's offenses now became dreadfully personal to Abby, and without full consciousness of her action, she clutched the small tintype photo in her pocket. *Please, dear God, stop this madness before the other two get mutilated – or killed!*

Since Christmas, Abby had been struggling with the restless agitation of feeling useless. Augusta Female Seminary was a private college and had managed to remain operating during the war while most of the male-only state colleges had closed. She was experiencing mounting conviction that she should be doing *something* even if she didn't possess the same blind patriotism of everyone else around her, another disparity that marked her as a misfit among her classmates.

The restlessness began earlier in the year with the conviction that her instructors had imparted all the wisdom and knowledge they had to offer. Though there were only a few more weeks remaining until her graduation, Davy's injuries provided the motivation she lacked to pack up and leave. So, despite the threats of more battles in the valley, Abby escorted Davy home to Winchester.

The two were barely settled in the manse when Jackson's troops were reinforced with General Richard Ewell's divisions and marched north to capture the Federal garrison at Front Royal, forcing General Banks north toward Winchester. The Valley of Virginia's forces pursued and met them there on May 25th.

When the first shouts of warning were heard, many of the neighboring residents, business owners, and their customers, as well as the occupants of the manse, gathered for an impromptu prayer meeting in the Presbyterian church basement. Davy had hastily been carried from the manse on a folding metal cot that now rested between Annabel and Abby. The faces around the room reflected a common aspect of terror as the sound of artillery blasts shook the ground, drowning out the minister's urgent petitions.

Each time a mortar burst and shook the walls, Davy clutched Abby's hand as the sound itself brought back traumatic visions to his over-stimulated brain. Then, mortified by his display of panic, he let her go, interpolating, "I should be *out there fighting with them*. I wish I were *with them now!*"

"I for one am glad I am *not!*" his sister retorted irritably after extracting her hand from his grip the fifth time. "And please spare me your *idiotic* sentiments."

"*This is utterly intolerable!*" she hissed to Annabel when the worst seemed to have blown over and the church mercifully still stood.

"Ain't that the gospel truff," was the low, grumbling reply between gasps. "I don' like all that shootin' an *boomin'* but I don' like bein' down heah in the *black dark* much *neitha! I don' like bein' shudup unda the groun' in the dark. If they don' lemme outa heah soon, I'm gonna go ravin' mad!*"

Joe Sturgis, the new church sexton, was the first to emerge from the shelter, followed by Annabel gulping air. Paul later reported to the manse evacuees that Jackson's army had routed the enemy, who were now running for the Potomac. During their flight through town, Colonel Donnelly's whole regiment was chased past the church down Loudoun Street, which accounted for the chaos and exchange of artillery fire they had heard at close range.

After securing the valley, Jackson's exhausted troops returned for a brief stopover in Winchester enabling Geordie and Edmund to spend the free time they were given at the manse. Edmund joined Geordie's efforts to raise Davy's deflated spirit but kept his primary focus on their sister.

During the late winter months Edmund had written Abby twice and in the second had shared the news of his father's death. It seemed important to him to have her comfort and there hadn't been time on the march through Staunton three weeks before. Finding Abby sitting alone on the front porch, he joined her.

"We will be leaving early tomorrow, Abby, but so much has happened and is still happening so quickly, we have not had the time for a private conversation. It surprised me to know you left the seminary when you were so close to graduating. Is it too late to go back now?"

"I was ready to leave and have no regrets. I learned everything they could teach me, and I want to start teaching *now*."

She looked up at him and remembered. "I am so *very sorry* about your father's death, Edmund."

She stood and took his hand. Gratified, he reached for her other hand with his free one so that she faced him.

"I confess I never had as high a regard for him as I do for the general and *your* father, but I loved him and regret not having the close relationship the boys and you have with yours," he admitted wistfully.

"You rarely talk about your family, at least to me," she commented quietly. "I hope *I* was not the cause of any estrangement between you."

He shook his head with a deep sigh, stroking the back of her hands with his thumbs, craving more of the familial comforts and camaraderie he'd found in her family circle. *Abby*, he was convinced, *had no idea how much he needed her touch, especially so as the war dragged on and kept them apart. Did she need him as he needed her?*

"I honestly cannot remember feeling the closeness to my family like you Grahams have, and I know it is because of your wonderful papa. I hope all four of you know how blessed you are."

She nodded with a pensive smile. Edmund had never met

Harry and she accepted without comment that their oldest brother seemed to have faded from the family circle like a ghost.

"I am not convinced Davy knows, but the rest of us certainly do. I hope my being home will, at least, be a blessing to *Papa*. He has given me permission to use the church basement for my school again... if there are any Negro children to teach. Annabel tells me that most of the mama's are afraid to let their children out of their sight now."

"You can teach white children, Abby. With your education you will be in demand by wealthy families wanting you to teach their children."

"*Negro* children need a teacher *too*, Edmund. If I could, I would open a school for Negros, both free and enslaved. No one should be enslaved, and no one should be denied the privileges and the joys of reading and writing."

"After the war, I would like to see things improve for the Negros. Since we have been forced into this war, maybe good can come from it, but we have *got* to win it first."

"The *only* good thing I could see coming out of it is total, legal abolition of slavery. You say you are fighting for Virginia and not to protect the institution of slavery, but it is the *same thing!*"

"Please, Abby, let's not argue about this again. I leave tomorrow to fight those who have invaded Virginia and are, at this very moment, converging on Richmond. I do not want to fight you too!"

Edmund's voice had risen but became gentle and pleading as he continued. "I love you, Abigail Graham, and I want your promise you will marry me when this war is over. Will you?"

"You also said you *respect* me, but how can I believe you? You do not want me to teach Negro children, and *they* are the ones I am called to teach. And I *know* you would disapprove of what I have done... and will *continue* to do to help fugitive slaves."

She watched the changes of expression on his face that settled into an intense frown.

"*Abby!* Teaching free Negros is enough of a legal risk! *Do you know what would happen if you were caught helping a slave escape?* And what consequences there could be for your father and brother? How can you say you care about *them*… about *me* and *do something like that?"* he demanded in an intense whisper.

"How can it be reasonable for you to willingly put *your* life in jeopardy for *your* cause and it not be reasonable for *me* to do the *same?* If you care about *me*, why not abandon the war and help me with *my* cause?"

He stood speechlessly searching her fathomless golden eyes, desperately looking for a way to reach her again. Abby, with a look of aggrieved consternation, stared back, and abruptly pulling her hands from his clasp, clinched them at her sides.

Did she really expect him to desert the army if he wanted to marry her? This lovely – yes, she was stunningly beautiful with fire in her eyes–woman he loved was stubborn as a pig-headed mule, and she was breaking his heart!

As he watched, the fire in her eyes was extinguished with the flooding of tears and she said softly but with conviction, "I could *never* be the wife you want me to be, Edmund. I am sorry, but I cannot give you the promise you want."

CHAPTER 9

JUNE 1862

There were several contributing factors in Abby's decision to leave Winchester. Besides the disruptive madness reigning in the town, "madness" had also infused the quiet manse now under the tyrannical domination of her brother Davy, who, although his burns and amputation site still caused him considerable pain, suffered the more serious wounds of the spirit.

Abby's relationship with Davy, although loving and loyal, had always been tinged with remnants of resentment held by Davy since her birth. Through no fault of her own, she had robbed him of his mother's coveted attention, and, though he recognized its unreasonable basis and succeeded in suppressing it most of the time, the loss of his limb appeared to have sparked the smoldering ashes.

Trying to please him became an exercise in futility, and Abby quickly tired of it. Her own restless spirit, grievously unsettled by her parting with Edmund and her disappointed plans to teach, balked at the designated role of scapegoat, and her father's admonition to practice patience and tolerance only added to her sense of culpability and list of failures.

She wanted to teach, but many of the free Negros had migrated north of the Mason-Dixon since the start of the war, and interest in sending the remaining children to school was demonstrably limited. In addition to the terror of battles raging through the streets, there had been instances of children being kidnapped and presumably sold to plantation owners further south, and everyone lived in a state of high alert.

The triggering event leading to Abby's departure came soon

after Jackson led his troops south to Cross Keys and then Port Republic before heading east to Richmond where he was urgently needed to help General Lee's army defend the capital city. Although Winchester residents seemed to be breathing a sigh of relief following Jackson's decisive victory in May, there remained the disquietude of ambivalence over the troops' departure. There was both relief they were gone and fearful regret due to the lack of protection.

It was past midnight, and Abby was asleep when she was wakened by Annabel's gentle shake. She carried no candle, and the room remained in darkness as Annabel whispered that she was to come, and without hesitating, she quietly obeyed.

Still in darkness, Abby silently followed Annabel through the back door, across the yard, and into the unlit cabin where she discerned a form huddled on the floor and instinctively knelt beside the trembling figure. It was a thin Negro woman with a swollen belly.

Squatting down on the woman's other side, Annabel explained in muted tones that the young woman, named Maisy, had reached the Bowers' farm but was unable to go further due to extreme weariness and her impending labor. Mr. Bower, the Mennonite farmer and Annabel's contact in aiding fugitive slaves, had urged her to hide Maisy at the manse until she was able to travel on.

It only took moments for Abby's brain to realize that harboring the fugitive placed her family at an increased level of perilous involvement. Davy wasn't aware of Annabel's and her activities as "*good Samaritans*" and, in his current condition, he would likely be less than sympathetic to the cause. There was no time to lose, and Abby made up her mind to act.

"It will be all right, Maisy," Abby whispered to the only perceptible feature of the dark face, the whites of terrified eyes. We are going to help you reach a place of freedom . . . freedom for you and your baby."

While Annabel sat with Maisy, Abby returned to her bedroom and packed a carpetbag, washed, dressed in the worn blue day gown, and tiptoed into her father's room. Kneeling beside his bed she woke him and explained the situation and her plan. With just a nod Paul rose, and she left him there to dress and meet her below.

The sun was barely over the horizon when Paul hitched the buggy and drove to the depot where he purchased two tickets to Harpers Ferry on the Winchester & Potomac line.

Casually explaining to the stationmaster that his daughter, accompanied by a servant, would be visiting his brother in Boonsboro, he inquired about a coach at Harpers Ferry that could drive them the eighteen miles there.

Hurrying back to the manse, he returned with Abby and Maisy and waited until the train disappeared down the tracks with the women safely on board. He had acted on instinct but now was left with the gripping fear of the perils Abby was facing. *Why hadn't he gone instead of her?*

He sincerely wished he had, but the truth of the matter was that *he was the one who taught and encouraged her to act on her convictions, not just profess them.* True acts of Christian charity always involved sacrifice–to walk by faith rather than sight. Just as he had entrusted his sons, he must entrust his daughter to their Heavenly Father's care.

On the journey, Abby did her best to credibly play the role of slaveholder, repressing her own inclination to attend her companion. Maisy sat quietly looking as miserable as she felt, and Abby considered it a miracle they were able to reach their destination without attracting suspicion.

After disembarking at Harpers Ferry, it took longer than Abby hoped to find a coach to carry them the rest of the journey to Boonsboro and it was late afternoon when they arrived. Once there, Abby had no trouble getting directions to "Doc" Douglas's house and surgery, a sprawling two-storied dwelling on the east side of town.

By the time the door opened in response to her knock, Abby was bodily supporting Maisy and was thankful when, without a word, the large, grimed-faced Negro woman deftly took Maisy's weight. The woman whom Abby surmised was Naomi led them to a small office, loudly calling, "Doc! You is needed *ri' ni!*"

The door inside the office opened and a look of surprised hesitancy gradually cleared as Seth recognized his niece.

"Abby? My, my, haven't you grown into a spit image of your mama! What are you doing here?"

Disregarding trivialities and pushing Maisy gently forward, she jumped right to the point. "Her labor pains have started, Uncle Seth. Will you help her?"

"Certainly," Seth replied brusquely, motioning with a nod to Naomi who followed him into the adjoining room and laid Maisy unceremoniously on the surgery table as Abby retreated to the front parlor.

Numb with exhaustion after the sleepless night and a day of travel, Abby had fallen asleep in a worn upholstered rocker but woke with a start when she felt a hand on her arm. Blinking several times in an effort to remember where she was, she found herself looking into a pair of gray eyes, crinkled at the corners as a broad smile lit his face.

"Are you Cullen or Corbin?" she asked, realizing belatedly she would not be getting a response.

"That would be Corbin," Uncle Seth's voice settled the question and he stepped out of his office wiping his hands with a towel. "Cullen is in the kitchen on nursery duty with the new arrival and the new mother is sleeping. I warned Corbin not to wake you, but the pleasure of your appearance seems to have overruled his good manners. Nevertheless, giving him benefit of the doubt, I believe he wants you to know it is time to eat."

"Are Maisy and her baby all right?" Abby wanted to know as she stood up to stretch and shake the wrinkles out of her gown.

"Right as rain," he assured her. "I am afraid our supper has gotten cold, but it is still on the table so let us eat. Cullen ate his earlier so he could cuddle the baby. He's always loved babies."

With a sigh he lowered himself into the chair at the head of the table and beckoned her to sit beside him as Corbin took the bench-seat opposite her.

After a brief prayer of thanks and several mouthfuls of barely warm stew, Seth picked up his initial inquiry.

"I heard about the ruckus in Winchester. Is that why you came? Did you all survive?"

"Everyone has been mercifully spared. I think Papa wrote to you about Davy who is home now, but Geordie is with General Jackson headed to Richmond."

She hesitated to say more, not entirely sure where his loyalties lay, sometimes not even her own. "Davy is morosely *wretched* and there is not much anyone can do about it. Papa is trying to keep the church from splitting, but, other than that, he is well and sends his love."

She paused to chew on a tough piece of stew meat and consider her words before going on. "You most likely know that much of the trouble in our church is over slavery, which Papa and I believe is wrong."

"Your church is not the only one having those problems, but is that why he wanted you to come here? Have you been *threatened*?" he asked as his anxiety rose. Corbin who'd been intently watching their faces responded with the same look of apprehension.

"No... oh, no. We have never been threatened, but we have tried to be... very cautious," she finished, searching his face for clues of his reaction. "What are *your* feelings about slavery, Uncle Seth?"

"Well, as for myself, I am not going to bother arguing with any fool trying to tell me what I *ought* to think about it. But my opinion is pretty much in line with your papa's, that I never would presume to own another human being. As a Christian and a humanitarian, I do not believe in mistreating any of God's creatures, man or animal. Is that what you're asking?"

"Yes, but how far would you go to help another human being... to be *free?*"

Seth was quiet as he contemplated and discerned the relevant meaning behind her questions.

"As a physician I will never refuse to treat anyone who needs medical attention. That is the oath I took when I became a doctor, and why I provided help to the poor woman you brought here today. But that is not all you're asking is it, girl? You want to know if I would *knowingly* assist a fugitive slave, and that is a question I never had to answer… before today, that is."

Seth pushed his empty plate away, and taking a pipe from his vest pocket, reached for the pouch of tobacco and box of matches on the sideboard behind him. Leisurely and silently he filled the pipe, lit it, and savored his first inhalation. Practicing the quiet patience she lacked with Davy, Abby waited until he was ready to continue while Corbin sat as still as a statue watching her.

"Well, I suppose since I have already done that very thing and am experiencing no torment of conscience, the *answer* is no longer *in question*. By the way the young woman reacted to me, I suspected she was a runaway, and it never occurred to me to be concerned. Whether or not she is a fugitive, I not only delivered that little mite, but welcome her to stay here till she's ready to leave of her own accord. I will not turn her out."

Relief flooded Abby's weary features. "Thank you, Uncle Seth," she exhaled and poured out the whole tale. During her monologue, she stopped only once to greet Cullen, who appeared like a silent ghost with a broad grin and settled down on the bench beside his twin, a small, blanketed bundle held tenderly in his arms.

"Well," her uncle concluded, "I am highly impressed that you made it this far, and would assume that right now you could use some hard-earned rest."

Abby could not agree more but insisted first on a brief visit with Maisy and her new baby boy Sammy before she was shown to the guest bedroom upstairs and hastily prepared for bed. But sleep didn't come soon enough to relieve her active brain.

It had been five years since she'd seen her uncle and the boys. Nearly a year after their visit to the Grahams in Winchester, Corrine began to develop symptoms of osteoarthritis in her spine, and thereafter travel became too painful. And, although both Abby and Paul hoped to return the visit, it had never been realized.

Seth, now sixty years of age, was as mentally sharp as she remembered, but his body and countenance had aged considerably. Even more pronounced than the normal changes of age in the twins were the differences she noticed when they were twelve. Though still lanky, Corbin's features and frame had filled out with health and strength while Cullen's had become more prominent with bones lacking the protective qualities of firm muscle. He wasn't grotesquely thin but unmistakably frail, nonetheless.

Abby hadn't asked but wondered if Cullen had been ill or perhaps was suffering from the effects of grief since Corrine's death the year before. However, just as before and now obvious to Abby even in the short time she been with them, what Cullen lacked, Corbin was ready and willing to supply. And his solicitude wasn't condescending in the least; it was a natural, instinctive response.

She wouldn't have described the twins as handsome like her brothers or Edmund, but with their sharply defined features, intense gray eyes, unruly shock of hair the color of crow's feathers, and complexion indicative of Native American ancestry, she would call their appearance striking. There was something extraordinary, unexpected, even feral about them that couldn't be explained by their deafness and limited communication skills. They had fascinated her five years before and even more so now.

The urgency of her mission and need to trust Seth had been her primary preoccupation, and she'd not asked about their reading and writing proficiency. She'd had no doubts about their intelligence and desire to learn since that afternoon in the manse, but her professional curiosity was definitely aroused by seeing them again.

With a sigh Abby turned over on the lumpy mattress and her thoughts turned to the morrow. Everything had happened so quickly the previous night she'd not had time to consider anything except getting Maisy out of the manse and away from immediate danger to the slave woman and the entire household.

It occurred to her now that she didn't want to go back to Winchester since she wasn't needed as a teacher and her presence only seemed to irritate her brother. *What other options did she have?*

A sob caught in her throat, and rolling over again, she fluffed the flat pillow into a precarious mound. She still wasn't entirely sure what all had transpired between Edmund and her, and in moments like this, she deeply lamented the way it concluded.

Edmund had comprised the other half of the plan she'd made for her life, and he was gone too, burned up in the fire the war had ignited.

The *damn war* had turned the world upside down. It had fallen apart before her very eyes like Humpty Dumpty, and *who knew how to put it back together again?* Abby liked firm, fixed rules and clear, reliable pathways that conformed to basic Christian principles of right and wrong and rational deductive reasoning–the way life was *supposed* to work but no longer seemed to be operating.

Abby had come to Boonsboro simply because it was the closest place north of Winchester where she had an association. Now, without a plan and no idea how to make sense of a world that held only lost hopes and dreams, it suddenly struck her that she was alone in a strange place with no familiar landmarks, nothing to guide her to–*who knew where? Dear God, how was she to know what to do now?*

Risking the loss of the little bit of loft in the feather pillow, Abby buried her face in it and cried.

CHAPTER 10

SUMMER 1862

After the fitful night Abby was awakened by a repetitive rap on the bedroom door, and without rising, called out, "Yes? Is there something wrong?"

There was no reply and the rapping continued so she stumbled to the door and opened it. It was Cullen, who, with a sublime smile, motioned her to follow.

Assuming his smile indicated no crisis at hand, Abby nodded and closed the door again to get dressed before answering the summons. When she descended and presented herself, Seth was waiting for her in his office. His silver streaked, shoulder length hair was loose, and his sharp blue eyes fixed on her face.

"I will be gone most of the day to see patients and wanted to speak to you before I left; otherwise, I would not have had Cullen wake you. Our young mother and baby seem to be getting along well enough, but she seems mighty anxious to be getting on her way."

Seth began packing his medical bag as he continued. "I think it would be best for her to stay at least two or three weeks to regain some strength and ensure young Sammy adds some weight, but I can understand her haste. She says she has some kinfolk around Philadelphia. Is there a plan to get her there?"

The sense of disorienting dismay from the night before settled back on Abby, forcing a deep sigh from her depths. The weight of responsibility felt so heavy she sank into a chair.

"I must confess I came yesterday with no plan but to get Maisy out of Virginia, Uncle Seth. She had come all the way from somewhere around New Market, and I could not bear to have her caught and taken back. I did not ask, but it must have been an intolerable situation to come by herself in her condition. I suppose I was just hoping you could help her." Her voice trailed off as she realized the audacity of her presumption.

He gave her a wry smile. "I try very hard to stay out of everybody else's business and just tend to my own so, if there are 'safe places' for fugitive slaves in this area, I am unaware of it. I would assume you got here without arousing undue suspicion, but I do not know how far you could get that same way. I have not heard of too many incidents of slave catching in these rural parts, but the further east you go, the more trouble you're likely to run into."

"Do you have any suggestions?"

He shook his head and getting up slowly reached for his hat. "I will give it some more thought, but, as I said, all this is new to me, girl. The only secrets I have ever felt obligated to keep, other than confidences of my patients, are those associated with the Masonic foolishness, and I have not been active in years. Apart from that, subterfuge has never been necessary; but I will work at it."

"Thank you, Uncle Seth, but I see now I should not have come, especially without even asking you. Maisy became *my* problem when I chose to leave home with her, and I should not expect you to resolve it."

"Maybe it was a reckless thing to do, and I am a bit surprised your papa allowed it, but it was also very brave, Abby. I have always had a soft spot for spunky women like your Aunt Corrine."

A cloud of grief settled on his whiskered face before he brusquely reminded her, "Don't hold me up now, I must be going. See if Corbin's got the horse hitched to my buggy, will you?"

Abby's inner agitation continued to plague her long after Seth left on his rounds. Her only peaceful moments came when she held baby Sammy, counting his tiny fingers and toes and kissing the soft fuzz on his head. She had never held a new baby before, and she marveled at his diminutive size. With the baby in her arms she could dispel all doubt about her impulsive actions and believe she had done well.

It was during one of these peaceful interludes that afternoon that the next step in achieving the goal fermented in her mind. Papa had insisted on giving her all the minted cash he had in the house that she'd intended to return. But acting on her plan would require a good portion, and she was now thankful to have it. It would be risky, just as the flight from Winchester had been, but at least she had the present advantage of time to prepare. And while she focused on the matter at hand, she could avoid thoughts of other troubles and perplexities.

During the next two weeks, all curious inquiries about them were quelled by the explanation that got her there; she was Doc Douglas's niece accompanied by the slave woman. The expanded version was as simple as could be convincingly contrived. She had been on her way to New Jersey to return her brother Harry's house slave when *said slave* started early labor, necessitating a detour through Boonsboro for assistance and an unplanned but delightful visit with her uncle and cousins. She would be continuing her journey as soon as the woman was allowed to travel and was presently unsure whether or not she would stop by again on her way back to Virginia.

This account appeared to be accepted with no signs of excessive skepticism, building Abby's confidence in the story's credibility. And, with such opportunities for rehearsal, she grew more comfortable with her roleplaying.

Meanwhile Abby enjoyed the company of Corbin and Cullen. She was impressed with their overall level of proficiency in reading and writing. And as she spent more time with them, she found she could pick up on some of their non-verbal language, though with considerably less skill than theirs to understand *hers*.

They spoke with their eyes and their bodies, using subtle hand signals as she had seen horse-trainers exhibit. In fact, Corbin especially was an expert in communicating with the family menagerie – the horses, Merlin and Molly; a billy and a nanny goat, Hershel and Bettina; and the mongrel dog, Gypsy.

It took persistent effort to earn the dour Naomi's favor, but

Abby worked hard to win her over by pitching in to help with household labors as well as patient care. Her commitment to achieve the goal was rigorously tested, but Naomi's respect was earned when she volunteered to sit on top of an extremely large, belligerent man's chest while Seth extracted a tooth broken in a taproom brawl.

Seth's supply of chloroform had run low, and the amount administered to the patient was quite evidently insufficient. Even with her contribution, it had taken the whole team to accomplish the feat, with Corbin and Naomi holding his arms, Cullen straddling his ankles, and Abby atop his chest while Seth inserted a wedge between his jaws and dug out the roots.

Abby had been exposed to ugly wounds when she helped Annabel dress Davy's burns and severed leg between Doc Patton's visits, and she believed that nothing could require more grit and strength of stomach than that nasty business. But the combination of two adverse occurrences as she sat on top of the volatile, stinking mound of corpulent flesh challenged that presumption.

When she initially attempted to find an effective place to put her weight and the patient began to flail, she slid off his chest and landed squarely on his privates, exciting the man into pleasure-inspired reverberations and vibrations before a red-faced Corbin pulled her off.

The second incident was less embarrassing but even more repulsive. As Seth was attempting to stitch up the excavation site in his mouth, the man hurled a purulent explosion of blood and vomit her way.

After order had been restored to the surgery and the man had been carried off, Abby had scrubbed herself raw and shared her belief that it had been a *bonding experience.*

Several days later, Paul's response to the note sent upon her safe arrival to Boonsboro brought Abby's thoughts back to what she had left behind in Virginia. Since then, Paul wrote, Davy seemed to be aiming his displaced anger at the church, heightening the stress Paul was already experiencing in his efforts to practice mediation and preach on the theme of brotherly love. He wrote:

> *"I have exhausted the systematic study of New Testament teachings on maintaining peace and demonstrating ones' love for Christ by exhibiting love for one another in the church with no substantial improvement in the rift here. At times I am tempted to despair, especially when I come home to Davy's angry ranting. However, I continue to pray, especially for him and for the Session member, that the Spirit would bring them to their spiritual senses and to repentance. I am still waiting for a response to my letter to the Presbytery for guidance.*
>
> *I pray for you also, my darling girl, that He would lead and guide you in the 'matter at hand' and in other decisions you must make. Of course, I would rejoice to have you here after the long years you spent in Staunton, but do not let your father's loneliness for you hold sway over your future. You must be ready and willing to follow the path your true Father has set before you. If He has not shown you the next step to take, then wait until He does. He has promised to complete the work in us, and He will do it.*
>
> *I have had no correspondence from Geordie since he left over three weeks ago but hope to hear something soon. The newspapers report they are somewhere around Richmond and that there are frequent skirmishes. Ben, as you know, is married, and as the chaplain to one of General Lee's regiments, may have to go with them once Richmond is secure. Keep them all in your constant prayers.*
>
> *Do not concern yourself with worry for us here in Winchester. So far, by God's mercy, there have been no further threats from the Union army to occupy Winchester. Our confidence is not in men but in our King, who reigns over heaven and earth."*

Suppressing her guilt of desertion, Abby put Paul's letter in the bureau drawer and out of her mind. She dreaded the feeling of being scattered between divided loyalties and obligations for causes and responsibilities she was incapable of fulfilling.

Life had been manageable with only one goal to pursue, completing her education to become a teacher. *Would life ever be that simple again?* Reigning in her gloom, Abby focused her energies into planning Maisy's escape.

Abby speculated that taking the train on a Sunday, when it would be filled with families, seemed to be the best plan, and Corbin drove Abby, Maisy, and baby, dressed in their best, to the depot in Myersville on the B&O line in Seth's four-wheeled curricle. There Abby purchased tickets to Princeton, New Jersey, to support her story but planned to disembark in Philadelphia. Telling untruths did not come easily to Abby, and it lessened her guilt to buy tickets to Princeton where Harry did, in fact, live. The absurdity was less important than grasping for moral high ground, as much as possible, she reasoned in an effort to find peace of mind – shaky ground at best.

Unforeseeably, there were many more Union soldiers on the train than families, and Abby tried to discourage as much friendly attention from them as she could without garnering more by protestations.

"I never seen a *real* Southern Belle before. Are they *all* as purdy as you?" asked a soldier in blue, leaning over the back of her seat with a mix of reverent awe and unbridled eagerness.

"Well, I really cannot say for sure, although I *do* appreciate your gracious complement, sir," Abby replied with feigned aplomb and bright smile.

Once the reserve was broken, a thick, blue-clad crowd of admirers surrounded Abby, vying for her attention, and she swallowed hysterical giggles rising in her throat as she wondered if Lucy and Caroline would be duly impressed with her sudden expertise. But she forgot her momentary triumph with two subduing thoughts in rapid succession – *Edmund*, and then the more immediate one, *Maisy*, trembling with fear and near hysterics in the seat beside her.

"Now, now, gentlemen. Where are your *manners?* Cannot you see you are scaring my girl? You will not like it *atall* if she gets to crying and carrying on, and her bitty baby too!" she warned them severely, still in the sugary tone.

Her own hysteria was now rising like bile in her throat, and she was quite sure they wouldn't think too highly of *her* if it happened to reach the right orifice and be loosed. A sudden flashback of the dental patient's revolting geyser did not help matters but madly fanning herself did, with the added benefit of prompting one of her devotees to open the window nearest her.

In spite of the unsolicited companionship, the journey progressed smoothly until a guard at the Baltimore depot approached Abby, requiring proof of Maisy's status. Struggling to hide her renewed trepidation, she again mustered an exaggerated air of southern charm, and giving him a look of pained distress and innocent appeal, ended the performance with a dazzling smile.

"*Oh dear me!* Nobody *told* me I would have to bring along *papers to prove she belongs to me*. Is it *absolutely necessary*, officer, sir? Next time I will *make sure* I have them with me. Oh, what would *my daddy say* if I get myself *arrested* and *put in the jailhouse? It gives me the vapors to even think about it* . . . ."

The guard gave her an uncertain appraisal and she added a flutter of her long lashes that seemed to be just the thing to tip the scales in her favor. And, after responding with extravagant appreciation and appropriate sobriety to his warning lecture, she breathed a most sincere sigh of relief when he moved on. Abby took the warning seriously. It was an extremely dangerous business, and she wasn't going to forget it.

It was late afternoon when the train pulled into the Philadelphia, Wilmington, and Baltimore Railroad Depot on Broad Street, and Abby herded Maisy, carrying Sammy in a basket, onto the streets of Philadelphia. In conversation with a Quaker couple on the train, Abby learned there was a meeting house on Arch Street, and hailing a cabriolet taxi, gave it as their destination.

With a mix of relief and trepidation, the exhausted young women approached two men in conversation outside the doors of the brick façade.

"Excuse me, Friends," Abby began, "we are in urgent need of assistance."

The Quaker congregants were duly obliging, and Abby and her companion were not only fed and provided lodgings for the night but also assured the Pennsylvania Abolitionist Society would help Maisy locate her kin.

The Friends refused Abby's offer of compensation the following morning, making her suspect that her sincere, though hesitant offer had been accurately interpreted by her hosts; she had very little money remaining and would need it for her return passage to Boonsboro. After bidding a tearful farewell to Maisy and the infant, Abby was collected by Friend Rutledge, who saw her safely back to the train depot.

Concern over the possibility of meeting the same guard at the Baltimore stop prompted Abby to change her appearance and demeanor as much as possible. She wore a plain skirt and high-necked shirt and, knotting her hair tightly at the nape of her neck, covered her head with a plain white Quaker bonnet in place of her stylish feathered one. When a response was required, Abby adopted the reserved manner of the Friends, using Quaker speech liberally redundant with 'thee' and 'thou.'

Upon reaching the Myersville station, Abby spent the last of her coins on transport by work wagon down to Boonsboro, arriving early evening as the sun was setting. If she had any reserve energy, she would have returned in triumphant victory of freedom over tyranny, but the stale odor of cigars and fear-induced sweat clung to her as when a high fever breaks, and she felt limp with fatigue.

The events of the last two days, the last two-and a half weeks, had drained her of every drop of vitality and all she wanted now was the lumpy bed with the flat pillow and twelve uninterrupted hours of sleep.

The following evening, as succinctly as possible, Abby recounted her adventure in varied forms of written and spoken word and pantomime and was met with appreciative applause by the twins and Seth's head wags. With the mission and its reporting accomplished, along with a boost of self-confidence that came with it, she suppressed the niggling unease of inner conflicts and focused on her future.

"I want to *teach*, Uncle Seth," she began. "Do you know of any opportunities for me here?"

"That depends on the amount of motivation you have, my dear. The Boonsboro school has a teacher, a Mr. Murphy, but the families on South Mountain do not always send their children. The boys go fishing up there and can acquaint you with some of the folks who might be interested in having you teach their children."

"I am prepared to teach *anyone* willing to learn. Is there a road up there or just trails?"

"Other than through the gaps, there are no roads. But I can get my buggy up and down most of the time, or at least close enough to walk to a patient's cabin when necessary. The boys go on foot, so you had better get used to walking if you want to go."

"I can do it if they can, Uncle Seth, but I hate to take them away from their duties here. If the trails are marked clearly enough, I could go by myself."

"Don't you even think about it, girl! There is a *war* going on, and, although we have so far been spared, there is no telling when it might come to our door. You are a brave soul, but if you want to go up South Mountain, you take one of the boys with you. Do you understand me?"

"Yes, sir," Abby replied meekly, though she had difficulty imagining anything more fear-provoking on South Mountain than she'd encountered on her trip to Philadelphia and back.

Over the next several weeks, Abby followed Corbin along the trails of South Mountain becoming acquainted with the Robbins and Garrett families, who worked together in a logging business. He also directed her to the Smith and Delaney families, who lived further up the rougher trails and subsisted off their small patches of cleared land. She approached other mountain families who declined her offer for a variety of reasons, but, on the whole, she was encouraged.

Among the four interested families there were eleven children between the ages of five and thirteen who could be spared from varied responsibilities for at least four hours, two days a week. Before beginning the formalities of teaching, Abby spent time with each family, establishing relationships and assessing each child's level of knowledge and potential for learning.

Winding their way further up the mountain slopes one afternoon, Abby and Corbin encountered a small group of Negros living communally in huts and tents, similar to the Native American tribes. Two wide-eyed young boys, carrying armloads of sticks, were the first to approach them, but did not respond to

Abby's greeting. Another child, after eyeing them from a distance, disappeared but returned immediately followed by an older man and several women in his train.

"Wha'cha folks lookin' fer?" the man warily inquired.

"My name is Abby Graham and this is my cousin Corbin. I am a teacher and will be teaching children here on the mountain, and I wanted to offer to teach *your* children as well." She looked around and smiled at the shy faces peering from behind the adults.

"We don' 'llow de chi'ren ta go no wheahs 'sep dey be wif us," the man responded firmly, but not impolitely. "An' we teaches'um wha' dey needs ta know ri 'heah."

"They would not need to leave your… um, village, sir. I know it is important to you to keep them safe and can teach them right here," Abby persisted. "They are very smart, I am sure, and might enjoy reading some of my storybooks." She did not want to offend them by assuming they were totally illiterate.

The man seemed to be wavering as he looked around at his "tribe" and then returned his steady, guarded gaze on Abby and Corbin.

"We don' know yous, ma'am. We don' trus *no* white folks and gets 'long jus fine dat way. But I thanks ya fo' ya offa jus de same."

"Corbin's papa is the doctor in Boonsboro… Doc Douglas, and would be willing to provide some medicines if someone gets sick." Abby wasn't ready to give up and was encouraged when the man repeated his silent deliberation.

Finally, with a sigh he shook his head. "We 'preciates ya offa, ma'am, bu' wez doin' aw'rat wif no white schoolin'."

Undaunted, Abby and Corbin made a second visit, this time sweetening the offer with a bottle of salve for burns and an eight-point buck Corbin had killed that morning with his hunting rifle, an 1849 Sharps breech-loader Seth was given by a patient who worked at the Harpers Ferry Armory, in lieu of cash. Seth had never used it, but Corbin gained proficiency with practice and considered the gun his prize possession. He made sure Abby understood his hesitancy to kill, but he deemed that her success in gaining the Negros' trust and favor justified the slaying that day.

In the end, Abby was granted permission to come once a week to teach the youngsters to read and write. She would come on Saturdays, obligating her to climb South Mountain three times a week, but Abby had no regrets. It was time to apply what she'd spent the last four years of her life preparing to do, and it provided what she feared she had lost – her sense of purpose.

CHAPTER 11

By late July Abby was again under the magic spell of teaching, relishing the rewards of watching young minds open, grasp, and use the knowledge she hand-fed them. For her it would always be a miracle, just as it was when Corbin and Cullen, making the connection between the crude drawings and the mystifying characters beside it, laughed in wondrous enlightenment.

What brought her even greater satisfaction was watching that first student become a teacher himself. Corbin frequently found ways to incorporate the wonders of nature in the children's lessons, such as offering something that started with each letter she presented. For the letter "A", he gave each child an *acorn* and an *apple*; for the letter "B", a *beautiful butterfly*; for the letter "C", a *corncob*, and so forth.

However, it was with the Negros that Corbin developed a special bond, learning their secrets of survival and sharing with them his own with actions rather than words. Whenever he appeared the children flocked around him, vying for the opportunity to hold his hand or be first to receive whatever treat he may have brought them.

Abby enjoyed the pleasure of watching the light shine in his slate gray eyes when the youngsters found something hilariously funny, or his delight in teaching them something new, such as how to make fishing flies with chicken feathers.

Corbin developed an especially close bond with one particular child, a ten-year-old fatherless boy named Gideon, born with a cleft-lip and palate. The boy was quick and eager to learn, and the brightest of the young scholars though his speech was markedly impaired.

One Saturday afternoon after the end of lessons, Abby

approached his mother.

"Mrs. Ruby, I have talked to my uncle the doctor about Gideon and he may be able to help him to eat and talk more easily. Would you be willing to let him go to Boonsboro with Corbin and me so that my Uncle Seth could examine him?"

Abby watched the internal struggle in Ruby's eyes for several moments before there was a shake of her head.

"No ma'am, Miz Abby. I been taken ker of dat chile fom da time he come outa me, an' kep um alive. I lossma husban' an' ma firs' two babies, an' I ain't gonna lose ma boy. I know he small, but he be aw'rat."

Gideon had come to his mother's side as she spoke, and Ruby held him tightly.

"I wanna go, Ma," he pleaded. His words were barely discernible but the message in his big dark eyes was unmistakable.

"No, baby, yo mama know bes' an' ya stays wheah I can sees ya. I trus' dees white folk bu' not all dem otherns. Ya gotta unda'stan… it ain't safe out deah."

After weeks of begging on Gideon's part and assurances on Corbin and Abby's, Ruby relented with the stipulation that one of the men accompany them. Old Tom Green was nominated and willing, and that evening there were two guests at the Douglas dining table for the Saturday evening meal.

Although it was the first time he had been away from the settlement where he was born, Gideon's excited anticipation, natural curiosity, and spirit of adventure quickly overcame his initial shyness. By the end of the simple meal of potato soup, which he polished off with relish even before Seth informed him there would be no breakfast before his surgery, Gideon kept up a lively chatter, peppered with inquisitiveness about everything that was new to him.

Old Tom (as he was called to eliminate any confusion between him and *Young Tom*, his son, and *Tom Too*, his grandson) was much more inhibited. As a young man he had lived in Lewistown, he hesitantly divulged when Seth tried to draw him out, but after supper, when Seth offered one of his pipes and a packet of tobacco,

Old Tom gradually became more communicative.

By the end of the evening, after Gideon had been tucked into Corbin's bed, since the twins were camping out in the barn for the next few days, and Old Tom had repacked the pipe with tobacco, he revealed the full story of how he came to settle in the heights of South Mountain. His family worked as tenant farmers and got along fine with the white family who owned hundreds of acres, until his sister Junie was assaulted by one of the overseers, and Tom's father Jasper confronted the man.

Given the time, place, and absence of justice, the result was predictably disastrous. His father was lynched, and the family fled over Catoctin Mountain before feeling safe enough to settle on the west side of South Mountain where, over thirty years later, they maintained peaceful, though impecunious lives.

"We don' ha' ta be treated wrong by *nobody*," Old Tom nodded in emphasis and drew deeply on the pipe. "We knows da Bible an' we tries ta live by it as close as we kin. An' we 'preciates ya gal comin' ta teach ow chi'ren, Doc. You's gotcha sef a real fine fambly."

"Thank you, sir. I think so too," Seth agreed with a brief smile.

Seth waited until the next morning before making a thorough examination, although he'd observed Gideon closely the previous evening. Gideon had the characteristic fusion of the upper lip and nostril and his palate hadn't fully developed in the back, but not as badly separated as Seth had seen before.

The boy, though small and malnourished, had obviously survived infancy without the ability to nurse, was given milk with something similar to a dropper, and had been able to feed well enough to subsist. Seth believed he could surgically improve the function of the lip and the palate, and explained the procedure to the boy and his guardian as simply as he could.

Without hesitation, Gideon nodded his approval of the plan and submitted to the pre-operative regimen that had already begun with deprivation of his breakfast. Both Corbin and Cullen had been trained to assist Seth when help was needed, and it was Corbin who stood on full alert, responding immediately to Seth's signals throughout the procedure, and who was first to emerge from the surgery to relieve Abby's and Old Tom's anxieties with a smile and nod signaling *success*.

After two weeks of enforced inactivity and bland liquids, Gideon was raring to head back to his mountain home to proudly show his mama his scars as well as his improvements. Abby and Corbin had continued their usual schedule and, between them and Old Tom, had dispelled the worst of the dire prognostications. But it was Gideon's triumphant return in one whole piece the next week that prompted cheers and tears of joy.

It also prompted a further act of trusting disclosure on the part of the community. They were harboring two fugitive slaves. Old Tom's wife Bonita told Abby there had been many who had sought asylum among them over the last nine or ten years, and, in fact, the numbers had been steadily increasing. Old Tom's father had bought his family's freedom, but the status of other settlement residents was unclear, and Abby did not ask questions.

Most sojourners had continued on into Pennsylvania in hopes of locating family members established in communities providing a measure of security, or others ventured farther, with even greater aspirations of reaching Canada – the *North Star* they called it, that mystical land of ultimate freedom. There had also been a few who had expended all their strength ascending the mountain, those who were sick and injured and now buried along with the settlement's own dead.

While Abby found deep satisfaction in her work among the young inhabitants of South Mountain, Paul's next letter, dated August 18th, incited her longing to see him and her anxiety for the wellbeing of the ones she loved. Even his efforts to communicate without risking censure, if the letter found an unintended recipient, filled her with sadness and pain.

> *Dear Daughter,*
> *My heart leaps with joy to know you are investing yourself and your gift of teaching in the education of those precious children. The Lord has indeed heard my prayers on your behalf, and despite present troubles, I give Him my wholehearted tribute of praise!*

I will not deny that Winchester appears to be the coveted possession of both armies and the citizenry never know from day to day who will be in charge. When the Union army occupies, resentment and resistance in many forms sometimes result in a disagreeable backlash.

There was a very unpleasant incident last Sunday when several Union soldiers interrupted our morning worship service. Several members were ready to attempt ejection, but when I interceded and encouraged our 'visitors' to stay, they left on their own accord.

Another result of Union occupation is an increase in the number of slaves taking their chance to escape. This side effect, of course, is a positive one to those opposed to the institution and quite frightening to the slaveholders. Again and again I have warned those congregants that are slave owners they will be brought to account on how they treat their fellow man.

It saddens me to report that our prodigal Davy's antagonism has not abated, and he has, in fact, resorted to some disturbing behaviors, and you would likely not recognize him. Before he was injured, he took pride in his military college-grade grooming, but now has allowed his hair and beard to grow into an unruly bush.

He is drinking heavily and is seeking the company of reprobates and prostitutes. Despite my prayers and efforts to offer the counsel of Solomon to his son, Davy is unwilling to repent and seek the full atonement waiting for him at the cross. Please continue to pray he will find the right path for his life, just as our gracious Lord has granted you.

Regarding news from the battlefront, I have received recent missives from both Ben and Geordie reporting intense fighting around Richmond that has mercifully ended with General McClellen's retreat. The news gives me additional reasons to thank the Almighty for his protection of our dear boys and Edmund.

I was encouraged to finally receive a reply to my letter to the Presbytery stating that a committee will be meeting in Harrisonburg at the end of the month and will be followed up by a letter of recommendations for addressing political divisions in our churches. The committee will be soliciting practical suggestions to be submitted before their meeting. Praise God for this ecclesiastic action!

Please share the letter and my love with Seth and the boys.

Love, your Papa

Abby wept when she read it, and her sadness lingered, prompting concerned looks and kind efforts by Corbin and Cullen to comfort her. The detail causing the eruption of tears was the mention of Edmund and it surprised her to realize the depth of her feelings. These intense but ambiguous emotions, mixed with homesickness for Geordie and Paul, were overwhelming and as hard as she tried to control it the tears would not cease.

When she appeared at breakfast the following morning with puffy, red eyes, Seth was still at the table and addressed the issue in his brusquely direct manner.

"Do you want to go home, Abby?"

Heaving a sigh as she sat down, she shook her head. "No, Uncle Seth. I mean... yes, I miss Papa terribly, but I don't really want to go. There is nothing for me there, and I believe I need to stay here. I miss Geordie too and am so sad because we cannot be together... and likely will never be again. *I hate this war!*"

Seth nodded and sipped his coffee. "There is enough violence in the world without going to war, and I have a terrible feeling this one is far from over. I surely hope Plato was wrong when he said, 'Only the dead have seen the end of war.'"

The depressing conversation was interrupted by Cullen who took Abby's hand, led her outside and into the barn. There she found Corbin kneeling in the corner beside Gypsy, with her litter of three new pups.

"Oh, how darling," she whispered, sitting down in the hay beside Corbin who placed a wiggling ball of light brown fur in her lap.

Watching her, he smiled at the look of delight on her face as she held the puppy tenderly against her chest. When she looked up and smiled back, he gestured to indicate the puppy was to be her own, and she nodded in acceptance of the gift. She named him "*Pax*" – the Latin word for "peace."

Peace, just as in the day of Jeremiah, was not to be found. The same morning Abby acquired a brief solace of peace in holding the small living creature, the armies of the Confederacy and the Union were meeting once again on the blood-soaked hills of Manassas. By the end of the following day, the blood of 16,500 more dead and wounded men would mingle with the blood and bones on those same hills.

The first week of August, Paul received a letter from Geordie.

Dear Papa,

I was anxious for you to know that Edmund and I are still alive and well, although our revisit to Manassas has further reduced our forces, as well as given us an even more bitter taste of war. I cannot even describe to you what I saw when a mortar fell not far from our line and unearthed the remains of those who died in battle less than a year ago. There were so many corpses! Bones and skulls came flying through the air when the mortar hit. I know there were a great many others who saw it, but we could not make ourselves speak of it. Maybe someday we will be able to help each other heal these terrible memories.

We all long for the war to end when we can be home to stay. I pray every night the Lord will help us and protect our family from harm. So many of our comrades will never be home again… so many buried along the way from wounds as well as diseases.

I am so very grateful to be with General Jackson, trusting in his brilliant strategic abilities to outwit the opposing generals, this time General Pope. After we captured the Union supply depot at Manassas Junction, we attacked the Union column east of Gainesville, drawing Pope's attention away from General Longstreet coming to meet us. Pope thought he had us beat until he realized the 1st Corps had arrived, and we trounced them handily back to Manassas.

I have given much thought to David the warrior, whose exploits are recorded in scripture. Somehow it gives me comfort to know he witnessed the same bloodshed and violence, and still could wholeheartedly trust in the Lord. And it gives me hope too that one day, like the divided Israel, our own country can be reunited under a leader such as David. That may sound very foolish to some, but I know you will understand what I mean, Papa.

My thoughts are also drawn to Abby. I am glad she has found a place where she can feel useful in teaching and am thankful she is not in Winchester, which I understand is having its own troubles. Edmond was disconsolate when we left with his hope of their engagement dashed. He loves her as much as I do, if that is possible, and I pray that when this war is behind us, he will become my brother by marriage as well as by deep friendship.

I continue to pray for Davy. Tell him if he does not get himself straight before I come home, I will do it for him by violence! He should be a comfort and help to you, not an added source of trouble and grief.

I covet your continuing prayers for Edmund and me but do not worry, Papa. As the General has so often reminded us, we need not fear to go into battle knowing our sovereign God is in control and will accomplish His purpose in and through us.

I send all my love to you... Your son Geordie

Although the reports of the battle circulated through the small town of Boonsboro, Maryland, Abby with Corbin at her side continued to climb South Mountain three times a week with her haversack of books and teaching materials. Abby had always loved the Appalachian Mountains that flanked the Shenandoah Valley, the Allegany's on the west and the Blue Ridge on the east. South Mountain formed the northern tip of the Blue Ridge and she claimed it as her own piece of glorious majesty. There was something mythical, even personified, about it in the way it flexed its muscles and spoke to her soul.

The more time she spent on the mountain, the more she learned and appreciated the vitality that spoke to her in every sound of animal, bird, and insect that was a part of the whole interrelated ecology. And it wasn't just the lively sounds of the things drawing breath that whispered to her in the language of the soul–the rushing sound of running water, the free-spirited wind that sent the leaves and trees dancing in its wake, and rain either gently pattering or pouring with reckless intemperance. It was all music in her ears.

But there were also times when she was forced to remember that her pleasure did not negate the reality that the mountain was not tame, no more tame than the lions she'd seen at a traveling circus when she was small. The lion tamer cracked a whip that made the lions *seem* to be cowering, but she had been close enough to the round cage in the circus tent to observe the way the lions regarded the man with the whip, and she had heard them roar.

She was astute, even at that young age, and knew that at any moment the lions could overpower the man. He dare not become complacent and forget the force and power of the beasts that roared and bared their teeth, waiting for the right moment to prove that he was just a *paper tyrant* after all.

There were no tawny-maned African lions or Asian tigers on South Mountain, but there were plenty of mountain lions and bears. Corbin took seriously his responsibility to teach Abby to pay close attention to signs, tracks, and noises that would indicate peril. Abby took these lessons to heart, and it pleased her to identify tracks before Corbin saw them.

There were a number of times during the summer Abby caught sight of bears and their cubs and sleek mountain lions sunning by a pool of water, and she allowed fear born of wisdom to guide her actions while still appreciating the exquisite delights the mountain shared with her. She believed it was her deep respect and admiration for the gifts that had earned her these rare privileges.

But the mountain had a way of showing off its own bared teeth and mighty roar when severe thundershowers popped up out of a cloudless sky, hurling Abby over the edge of terror. And it was these occasions that reminded Abby of the restrained power and treacherous unpredictability of the circus lions in the roaring thunder and lightning flashes of gnashing teeth.

More than once she and Corbin were caught in the onslaught of a storm as they threaded their way down the mountainside, when a lightning bolt struck a nearby tree with blinding light and deafening sound, sending chards of debris in every direction and Abby into Corbin's arms.

But the terror provoked by the awesome powers of creation was minor in comparison to the destructive horrors of war she would witness when the opposing armies met for the first time on Maryland soil.

CHAPTER 12

SOUTHWESTERN MARYLAND,
SEPTEMBER 15-17, 1862

The first sure sign of impending trouble was the influx of Confederate troops marching west through Boonsboro. But the first Confederate casualties in the skirmishes leading to Antietam Creek were carried into Doc Douglas's surgery on Monday morning, August 15. The news was acutely disturbing. The evening before, Union troops had broken through both Turner's and Fox Gaps on South Mountain, which had been guarded by Confederate General D.H. Hill, and General Lee was now preparing for a full scale confrontation near Sharpsburg, less than seven miles south of Boonsboro.

Just as Seth had ominously predicted, the war had come to their door.

Quickly calculating the supplies on hand, Seth shook his head. He would be out of most everything in no time if a major battle was coming, but turning his attention to his current patients, he began to do all he could. Abby and Naomi attended the less critical ones, cleaning and bandaging flesh wounds, while the boys assisted Seth in the surgery.

As she worked, Abby's thoughts wandered frequently to the families on the mountain. *Were they all right?* She fought impatient urges to check on their welfare until the last of the wounded still fit for march had gone, and then she sought Corbin.

The Negro settlement was strategically located far enough from the gaps to presumably remain inviolate. Her concern was for the other families. It was after 3:00 but Abby calculated she could get to the Robbins' and Garrett's and back before it became too dark to see.

"I am sorry, Abby," Seth said firmly, "but I cannot allow you to go alone and I can't spare either of the boys. I need Cullen to stay here with these men, and I want you and Corbin to go with me to Sharpsville to get additional supplies. I fear that by tomorrow there will be more work for us than we can handle, so we must prepare while there is time.

"I have made a list of what we will need, and I want you to record what we will be given and how much as Corbin and I pack our cases. We will need to make a fast job of it to get back home before dark."

With Seth's words, Abby's thoughts shifted to the boys in gray. *Where was the Stonewall Brigade?* She had asked one of the medics this morning and was told they were not with the troops that moved through. Though they'd been spared the mêlée on South Mountain, they would surely be summoned for a major battle.

While she contemplated these possibilities, Corbin hitched Molly to Seth's buggy and saddled Merlin, adding extra saddlebags before mounting and following behind the buggy as they quickly headed southwest.

"Uncle Seth," Abby directed her wondering thoughts to seeking her uncle's. "I know you object to slavery and do not seem to have strong political leanings one way or the other, so… are you taking sides now?"

He responded with what sounded like a laugh but not one indicating amusement.

"That is a rather opportune question to ask, Abby. I have always known you to be uncannily perceptive." He gave her a quick sideways glance and shrugged his shoulders.

"The truth is, I have been asking myself that very same thing and I admit I am still ambivalent. The only answer I can come up with is that whether consciously or not, I have always considered myself a southerner… though a *Marylander* for over forty years now. Marylanders have typically been a bit confused about their identity, with the exception of the Allegany folk, of course. Their primary loyalties will always lie with their family rather than any government.

"But I am avoiding your question, aren't I?" Seth gave Abby another sideways glance and wry smile. "You are right. I am *not* a politically motivated man and will not allow *any* government to dictate my conscience.

"But I am nevertheless a southerner and, though I will not *fight* with them, I *will* take a stand with them. I am willing to help a wounded man on either side of this bloody disaster, but when I am directly faced with a choice, as I was when you walked through the door of my surgery with the fugitive slave woman, I pray for wisdom and follow my conscience. That is as close to an answer as I can honestly give, Abby."

Hearing her deep sigh, Seth patted her hands clasped tightly in her lap. She said nothing but continued to consider his words and apply them to her own internal tug-of-war. Somewhere in her subconscious, she was aware that Corbin had drawn Molly close to the buggy beside her but had dropped back again. She'd become accustomed to his attentive, though non-intrusive presence, similar to that which he gave his brother.

When they reached the outskirts of Sharpsburg, they were directed to the station west of the city where hospital tents were being erected in readiness to receive the wounded. Seth left Abby holding Molly's reigns while he sought the medical quartermaster to request supplies.

Glancing up at Corbin who stayed mounted Abby observed the tension in his taunt muscles and his eyes focused on the ground. She wondered what he was thinking. *Did he ever question Seth's directives, or did he exercise complete trust in his adoptive father's judgement?* She could detect no clues of his thoughts in his watchful but expressionless features and those grave gray eyes.

After consultation with the quartermaster, the Chief Surgeon, and an officer on General Lee's staff, Seth's plans had changed considerably. In anticipation of General McClellen's troops approaching from east to west, General Lee was placing his lines along the west side of Antietam Creek leaving Boonsboro on the other side of the Federal lines.

Since Seth's offer of his services from his surgery was now impractical, if not impossible to deliver, the only other option was to join the army physicians there at the field hospitals. Hesitantly, Seth agreed to return the following morning with his surgical assistants, as well as the three remaining patients.

The proof of Abby's strong will and determination was demonstrated by her presence with the medical team the following morning that started out for the Confederate basecamp in the borrowed buckboard wagon. Even Seth's efforts to forbid her coming proved ineffective against her resolve to go.

"Yesterday you admitted you have to follow your conscience and *that is what I am doing!* Besides, I have helped you before. I cannot do all the things the boys can do, but I *can still help you in a great number of ways.* If you will not take me with you, *I will walk there by myself!*"

She had threatened and he had no choice but to relent, grumbling to himself that the girl was too smart and too stubborn for her own good. Besides the obvious risks of battle, Seth knew her hatred of war and had argued with her from that position. Still, Abby was drawn by a power she herself did not fully understand but could not resist.

If Geordie and, yes, Edmund needed medical attention or even a cup of water, she would make sure they had it! If she died trying to give it then so be it. It was as simple and straightforward as that, despite her fears that seemed to be gnawing like rats on her entrails. *What could be any worse than the experience she had in the Shockoe District of Richmond?*

Her uncle's immediate worries increased on their journey, often having to pull their wagon off the road for marching Union troops, artillery and supplies overwhelming them from the rear. Nevertheless, her presence with them may have added credibility to his explanation to a mounted officer who stopped them.

"What is your business, sir?"

"We have had an outbreak of influenza in these parts, and I am taking these patients to the hospital in Sharpsburg. I advise you not to get too close," Seth warned with a growl as Abby, hiding the patient with the head wound covered by her skirt, feigned a sick look and coughed in the officer's direction.

When she groaned and swooned, Corbin put his arms around her and began to cry pitifully while the two blanket-wrapped patients lying in the wagon bed added unfeigned moans and Cullen joined in with coughing spasms.

Quickly backing away, the officer barked, "I advise you to turn around now, but if you are determined, stay out of the way and *don't hold up our wagons!*"

Their progress was slow as tension continued to mount each time they were waved aside by the oncoming Union army that literally surrounded them. Once they were able to get beyond their lines, Seth urged the horses forward through the streets of Sharpsburg.

Many of the citizens were packed in loaded wagons, and headed southeast over the Potomac River towards Shepherdsville, creating another logjam and the delay of Seth and his party's arrival at the center of the field hospital area of camp.

While Seth transferred the patients and became acquainted with the medical staff, the twins and Abby helped to organize supplies and line up barrels of water on the handcarts ready to distribute to thirsty combatants. When the opportunity arose, Abby gingerly approached one of the medical officers standing under a tree puffing on a cigar.

"Excuse me, sir. Is General Jackson's brigade anywhere close by? My brother is one of his officers and I would like to find him, if I can."

"I believe the general and his men are on their way from Harpers Ferry but likely won't arrive until this evening. What is his name?"

"Geordie... Captain George Graham."

"Is *he* one of your brothers?" the doctor inquired, tipping his head in Corbin's direction.

"No, sir, my cousin." She hesitated but felt compelled to answer the question behind the doctor's query. "He and his twin brother cannot hear or speak but they are very competent surgical assistants to my uncle."

After a hasty meal in the medical staff's mess tent, Abby wandered through the camp hoping to catch sight of General Jackson and his officers, but it was after dark when she was told of their arrival and, by then, was hesitant to stray from the medical encampment. Even though she wore a Quaker bonnet and plain modest clothing, Seth had warned her she could be mistaken for a "camp follower."

Doc Douglas and his young companions were provided a tent for the night but, due to her own agitation and his snoring, Abby was unable to sleep. Sometime in the night she gave up and, taking a blanket, curled up under a tree and fell asleep for what seemed a short time before stirrings in the camp woke her again.

Her first disoriented thoughts failed to provide any relevant information except it was raining and she was completely covered in a tarp. Peering out into the dim light of dawn, she recognized the form of Corbin coming from the direction of the latrine ditch and became acutely aware of her own pressing need. Unfortunately, an army camp provided no special accommodations for females, and covering her head with the blanket, she headed for the nearest scrim of trees.

The sense of disorientation remained with her through the day as the deafening sounds of heavy artillery became constant, and though the skies had cleared, the smoke from the guns shrouded the camp in a foggy gloom. The few occasions Abby's knees forced her to sit on the ground, she looked around in dazed wonder and assumed she must be caught up in a terrible dream. Nothing was familiar; nothing seemed real.

While on her feet, she passed jugs of water to the wounded lying on the ground, everywhere, in every direction. And more times than she could remember, she realized that the mouth of the man into which she poured water was no longer in need of her ministrations, arousing an irrational sense of shame for needless waste.

The only familiar sight able to restore nominal sensibility, even momentarily, was the figures of Corbin and Cullen taking shifts at

Seth's side in the surgical tent. Seth himself was coming to the end of his endurance and sat on a stool as he operated. By mid-afternoon, he was forced to stop when his hands shook with exhaustion to the extent that he could no longer hold a scalpel.

But the broken bodies arriving on stretchers stacked in ambulances continued to pile up as the action moved southward along Antietam Creek. Abby had no idea how the battle was going but wondered how there could possibly be anyone left to fight. Regardless, the longer the noise of guns and artillery fire continued, the more she dreaded its silence. It blocked out the screams and groans of mutilated and dying men, and she envied her cousins' deafness.

It was much later that she identified the source of impetus that kept her on her feet, kept her moving through the maze of battered, moaning flesh, shooing flies away from the faces and offering what little she had to give. Below the thin layer of consciousness, she was looking for Geordie and Edmund, hoping, yet terribly afraid she would find them.

Eventually the sounds of battle ended, and without conscious assent, Abby joined the cavalcade of ambulance wagons on the field harvesting corpses, their geographic affinity indistinguishable by the uniform, all soaked in the dark color of blood. The area was also populated with several wagons from the Union side silently performing the same insalubrious duties. Some wagons were for the *already* dead; the others, moving more slowly, gathered the fallen still possessing an ounce of discernible breath to be delivered to one of the field hospitals. Those beyond hope of resuscitation were to be consigned to the burial detail.

Cullen and Abby, each with a jug of water, followed behind the last Confederate wagon gleaning the remains of the day in the area along Sunken Road that had seen some of the heaviest exchange of fire and hand-to-hand combat. Having escaped into deep mental disengagement Abby didn't notice Cullen, who had picked up and was wearing a gray Kepi, wandering down toward the creek bank looking for more living casualties until she heard the volley of shots from the opposite side, and looked up to see his body jerk and drop.

The sense of unreality persisted as the jug dropped from her hands and she ran to him, calling to the ambulance attendants who had dived under the wagon. When no further shots came, the two young medicos assigned the post-slaughter detail cautiously approached and found Abby cradling Cullen's bloody head in her lap with an expression of incredulous shock. She resisted when they tried to take him, but anxious for their safety and hers, they tossed both bodies into the wagon bed on top of the other wreckage and hurried back to the center of camp.

Corbin had remained at the hospital station to load patients into wagons for transport across the Potomac to Shepherdsville, and he was searching for them when he recognized the white Quaker bonnet Abby was wearing. He reached the wagon before he saw her face – and instinctively knew whose body lay inert beside her.

It was his wailing that roused Abby from the dissociate state of mind separating her from the unbearable reality of Cullen's death. The sounds lacked distinctly human qualities, like the bellowing of a kine for its lost calf, the howling of wind through a subterranean cavern, or deeper and more unnerving still. It brought to Abby's fractured senses the imaginings of the cursed, bloodied ground at the foot of the cross, *groaning* for the resurrection and beyond – the *recreation of new heavens and earth!*

It also brought chills down the spines of the two corpsmen who, startled past thought, brought the wagon to an abrupt stop before reaching their destination, the mounds of dirt hastily unearthed to accommodate the dead. By the time anyone could move, Corbin had wrapped the body of his brother in his arms, sunk to the ground with the lifeless load, and begun rocking and crying in agony of grief.

Responding to his cries, Abby fell out of the wagon and huddled down beside him, wrapping her arms around his neck. The scene attracted a small crowd, and it wasn't long until Seth knelt on Corbin's other side, and silently waited until the keening subsided.

By this time, it was growing dark and Seth contemplated how best to take care of his remaining family. They were in a grossly sad state, but he hesitated to stay any longer although the chief army surgeon, after his strong-armed tactics failed, had begged him to stay. But they had done their part and made their sacrifice. It was time to go home.

CHAPTER 13

Days later Abby was still trying to process the events that completely surpassed any other experience or imagining in the eighteen years of her life. Although she hated the war theoretically, nothing had begun to prepare her for the full measure of its horrendous realities. The events of that day had irrevocably changed her, and nothing would ever be the same. The one and only thought offering consolation was that among the dead and wounded, she hadn't found Geordie or Edmund.

Before Seth led Corbin and Abby from the battlegrounds that night, they had climbed down the bank and washed themselves in the river, Seth and Corbin still clothed and Abby stripped of her bodice and skirt in an effort to wash the blood from her underclothes. This ritual cleansing, as well as the slow journey back home, was done in utter silence. There was nothing to say.

Abby bathed several times during the week that followed, trying to erase the smell of blood clinging to her body and the metallic taste of it in her mouth, but the assault on her sensorial memories could not be scrubbed away with soap and water. It was the same foul odor and taste she'd experienced in her parents' bed, the morning her mother died. She felt the need to pray for spiritual cleansing, but the thought that it could only be obtained through the *blood* –being *washed in the blood of Christ*, suddenly became alarmingly offensive.

Even sleep provided no respite from the horrors Abby had witnessed. Nightmares plagued her with visions of Geordie, Edmund, Cullen, and even Davy and Paul, soaked in blood, dead but calling to her from their open graves, begging for her help, but though she tried in desperation, she could do nothing effectual. There were several nights her screams brought Seth to her bedside, requiring him to wake her completely to convince her the sweat drenching her body and soaking her nightgown wasn't blood.

Her heart ached to see her father. *He would know how to help her.* But when she tried to write him, she couldn't find the words. There was no vocabulary to adequately describe the scene of battle, the exhalation of Cullen's last breath, Corbin's depth of grief, the mound of earth now covering Cullen's body in the Salem Church cemetery. Only in her presence could he feel her pain, could he touch and relieve it. But war now separated him from her, by geography and by experience.

Abby knew that to survive she must find ways to release her pain, and mercifully there were two resources. The first was her puppy Pax now weaned and incorrigibly rambunctious. Thankfully, Pax was quickly housebroken, and despite several episodes of destructiveness, including the gnawing of Seth's favorite pipe, he was a positive distraction. The puppy also provided comfort through the night since Seth permitted the ball of fur to sleep in Abby's bed.

The second source of solace was the days she spent on the mountain, her troubled soul nourished by the beauty and the love of the children for her and for learning. The first week after Cullen's death she had no energy to make the climb, but the following week she succeeded twice.

As was his essential self, Corbin's grief was deep and silent. Several times, Abby tried to draw him out, to interact with her, but he only shook his head and moved away. She missed him. She grieved with and for him, but he remained unreachable, which only intensified her sense of loss and feeling of lostness.

Abby never doubted Seth's affection for Corbin and her, but he was not by nature demonstrative or expressive with his feelings. However, Cullen's death, less than two years after the loss of Corrine, seemed to have a deep impact. He didn't hide his tears as he sat in the old rocker after supper smoking his alternate pipe, silently and mindlessly staring at the pages of the open book in his lap. And frequently he put his arm around Corbin's or her shoulders as if he craved as much as he offered affection and comfort.

Seth said nothing about Abby's going alone up the mountain, but after she left, kept a watchful eye on Corbin until he slipped silently away to follow. Seth had to trust that in spite of Corbin's emotional withdrawal, he would take no chance of losing Abby. The armies had withdrawn, but not potential dangers.

Two days after the battle at Sharpsburg, Zedekiah Smith, a local known primarily for shady dealings, appeared in Seth's surgery with two wounded cavalry horses. After examining the animals to determine the extent of the injuries and some dickering, Seth paid the huckster thirty dollars for the horses and saddles.

Seth, who was quite low on medical supplies anyway, made a hasty trip to Fredrick to replenish his stock and, with the assistance of Corbin and Abby, since Naomi was deathly afraid of horses, the bullet fragments were carefully removed, and the equine patients pulled through.

"I bought these animals for Corbin," Seth later admitted to Abby. "Of course, I was worried about them too. I hate to see anything suffering and knew Smitty would have let them die if I hadn't. But watching Corbin suffer is much worse."

"Is that why you left him with all their care after you performed surgery?" In her own state of lingering apathy, she had barely noticed, but she recognized the wisdom of her uncle's efforts. Corbin loved animals and had a positive way with them.

"Yep," Seth sighed, "but I do not know if it is working."

The additional animals crowded the small barn to the extent that a decision was required, and the next week Abby led the two goats up South Mountain and left them at the Negro settlement.

Abby was headed back after spending half the day teaching the Smith and Delaney children, her thoughts on how she might be able to make some simple storybooks for them to keep, when she was startled by the simultaneous noises of rapidly approaching footsteps behind her and a hoarse, cracking voice.

"*Abby, RUN!*"

Though alarmed and confused, Abby instinctively obeyed, almost tripping and sliding over the rocky path covered in fallen leaves until she dared to duck behind a large cedar and catch her breath. The loud shouts she'd heard after the command had ceased, and the only sound she could hear now was her own heartbeat and rapid respirations.

Peeking out, she could see nothing posing a threat, and as fear dissolved, her curiosity emerged. Cautiously Abby started back up the trail, stopping every several yards to listen. Reaching the turn in the path approximately where she had been given the command to run, the ground was disturbed as if there had been a struggle, and a shiver ran down her spine.

She listened for the ordinary chatter of birds but there were none, only an ominous silence. Just before panic set in again, her attention was arrested by another source of reverberation somewhere off the trail, a human sound. Someone was breathing heavily as if at labor, and suppressing her fear, she slowly crept through the trees and undergrowth.

Corbin was gathering large stones in a ravine below her, approximately fifteen to twenty yards off the trail. As she came closer, he stopped his work and looked up, and his eyes tracked her as she made her way down into the ravine and came to stand in front of him. There were bloodstains on his hands and shirt but no discernible injuries.

After a moment of intense eye contact, Corbin turned back to his work. Grabbing his arm, Abby pinched until she had his complete attention once again and demanded, *"What are you doing?"*

He pointed to the pile of stones several feet away, and when she looked closely, recognized the body of a man partially hidden under brush and stones he had gathered, ostensibly, for this purpose. She dumbly stared at it for several moments before returning her fixed gaze on Corbin's face.

"Deserter?"

That was all she was interested in knowing. It didn't matter which army, and under the current bizarre circumstances, it seemed absurdly irrelevant anyway. She just needed time to grasp what was slowly rising in her consciousness.

He shrugged and tried again to resume the task of concealing the corpse when he was hit in the gut, then pounded on the chest with both her fists. When he gripped her arms to stop the barrage, Abby burst into angry tears.

"*You . . . you deceiving liar!*" she screamed. "You can *talk!* You told me to *run, didn't you? You can hear too, can't you! Tell me WHY? I want to understand WHY?*"

Corbin shook his head and sat down on the damp ground with a deep shuddering sigh. When his silence continued, she nudged him with her foot and gave him an impatient glare.

Clearing his throat hard, he glanced up at her.

"I . . . doubt I can." He said it slowly, his voice cracking, his elocution poor and his tone bitter with despair, laced with resentment.

"You had better *try*, or I will *beat you to a bloody pulp!*"

His response to her words was another shudder and a stifled sob that dissipated most of her anger, and she added, "But, if you are having trouble with *that*, you can tell me what happened *here*."

Relieved she had stopped crying and hitting him, he glanced up at her again, this time in subdued resignation. He swallowed and cleared his throat before making another attempt to speak.

"He was following you… to *attack* you. I hit him with a tree branch. I didn't want to *kill him*, just wanted to run him off but he… he *pulled a knife. Why did he have to do that?*"

His genuine distress brought Abby to her knees beside him.

"You are right, Corbin, he should *not* have, but you were *forced* to protect yourself. If you had not been here, he *might have killed me!* You *had* to stop him. But he could have killed *you! Thank God he didn't!*"

The thought of the deserter not only attacking Abby but possibly killing her, startled him and he seized her tightly; then just as suddenly, he let her go. The spontaneous embrace seemed to be more unsettling to him than it was to her, and he abruptly stood and picked up another stone. Abby, with a long exhalation, also stood and joined in the labor until the corpse was completely hidden.

They were both still panting with the exertion when Abby removed the canteen strap from around her neck, took one of Corbin's hands, and washed the blood from the one and then the other.

"You are not hurt, are you?"

He shook his head as he turned, climbed out of the ravine, and picked up the haversack where she'd dropped it.

"Let's go home," he whispered hoarsely and led the way back to the path.

They did not meet the other's eye or speak again until they were crossing the field toward town.

"Are you going to let Uncle Seth know *you can...*?"

Shaking his head Corbin answered, "No . . . not now."

It was an obvious effort for him to speak, and it required full attention to understand him, but Abby was hearteningly amazed at this unexpected discovery.

Not another word was exchanged that evening, and Abby decided not to pressure Corbin for a complete explanation until he offered it. It was a mystery, and she hoped it wouldn't be too long before she had answers. At least, she consoled herself as she lay in bed that night, she had broken through his wall of grief and, by so doing, had loosened the vise-grip of pain in her own heart.

Saturday of the same week, Corbin went with Abby to the Negro settlement on the mountain and was greeted with sympathetic tears and welcoming smiles. Abby had told them about the loss of his brother and today they expressed their sorrow not only with their hearts but with an assortment of gifts – from a plate of hoecakes to a rabbit's foot to bring him luck.

Gideon's offering was a skunk's tail that Corbin was assured would provide complete protection, though Corbin now carried the rifle as well as his hunting knife. He was visibly touched by their kindness, and Abby was gratified.

There had been no further verbal communication in the three

days since the averted attack, and on the downward trail, Abby left the path and stopped at the top of the ravine. She was relieved to find nothing had disturbed the pile of stones but continued to stare down at it when Corbin appeared beside her.

"Tell me now," she urged in a strained voice.

"Not *here*," he mumbled, and she followed him along a deer path until they came to the bank of the creek where it formed a large pool at the bottom of a fifteen-foot falls. It was a beautiful spot, and she breathed in the serene site before sitting on a boulder beside him and waited.

"This is where we came to fish," he haltingly began in a wistful tone. "After a hard rain the sound… of the falls is so loud I could… make as much noise as I wanted. When I was by myself, I could *sing, scream, cuss*, and no one could hear me.

"When he slept… I would whisper to him, but softly so ma and pa could not hear, and he would not know. But I always wondered if he *did*."

Corbin had been looking into the pool but now turned and gave her a pleading look.

"How *can* I explain it? It *wasn't right* that I could hear, and he could not. So, I used my ears to take care of him, to protect him but…."

His hoarse voice trailed off as he labored to stifle a rising wave of grief and regret.

Abby gazed at him in sympathy and wonder, and she took his hand. It amazed her to contemplate the choice he had made, even if it hadn't been a fully conscious one at such a young age, to suppress the normal reaction to sounds and response to spoken language in order to fully identify with his brother's limitations. It was truly a mysterious peculiarity of nature that could instill such an inextricable connection between identical twins.

As if reading her thoughts, he continued in a dispassionate tone. "It was fairly easy when we were with ma and pa Logan. I did not want to hear pa's yelling and cussing. I wished we were invisible too, so he couldn't beat us. I tried to take Cullen and run away once."

He paused to clear his throat again.

"I always wondered if he killed ma when she gave us to the Douglas's because I never saw her again. Pa... *doc* threatened to call the law if he ever came back around, and he must have believed it because he never did. But it could have been because he was glad to be rid of us."

He exhaled a deep sigh and sank into silence. Abby could think of nothing to say, so she continued sitting beside him until he rose and pulled her up by the hand she still held.

CHAPTER 14

Three weeks after the disastrous battle, Abby received a letter addressed in Geordie's bold handwriting. When she opened the envelope, she found there were two letters, one of them from Edmund causing her heartbeat to escalate. She read the one from Geordie first.

My dear little sister,

We have just learned from Papa that you were with Uncle Seth and the twins at Sharpsburg! Our first thoughts were of deepest regret of being so very close to you without opportunity to see and kiss you. However, our second and most dreadful thoughts were of you in the midst of such grim brutality and danger. I asked myself why Uncle Seth would allow you to go but the question seemed foolish when I considered it was you of whom I referred... my darling, daring girl. But what in heaven's name possessed you?

Please give Uncle Seth and Corbin my deep condolences in the loss of Cullen. I can only imagine how his death has added to the suffering you all endured that awful day. I trust you are truly safe now and plead with you not to repeat such a fool-hearty escapade. I have always encouraged your spirit of adventure, but I would never encourage you to do anything that would put you in danger of bodily harm.

Even though Papa is in Winchester, it has never been my home. I feel more 'at home' in Lexington than in Winchester, but as I told you on our journey there five long years ago, 'My home will always be where you are, Abby, no matter where that is.' You must stay safe, dear one. I will need a home to come to when the war is finally won. Pray for us that it will be soon.

We are now headed back out of the Valley and we never know where our next engagement will be. We are all very tired. I long to see your face and know how you are doing. Write to me, Abby.

Your loving brother, Geordie

Thinking of Geordie brought tears to her eyes and an urgent longing for him that gripped her like palpable pain.

"Please, Lord, end this damnedable war and bring him back home safely to me," she prayed in a whisper.

Abby was in such deep contemplation, sitting on the porch steps to read her mail, she hadn't noticed Corbin watching her as he walked one of the rehabilitating horses around the yard. He noticed her hesitancy as she unfolded the second letter and began to read.

Dear Abby,

I am writing with the hope you may still have enough regard for me and our friendship to read this note I shall enclose with Geordie's. And I shall refrain from scolding you for the danger to which you exposed yourself in Sharpsburg, knowing he has done a thorough job of it, though you cannot possibly imagine how greatly I am tempted. It was the worst battle we have been through!

Instead, I will risk baring my heart once again and tell you of my regrets concerning the last time we saw one another. You were justified in pointing out my egregious arrogance and lack of respect for you and your 'cause.' Please forgive me, Abby, though I continue to beg you to exercise prudence, just as Geordie and I seek the same so that we can come back to you.

I have to believe the Lord in His mercy will show us who humbly seek Him the way to stop the killing and grant us peace. When it is granted, I have to believe that we can find enough common ground on which to be united. I cannot, and, in fact, I <u>fear</u> to give up this hope lest I be in despair.

With love always,
Edmund

The combined emotional reaction to both letters broke the dam in Abby's soul, and she burst into tears and found she couldn't stop. With the flood came all the horror and impotent sorrow of the battlefield, the senseless death of Cullen, homesickness for her father, Geordie, and Annabel–and *Edmund.*

Fearing she had received bad news, Corbin came to her side on the step and tentatively patted her back, making soft, comforting sounds. When the sobbing slowly ebbed to sighs and soft moans, he whispered in her ear.

"Has something happened to your family?"

Shaking her head, she looked up and gave him a faint smile.

"No, at least as far as I know everyone's still alive and accounted for. I miss them so and . . . and *Edmund*. And I *hate the whole damn war!*"

"Edmund . . . Geordie's friend . . . and *yours*?"

Abby nodded with a sigh, keeping her voice in a low whisper. "He wants to marry me but his family has slaves, and he does not accept what I have to do, though he *is* trying, I think."

Without conscious thought her hand sought the tintype photograph in the pocket of her skirt. Corbin eyed her intently until with a flush she stood, the letters dropping from her lap onto the ground. She waited as he slowly picked them up and handed them back to her.

"Thank you," she whispered, then added with a shrug, "It does not matter now. The only thing that *does* is that we all do what we have to do and somehow *survive*. The way it is going though, most likely, we will *not*."

After the battle at Sharpsburg, Maryland, and General Lee's troops moved east of the valley, Winchester again was the target of Union covetousness and also propaganda. Five days after the battle, President Lincoln issued the Preliminary Emancipation Proclamation, announcing that all slaves in areas still in rebellion within one hundred days would be granted freedom.

After reading the text of the Proclamation in the newspaper, Paul contemplated the impact. Secessionists would consider the act just another empty bluster, an attempt to make the war an issue of slavery rather than the autonomy of the states, the cause for which most Virginians were fighting.

But, regardless of the personal provocation that brought Southern *and* Northern men to arms in May of 1861, by issuing the Proclamation, Lincoln would succeed in turning the focus of the war, at least in popular opinion, to the abolition of slavery. For those who opposed slavery, the measure immediately provided new hope, and that included the Reverend Graham and his housekeeper Annabel.

"What do your friends think of Mr. Lincoln's Proclamation,

Annabel?" Paul asked that evening after supper.

"They don' know what ta think 'bout it all, Precha. Does it mean *eva'body gonna be free then?*"

"The way I understand it, if the Confederacy does not surrender within one hundred days, the slaves in the ten states will be *declared* free. Logically then, *if* the Confederacy *does* surrender and therefore is no longer 'in rebellion,' the order is technically nullified and the status of slaves is unaltered. The only way it would become effectual is *if* there is no surrender and the Union troops' occupation is dominant enough to enforce it. Although both sides claim the victory at Sharpsburg, I do not believe the Army of Northern Virginia is ready to surrender anytime soon."

"This war is a *bad* bidness, but I know one way or t'other this slav'ry *gotta en'!* Mo 'an' mo' colored folks ni comin' th'ough heah ever'day, 'specially when the Union army be heah."

"The Proclamation states that if a slave joins the Union Army, he is *free*, but it is not clear about the women and children who obviously are not able to serve. And, since it only applies to the ten Confederate states, are Maryland and the states above the Mason-Dixon still under the mandate of the Fugitive Slave Act? There are more questions raised than are answered in this document."

He shook his head and sighed. "It seems to me, though I wholeheartedly support the sentiment, Lincoln's Proclamation, as it stands now, is only political verbiage when it comes down to it . . . it has no teeth!"

"I reckon we jus' keep a doin' what we doin' an' keep a prayin' ta the good Lawd fo' mercy."

"*Amen* to that, Sister Annabel. I wish we could hide fugitives in the church basement, but the whole property has been ransacked so often, I know it is not a safe place. I would ask the Ladies Circle to donate some of their blankets, but I have found them inflexible in their commitment to the Army of Northern Virginia... and I cannot deny the need there is as great there as it is for our refugee friends. Cold weather will soon be upon us."

An' the cost o' food is sa high, we kin barely afford ta feed ow own sef, an' the folks you invite fo' dinna. It sho keep us prayin' what the Lawd taught bout askin' fo' ow *daily bread!*"

"He has never failed us yet... nor will He."

As a father, Paul's most fervent prayers were for his children. His letters to Harry had become less frequent simply because there was little to tell. And because there had been no reciprocation since his letter almost a year-and-a-half ago, Paul could only hope for reconciliation after the war.

The infrequent letters from Ben were very encouraging and filled his heart with praise to the Lord. Ben who had received permission from senior pastor Dr. Hoge, now taking a less active chaplaincy role since the Seven Day Battle, had joined the 2nd Company of the Richmond Greys, one of three companies of the Richmond Howitzer Battalion, as their unit's chaplain.

Through his most recent letter, Paul learned Ben was very happy in his marriage, and although he hadn't been with General Lee's forces at Sharpsburg due to a case of influenza, the Lord was blessing his efforts, and a great many of the troops were responding to the preaching of the gospel. He wrote that chaplains assigned to other units were experiencing the same result, and he expressed sincere thanks for the work of the Spirit among men facing their mortality.

Geordie was the most faithful correspondent and continued to be a consolation to Paul in a number of ways, not the least of which was the confirmation of his living status. And Edmund, more often now, also included a letter in with Geordie's. Most importantly, their letters provided Paul with affirmation of their spiritual wellbeing.

Collaborating Ben's experiences, Geordie wrote of General Jackson's commitment to the whole 2nd Corps' spiritual needs, not only by recruiting chaplains to hold regular Sabbath services, but also by purchasing and distributing Bibles and tracts. Geordie and Edmund were continually blessed by the services led by Chaplains Tucker Lacy, Robert Dabney, and William Pendleton as well as Bible studies and prayer meetings Jackson promoted. And all were blessed and encouraged by the devout general's prayers, both public and private.

Most of the letters Paul received from Maryland came from Seth, who had begun writing faithfully since Abby's fateful arrival with Maisy. The missives he received in Abby's own neat script primarily contained her yearnings to see him and frustration at her inability to adequately express herself with pen and paper. Nevertheless, it comforted her father to know, through Seth, that she seemed to be slowly healing from the wounds inflicted on her soul on the banks of Antietam Creek. Paul's prayers continued to be lifted on her behalf for spiritual restoration.

Paul's greatest heartache was the condition of Davy's soul.

While his father was on his knees in prayer for him, this youngest son was, more often than not, sitting in Tanners Roadhouse on the outskirts of Winchester singing bawdy songs in exchange for a mug of beer or begging Rosie Lafay for a night in her bed upstairs. He'd spent every penny he had buying her favors and was now dependent on her generosity or, as he preferred to believe, his ability to please her in that bed.

Davy hated Winchester, he hated God and the church, and he hated the Union soldiers who came intermittently to the roadhouse, especially those who paid for Rosie's attentions. He tried to hate his father who had evicted him from the manse a month earlier, but he couldn't quite develop it. *Who could truly hate the kind, gentle preacher – or Geordie either?* The rest of the family and the whole human race, with the exception of Rosie and perhaps Edmund, Davy had no trouble despising. In fact, he found it came naturally.

Most of all, Davy hated himself and the empty right leg of his trousers pinned up to the stump. It bothered him much more than it seemed to concern Rosie who assured him many times that his leg was not the part of his body she held in esteem. She had never lain with a man who cared about her pleasure as Davy did, and she thought she might even love him, at least when he wasn't drunk and weepy with self-pity. However, even then she refused to judge him, reasoning that she'd never had the things of value he had lost – things like a good home and family, education, and reputable career.

Her own mother, Collette, was a mulatto and had often told Rosie stories of her childhood in New Orleans where she had been born into a Creole family before being consigned to the auction block at age twelve and sold to a gentleman from Virginia. The gentleman, Robert Winslow, the owner of a large tobacco plantation near Culpepper, was also Rosie's sire. And he had granted freedom to mother and daughter in his Last Will and Testament.

From the time of her purchase, Collette was secluded from most of the other household slaves and her sole function was to provide sexual gratification to the "Massa," whose wife had already done her duty by producing an heir and a spare one, to boot. Winslow sired four more children by Collette before Rosie's birth, but had not allowed her to keep them after they were weaned. It was the one concession he made in the bargain with his wife, and he honored it despite his young consort's tears.

According to her mother's account, the validity of which Rosie had doubts, she was an exceptionally beautiful and light-skinned baby, and Collette threatened to put a voodoo curse of impotence on the man if he deprived her of his latest issue, and he had complied when he could not sustain an erection. The story also purported that, in the same way, her father was compelled by fear of an even worse curse to set them free at his death.

Regardless of the motivation, freedom hadn't been a positive experience for them, and without family and a strong will to survive, her mother hadn't. Rosie evidently had inherited a robust will to survive from her father's side; she used that will, along with her light complexion, dark curls, comely features, and full lips and breasts, to support herself.

Intrigued by the knowledge she was part French and never having an official surname, Rosie chose the name "Lafay" when she started in business. She would have preferred the name Lafayette, but she wasn't sure of the spelling. Her name was one of the few words she could confidently write, and she enjoyed doing it with a singular flourish.

Instinct more than experience taught Rosie to hide her racial heritage, and she did, even from Davy. It wasn't because she was as much ashamed of it as for expediency's sake. She was a natural pragmatist. It occurred to her after she and Davy became lovers that, although she would appreciate an academic education, she valued her basic common sense more.

Nevertheless, she didn't hesitate to take advantage of Davy's schooling, and she was more than willing to barter her attentions for his reading to her, especially during the lull of mornings. Since her own literacy skills were limited, and no one in her past had the ability or the desire to read to her, finding such an educated and agreeable source was a luxury she rapidly became accustomed to having around.

Rosie's favorite book and Davy's least, was *Uncle Tom's Cabin*, a gift to her from a Union soldier, and it was the one she always demanded to hear when she was irritated with him. The sad parts of the story always made her weep, and she found it purgative, though she never thought to ask herself *why*. Engaging in self-analysis would never occur to her any more than shedding tears for herself would.

Davy much preferred reading the old favorites his father encouraged him to take from their home library, Defoe's *Robinson Crusoe*, and Scott's *Rob Roy* and *Ivanhoe*. Paul had insisted he take *The Pilgrim's Progress* and his Bible, and after he'd read the others, Rosie demanded to hear those as well.

Davy was also gifted with a beautiful tenor voice, which was the primary reason Jerome Tanner allowed him to hang around the roadhouse when he had no money to spend. Jerome was a good businessman, and Davy was usually good for business if the drinks he consumed were limited and he was able to remember the lyrics to the tunes the customers wanted to hear. However, there were also occasions that prompted Jerome to throw him out.

"*Damn you*, Graham! I told ya to let *me* manage the customers! I don't need, or appreciate, your '*help*'!" Jerome bellowed as he threw the crutch at Davy whom he had just deposited in a muddy puddle outside the tavern.

"Then you need to do a better job of it, Tanner! Did you see that bastard squeeze her ass and hear what he called her?" Davy demanded angrily, slinging dirty water at the proprietor. "You were not anywhere around when he did it!"

"*You stupid bastard!* I put up with you 'cause she asked me to, but I don' know how much longer I can stand it! If Rosie can't handle a customer, she calls me. She don' need no damn bodyguard, especially not a damn *cripple* who don' have the sense not to start a brawl just 'cause some fella wants to have a *feel* before he buys!

"Rosie is the best damn whore I ever had. She knows how to *not* get herself knocked up, she's clean and don't drink, and she pays me half her earnings without whining. She's a winner, Graham, but she is *my* damn whore, not yours!"

Inexplicably, Davy didn't seem to mind when the transaction of Rosie's business dealings upstairs was only that–an impersonal, professional transaction, and that's the way Tanner preferred it as well. Tanner was leery of her attachment to Davy, and his to her, but as long as Graham behaved himself and did not interfere with her business, he would allow it. *Maybe,* Tanner thought, *he'd finally gotten that through to the son-of-a-bitch.*

Although his father had no way of knowing, it was actually in Davy's best interest to spend his time at the roadhouse rather than feeding his anger on other more dangerous exploits–specifically, waging his own private war against the known Unionist citizens of Winchester. Davy became the strategist behind a group of rebel-rousers who lacked the sense not to brag in public about deeds such as petty thievery and dumping human and animal waste into wells. In fact, when Union troops occupied the city during the late winter of that year, Davy Graham was the only true Confederate to appreciate their presence, which provided a wealth of opportunities to exercise his infinite creativity for destructive mischief.

CHAPTER 15

Other than the comings and goings through the surgery, Abby's primary interaction with the citizenry of Boonsboro was on Sundays at Salem Church, and she was always greeted with sincere, though reserved friendliness. Seth was loved and respected for his medical attentiveness and honorable reputation, and the community had developed an ungrudging, though circumspect, indulgence toward the peculiarities of his family.

Salem Church was unique in several ways and was a church Abby wished her father could pastor instead of the strife-filled church in Winchester. Salem Church was a combined congregation of Lutherans and a small Reformed church, and, though there were minor points of theological differences, the members had become proficient in the practice of tolerance within the body. This applied forbearance also appeared to moderate political and ideological variances, and peace was maintained, at least within the plastered walls.

There was one exception to the cordial yet distant courtesy with which Abby was handled at Salem Church; it was tendered by Mrs. Dorothy Mathis, a widow in her forties, whose husband had been the town's mayor. Her son Robbie was in a Maryland Confederate regiment, and her daughter Maureen was married to a minister in the Lutheran Church, now living in Harrisburg, Pennsylvania.

Dorothy was renowned in the community for her gardening skills and for her generosity in sharing her produce. She often popped by the Douglas home with a basket of collards and sweet potatoes, and, if Seth could spare the time, she was invited in for a chat and cup of coffee.

In Dorothy, Abby found a kindred spirit, someone who understood the ubiquitous tension of divided loyalties within one's family and even within one's conscience. And she was the only person outside of the Douglas household whom Abby trusted enough to confide about her relationship with the Negro community on the mountain.

When Seth's arthritis flared up as the colder, wetter weather set in and help was required in the surgery beyond that which Naomi's goodwill would take her, he needed Corbin. Nevertheless, knowing the hazards of confronting army deserters as well as nature's own, he opposed Abby's going on her teaching circuit alone.

A compromise was reached when Seth agreed for Abby to go by herself on the days she spent with the Robbins, Garrett, Smith and Delaney children, and Corbin would accompany her on the longer distance to the Negro settlement on Saturdays. Abby would also be going now on horseback.

Abby was, in fact, delighted with the opportunity to ride, and with the two fully rehabilitated cavalry horses, it seemed a sensible thing to do. The only issue of contention was her riding attire, for she had not forgotten the comfort and practicality of Edmund's riding breeches. Riding sidesaddle, even if Seth had owned that style, might be fine on relatively smooth, level ground, but did not provide a secure perch on rough mountain trails.

Her determination again trumped Seth and Naomi's dissent, and despite dark looks and mumbling, Naomi fit two pairs of Cullen's trousers as well as one cotton and one wool shirt to Abby's smaller frame, in addition to his heavy buckskin jacket. She also acquired a pair of worn riding boots, only slightly too large, from the bounty Smitty Smith gleaned around Antietam Creek.

Before riding alone up the mountain trails, Corbin rode with Abby on the other mount until she was confident in her ability to handle the gentler of the two horses. She named her steed *Mercury* and the more skittish horse was acclaimed *Mars*.

Although she swore she would never use it, Corbin also insisted she learn to shoot the valuable pistol Seth was given for his medical services at Sharpsburg, a volvanic lever action, .31 caliber pistol taken from a Union officer. With an hour of practice, she managed to hit a bucket at twenty yards and Corbin awarded his approval to her performance.

The first week of November, Abby, astride Mercury with pistol and her teaching materials inside the saddlebag, arrived without incident at the Garrett's four-room log cabin on South Mountain. She returned that afternoon to the two-storied frame house east of town wearing the smug look of success.

On the second Saturday in November, Abby and Corbin rode into the Negro community and discovered new faces. Old Tom explained, with appropriate signs and gestures aimed at Corbin, that the former harbored fugitives had moved on toward the Pennsylvania border, but a new group of four family members, including a woman and small child, were now with them.

Due to the hot, dry summer and a fire started by a lightning strike near the patch of corn and beans, provisions in the community were already running dangerously low, and with the coming of winter, there would not be enough to feed the new arrivals even with the additional two goats. Abby's first thought was to supplement their store with whatever could be spared from the Douglas home, and her second thought was to seek a donation from Dorothy Mathis.

That was not the assistance that was requested, however; the fugitives wanted her help in crossing over the Mason-Dixon. Abby's only crossing of the "great divide" had been by train with Maisy. The very thought of repeating that harrowing journey caused her to quake, and all she could do was agree to consider how it might be done.

On their return route that afternoon, Corbin led her off the trail until they came to the spot by the pool and then dismounted. Following his lead, Abby joined him as he sat on a rock and gazed at the rippling water in silence. After waiting for him to come to some decision her patience was eventually exhausted.

"What are you thinking?"

"I am wondering how to help them. We *should*, you know." His voice had lost most of its hoarse tones, though his pronunciation and some of his sounds still held an odd quality.

"I agree," she nodded, "but taking *one* slave woman on the train is one thing, and taking a whole family on foot through the mountains in the cold is another." She shivered as the rock chilled her bottom through her drawers and woolen trousers.

"Pa collects maps, and I think he has one of the ridge. That would be the safest way to avoid the slave patrols. If I can get them to Sabillasville, a Quaker family there named Grable that Old Tom was told about could get them the rest of the way to Pennsylvania."

He paused before quietly adding, "I do not expect you to go with me, Abby."

His last words raised another question, momentarily distracting Abby from the current discussion.

"Why not tell them and Uncle Seth that you can hear? Does it matter so much now that Cullen is gone?"

Her question seemed to agitate him, and he stood as if to go. Grabbing his leg to detain him, she persisted. "Tell me!"

"Because I refuse to fight! If everyone knew I am not deaf, they would expect me to *join the damn army!"* He was almost yelling, and it startled her.

Not waiting for a response, Corbin remounted Mars. "Come on. I need to find that map."

Abby approached him and took hold of Mar's reins until Corbin met her eyes. "Then you will need me, and I *am* going, so do not even try to stop me."

With a sigh he gave her a look of resigned vexation. "Why am I not surprised? I do not know why I bothered to suggest you shouldn't."

Seth had done his best to dissuade them but to no avail. In the end he'd joined Corbin in studying the map of the northern end of the Blue Ridge and handed over his compass. The exact mileage was incalculable since it involved ascending and descending hundreds of feet in elevation, most likely without distinct trails to follow, but they calculated it to be approximately twenty miles.

It would take at least a day to get to Sabillasville in the Harbaugh Valley on the east side of the mountain, and another day back by crossing over the ridge through the pass and returning on the road through Smithsburg and Beaver Creek. These calculations were based on the presumption there would be no trouble along the way, which was by no means guaranteed.

Samuel and Rufus were brothers, and Minnie was Rufus's wife. Minnie was extremely apprehensive about getting on Molly, the additional horse Seth agreed for them to take, but, with much coaxing, she was mounted with the infant girl Talley strapped to her chest with a woolen shawl. Rufus and Samuel followed behind the two lead horses heading north through the cold, filtered sunlit morning, and Abby took the rear on Mercury.

There was little talking, the only sounds besides the traipsing of feet through the leaves and heavy breathing was the occasional cry from the bundle around Minnie's middle. The cries stopped and slurping sounds began when a breast was produced. After three hours of trekking, the group stopped beside a creek for a short rest before resolutely resuming the trail to freedom.

Predictably, the going was difficult at some points, requiring Corbin to scout the terrain for a passible way forward while the others took advantage of the opportunity to rest and take nourishment. By the time darkness was falling, the Negro men were stumbling with exhaustion and Abby called to Corbin to halt.

"How much further do you think it is?" she asked, anxiously assessing their haggard troop. She knew Corbin would not be concerned that their *passengers* or *baggage,* terms referencing the Underground Railroad, were aware of his communication skills.

"I am not sure," Corbin admitted. "But I expect we should soon intersect the pass trail across the ridge and, then going east, it should take us to Sabillasville. We don't know if there are patrols around and I am not anxious to increase the risk by taking the open trail any more than is necessary. What do you think?"

"I think we should find the pass into the valley even if it means increasing the risk of running into a patrol. We can stay off the trail as much as we can, and the darkness will be useful as long as we can see where we are going. When we get close to Sabillasville, I will go into town by myself and find the Quakers' farm."

After considering it in silence, Corbin hesitantly agreed and led them eastward as the elevation continued to decline. Although the skies remained partly cloudy, the moon made its appearance intermittently, and, with relief, they found an established trail leading in the direction they needed to go.

By the time the faint lights of Sabillasville came into view, the night had grown progressively colder, and the wool blankets, wrapped around the shoulders of each of their party, could do little to reduce the sharp, biting chill. Keeping to the side of the road they stumbled into a pumpkin patch, a clear indicator of a farm, and Corbin instructed the rest to hide while he looked for an outbuilding that might provide shelter as well as concealment.

It wasn't long before he returned and led them to what appeared to be an unoccupied tenant shack on the other side of the pumpkin field, near a crop of trees where the horses could be hobbled and hidden. Once their companions were settled inside, Corbin and Abby again strategized.

"We cannot wait until it's light," Abby insisted. "It is not too late to ask at the farmhouse for the whereabouts of the Grable family. It cannot be far now."

Reluctantly he nodded and watched Abby head back to the road looking for the lane leading to the house.

Besides Cullen's altered clothing, she wore his wool stocking cap with her braid tucked inside, but as she approached the house with lights shining from a back window, most likely the kitchen, she pulled off the cap. It was time to be identified as the female she was.

A man, alerted by the barking of his dog, suddenly appeared on the front porch, a lantern in one hand, a rifle in the other.

"*Who is there?*"

"I am sorry to disturb you, sir," she called in a voice she hoped didn't shake with the fear and cold she felt.

"I am looking for the Grable's farm. I am a teacher to the mountain children and was told they might be able to donate some materials." She had devised this story along the way and hoped it sounded credible. "I know it is late, but I became lost on the way."

The man seemed to ponder longer than necessary, she thought, before he lowered the rifle and invited her inside. The front room was dim, but Abby could see into the room at the back where a woman and two children sat silently at a table. Her mouth watered and her stomach growled at the smell of warm food.

"You are mighty foolish to be out by yourself, young woman," he said, propping his rifle against the wall and giving her another look of disapproval as he appraised her attire. "What is your name?"

"My name is Abigail McGuffey," she answered. "Do you know the Grables?"

"I do. They live about two miles north of here. If you get back on the road, there is a lane about a quarter mile towards town that you can take, and it goes right by their place. His wife and daughters make quilts, and there is a sign on the house that says they are for sale."

"Thank you so much, sir. What did you say your name was?"

"Reinhart. Marcus Reinhart." He gave Abby another sharp glance and shook his head. "I hope you make it."

"Thank you again, Mr. Reinhart. I will be just fine once I get there." He followed her outside and watched as she mounted, still shaking his head.

Abby again made her circuitous route back to the tenant shack, giving Corbin warning of her return with a whistle. She stayed only long enough to let him know where she was going, insisting that there would be less suspicion aroused if she were alone.

Locating the Grable's farm without incident, Abby was relieved to see a light in an upstairs window. Without hesitation, she knocked loudly on the front door, opened several minutes later by a man in nightshirt and cap holding a lit candle.

"Are you Mr. Grable?" she asked before he could speak.

"Yes. And who might thee be, child?"

"Can you help me to get some *baggage* to the *train?*"

He took in her appearance, including the fact that she was shivering convulsively.

"Come in, dear Friend, and I will get thee something warm to drink. And yes, I might be able to assist. How many *bags* have thee?"

After a brief further inquiry, and while Abby gratefully drank a cup of tea, Mr. Grable explained the advantages of waiting until dawn to collect the baggage, when his wagon would be less conspicuous on the road.

"Will they be safe until then?"

"I hope so. My cousin is with them, but I should go back now and let them know."

"Tis not safe for thee to go back out again. The patrols are out most nights, though 'tis cold. The Lord kept thee safe coming here, but as Christ rebuked the devil, *'Thou shalt not tempt the Lord thy God'* by unnecessary testing of His providence. Thee will stay here tonight and we will retrieve thy baggage in the morning. Hopefully, we will not run into anyone who will question what a good Quaker might be doing out so early on a Sabbath morning with his wares."

Mr. Grable woke Abby at dawn and followed her in the wagon loaded with quilts until they reached the pumpkin patch, where the refugees were loaded and covered with quilts. He left a parcel of food with Abby and Corbin and parting words.

"May God bless and keep thee, dear children. And if I can be of further service, do not hesitate to come again."

CHAPTER 16

Anxious to return, Abby and Corbin immediately turned the horses west for the strenuous ascent to the heights of South Mountain. Halfway up the trail it began to sleet, making the slope even more treacherous and the trail more difficult to follow. By noon, with the higher elevation and drop of temperature, the sleet turned to large flakes of wet snow, obscuring the trail and their vision.

Abby kept from freezing by reminding herself of how hot it had been in September when she had tried to keep the wounded, dehydrated soldiers alive with her jug of water. They had long since lost the trail, and she was ready to abandon all hope of ever being warm again when she heard Corbin's cry. Barely visible through the blinding white was the shape of a structure, a rough-hewn log cabin.

It was in poor condition, obviously abandoned for some time. The one room was approximately fifteen by twenty feet in size with the only openings one broken window on the side opposite the stone fireplace and the door, hanging precariously on its rusting hinges. With the noise of opening it and the scant light from the outside, Corbin could see the scurry of several rodents. But he could detect no gaping holes in the roof, and the stone and mortar chimney on the outside and fireplace on the inside didn't seem to be crumbling.

Gratefully they entered, bringing the three horses in with them. It was a tight fit, but the animals appeared to be as thankful for the shelter as the riders, and Corbin hobbled them on the opposite side of the room from the hearth. Snow was falling through the chimney, indicating it wasn't blocked, and Abby joined Corbin in breaking the less-than-sturdy table and two chairs for firewood.

Once the small flames began to warm the frigid air, Abby broke the silence by asking, "What is that peculiar smell coming from?"

"It's whiskey. My pa Logan used to smell like that. There is obviously not any here now, but I wonder if this place was used to store barrels of homemade corn whiskey. Mountain folk make their own, you know."

"It does not smell like the kind my papa has. Though he rarely drinks it, I liked the smell on his breath when he kissed me goodnight. I do not ever remember him buying it, but he often got a bottle as a gift during the holidays. When I had the croup, Papa would give me a spoonful mixed with honey. I do not think his was made from corn though."

"I never saw my Pa Douglas drink it, but I think he did before Cullen and I came. I heard ma once tell him that we had seen what happened when our first pa drank, and she didn't want us to ever be afraid of him like we were of Coon. Since Ma died, Pa keeps a bottle in his office desk and pours a nip now and then in his coffee. And I know he prescribes it for coughs and such."

"Oh well, I trust you to know what corn whiskey smells like. It is not too bad, and the smell of the firewood will make it less so."

Turning to the chimney she observed, "This wood is burning up quickly and we should bring more inside before it does."

"I will go if you unsaddle the horses. We are going to be here a good while." Corbin picked up a blanket to hold the wood and left.

Less than an hour later, the little floor space left was covered in drying split logs Corbin found behind the cabin and they were eating the remains of summer sausage and biscuits Mr. Grable had provided. The dozen apples he supplied were divided between the three horses.

"You did not seem to mind Samuel and Rufus knowing you could hear," Abby sleepily mused as they lay side-by-side on the floor. "Why not let the other Negros know?"

Their heads were closest to the warmth of the blaze, and Corbin could easily reach the sticks of firewood he would need to feed it through the night.

"I likely will soon. It is a bit awkward, but I suspect they won't think much about it, just as Rufus and his brother didn't. I do not think they *expect* to understand why white folks do what they do anyway. I cannot imagine they would question why I am not in the army."

Abby was quiet and he thought she might be asleep when he asked in a low voice, "Do you think I am a coward?"

"No, of course not." She sat straight up to meet his eyes. "What you just did for Samuel, Rufus, Minnie, and their baby proves you are no coward, Corbin."

"I didn't do anything that required bravery," he objected, his voice still a soft whisper. "They are the brave ones, and so are you. You are the one who took all the chances. You are the bravest person I have ever known."

"I am not brave; I'm a *lunatic*." She said it in half-jest, but he heard the quiver in her voice. "At least, that is what Mr. Reinhart pointedly implied last night."

"Whatever you are, Abby, I like you just fine."

"I like you just fine too, Corbin."

With that mutual admission hanging between them, the conversation ceased.

By morning, the snowfall had stopped, and still shy after last night's declarations, there was little exchange between Abby and Corbin as they led the horses from the cabin and saddled them. Before leaving, Corbin cleaned the improvised stable and gave the cabin a more thorough inspection while Abby watered the horses, filled the canteen in the icy spring, and folded the bedrolls.

Hearing her name, Abby re-entered to discover him missing, until she noticed a section of floor removed; she looked down at the same time that her brain registered the stronger smell of corn whiskey.

"This is where they hid it," Corbin reported through the floor. "It took a lot of work to dig this out. It's over four feet deep and about six-feet square, which would hold a good many kegs."

His head popped up and he hoisted himself back through the opening, replacing the planks as he'd found them. "I am gratefully surprised it didn't cave in with the weight of the horses."

The sunshine directly on the snow was as blinding as the blizzard the day before, but in the denseness of the forest, they could see well enough to head southwest, Corbin stopping every fifteen to twenty yards to cut a mark in a tree trunk with his knife.

"You never know when we might want to come back," was all the explanation he offered.

Cold to the bone, Abby wasn't the slightest bit interested in the prospect. But she continued to follow him even when it was clear he didn't plan to take Seth's advice about crossing the ridge at the gap and return home by the road through Smithsburg. She trusted him, and that was enough to keep her from questioning.

It was nearly suppertime when Seth heard the sounds of their return and hurried out to meet them. With waning patience, he waited until they had eaten before requesting details of their journey, and then he sent them up to bed following his prayers of thankfulness for their success and safe homecoming.

Feeling obligated to make Paul aware of Abby's activities, he wrote, *"You have reason for pride in your daughter, who safely delivered some valuable supplies to a Friend north on the mountain. Of course, Corbin was with her, and the Lord graciously kept them safe. Hopefully, there will be no need for further dispatches."*

Paul read and interpreted the letter almost two weeks later with weak knees. He'd become resigned to the arithmetic of survival on the battlefield – many church families had lost loved ones, but the thought of Abby once again putting herself at risk was frightening. Nevertheless, when it came down to it, he wasn't sure he would stop her even if he could. She was fulfilling her calling, and his faith demanded he leave his precious daughter in the hands of the sovereign King.

The promised letter from Mr. John F. Baker of the Lexington church came by the same post. Mr. Baker had been one of the official representatives of the Shenandoah Presbytery at the charter meeting of the General Assembly of the Presbyterian Church of the Confederate States of America in Augusta, Georgia, the year before. Paul hadn't attended, due to the recent battle in Kernsville on the outskirts of Winchester.

Mr. Baker's letter stated briefly that several of the responses from one or two other ministers reported similar problems, but no operative solutions. Other respondents confessed they stood solidly on the conviction of support for the Confederacy and the issue of states' rights, and they advised those few who dissented to "go up to the Northern church."

Mr. John Baker and Dr. William White, the pastor of the Lexington church, had discussed the matter at length and could only refer Paul to one of the resolutions passed by the General Assembly, an addition to the second section of the eighth chapter of the "Form of Government."

Judge Swayne had introduced the motion in response to the Gardiner Spring Resolutions, which made support of the Federal government a matter of religious duty, and it was passed by the General Assembly in Philadelphia the year before, resulting in the separation of the denomination into two geographic bodies. The policy of the new Southern Assembly read:

". . . They shall not indulge in the discussion of questions of state, or party politics, or controverted questions, pertaining to civil government and policy."

"I apologize for the length of time you have waited for practical solutions for the schisms in your church, Paul," John Baker wrote. "It seems we must depend on our own divinely guided conscience to see us through these times."

As a minister, Paul had always been dependent on his private devotional and prayer time, enriched with the writings and recorded prayers of pastors in ages past who had faced greater trials than he could imagine. Among his favorites were Augustine, the heroes of the Reformation, and the Puritans. So, the following day he spent praying and fasting, seeking that "divinely guided conscience" in the Word, and in the writings of his " dear dead friends."

The monthly session meeting was scheduled the same week, and in recent months, he'd found himself dreading the inevitable conflict over which he had no control, but he often wondered if the combatants took some perverse pleasure in it. In fact, he suspected the only reason the church *hadn't* splintered was due to each Session member's stubborn determination not to be the one to leave.

After his day of prayer and fasting, Paul now approached the Session with a spirit of deep repentance and new resolve. He opened the meeting with a prayer of humble confession that included a quote from the pen of a Puritan Father... *"I thank thee, oh Holy Father and Divine King, that Thou has given me 'sensibility enough to feel the hardness of my heart, spirituality enough to mourn my want of a heavenly mind. I confess and bewail my numberless failures, my neglect of opportunities for usefulness. O recall me to Thyself, and enable me to feel my first love, and may my improvements correspond with my privileges' to know and serve Thee in bold humility and wholehearted allegiance. Amen."*

He then addressed them, "Brethren, I implore you to seek forgiveness and the freedom found in reconciliation with our one and only *King Jesus*. We have allowed our emotions and political fidelities to cloud our sight, claim our loyalties, and defile our judgment. From now on we will *only attend to the business of His Kingdom!* If you do not agree that this is our only legitimate duty, then I will promptly submit my resignation."

On the Sabbath morning three days later, the congregation was just as amazed as their Elders had been. Their gentle, scholarly pastor had become a fiery preacher!

His Old Testament text was the second chapter of Daniel, Nebuchadnezzar's dream and the interpretation, the prophetic description of the coming of Christ's kingdom that would shatter all earthly kingdoms. His New Testament text was Mark 1:14-15,

". . . Jesus came into Galilee, preaching the gospel of the kingdom of God, and saying, *'the time is fulfilled, and the kingdom of God is at hand: repent ye and believe the gospel.'*

"With Christ's incarnation, the kingdom of God was no longer geographical, that is *Israel*, as He explained to the woman of Samaria after she referred to Jerusalem as the only legitimate place of worship. But, *'the hour cometh, and now is, when the true worshippers shall worship the Father in spirit and truth: for the Father seeketh such to worship him. God is a Spirit: and they that worship him must worship him in spirit and in truth.'*

"The kingdom of God disregards earthy boundaries. You must choose in whose kingdom you will stand… one established by men or Christ's. You cannot serve both. And I remind you, no political government can save you, cannot sanctify you, cannot give you lasting peace and eternal life.

"This is *His* Kingdom, His universal Church, over which the gates of hell can never prevail, or even anyone sitting here today who would see this church divided before willingly and humbly putting aside all political opinion as the ephemeral, mortal doctrine it is! No matter which side wins this terrible war, it will ultimately fall, just as Babylon, Assyria, Greece, and Rome, and all other powers on earth.

"Christ commands us to seek *His kingdom first,* for those who choose to obey him will never suffer defeat. Let us repent and then be about His kingdom work. Only then can we dare presume to expect His blessing."

After the service there was a subdued quiet as the congregants filed out of the sanctuary. As Paul stood at the door, many offered their hand with a solemn nod and "Thank you, pastor," but with no pursuit of discussion.

"Ya told um rat, Pasta," Annabel opined with a firm nod when they stood alone on the church steps. "Ya sho told um rat!"

For the first time in over a year, Paul walked back to the manse praising God, overwhelmed with a sense of the King's pleasure resting on him.

CHAPTER 17

December blew into the Shenandoah Valley with a cold, bitter wind that swept east as General Lee and his officers met to confer in anticipation of an offensive by the latest commander of the Federal Army of the Potomac, General Ambrose Burnside. General Burnside fared no better than his predecessors, and although the city of Fredericksburg suffered through the ensuing bombardment as well as the looting by undisciplined Union soldiers, Lee's army won a decisive victory on December 13, sending the Union Army in retreat across the Potomac into Maryland.

Paul learned of the battle in more detail from the letters he received from Ben and Geordie. It was Ben's first combat experience as a military chaplain away from Richmond, and he wrote:

"If it had not been such a needed victory for our brave men who indeed fought valiantly, it would have been a travesty of grief. We could not believe the Union command would continue sending battalion after battalion of their soldiers across the field to be shot down by our artillery and rifles.

Truly, dear Papa, the stupidity must have grieved our Lord as well, for in the night, the heavens came alive with the most amazing colors, rippling through the sky with bands of light. I cannot describe with what awe we gazed on it and wondered. Someone told me that General Lee said, 'It is well that war is so terrible, or we should grow too fond of it.' As for me and the ordinary men among whom I live and serve, it is hard to imagine anyone growing fond of war. Nonetheless, it was encouraging to be reminded so vividly that night of His glorious presence.

I find myself most occupied with the troubles of my men, keeping me very humbled. One man recently received news that his wife died in childbirth, and another that both his parents succumbed to influenza. We are faced with death constantly, if not currently in battle, then in our dreams, and I can hardly imagine the grief and guilt that comes when a man is at war to protect his home and family, and is not there to keep them safe, even if he could have done nothing to prevent the tragedy.

Death also comes into our camp with the measles, pox, and dysentery. Hardly a day passes that I do not conduct a funeral and write letters to the families. If not for the assurance of my calling, I dare say I would likely go back to my church duties in cowardliness and discouragement. Nothing could have prepared me for the reality of war, and I am not even a combat soldier!

We are now fairly sure of some leave time so we might go home for Christmas. I miss my darling Fiona more than I ever imagined and hope to be with her and the MacLarens soon. You are continually in my prayers and I long to see you."

Geordie's letter also brought Paul joyfully to his knees in thankfulness to the Lord:

"I shall be home for Christmas, Papa, even if it will only be for three days. Edmund will be going to Charlottesville to see his mother, so I trust Abby will be willing to come home while I am there. Edmund continues to hope the end of the war will give them a chance for reconciliation."

Abby also received a note from Geordie encouraging her to come home to Winchester for Christmas. She had been in Boonsboro over six months and the thoughts of seeing her father and Geordie prompted a profoundly positive response. The only question for continued consideration was *how* she was to get there.

Trains were now unreliable and could be unsafe, and it was winter, making travel by horseback or buggy difficult as well. The distance between Winchester and Boonsboro was almost fifty miles and any woman but Abby may have found the challenge too daunting. Nevertheless, after much discussion and compromise, it was agreed that Corbin would ride with her on horseback, breaking the trip at Ranson instead of the heavily trafficked Harper's Ferry. In regard to other variable factors, they would pray for cooperative weather and avoidance of military skirmishes along the way.

Geordie was the first to arrive at the manse on December 23rd, and Abby and Corbin reached there before dark. The joyous reunion went on for some time before the family could settle in for the meal faithful Annabel had prepared. The travelers were exhausted but Abby, reliving the events of her life since leaving the shelter of her father's house, had difficulty falling asleep.

Abby was still in her eighteenth year, but the events of the recent past had shaped and aged her almost beyond her own recognition. After tossing and turning for over an hour, she gave into frustration, got out of bed, lit the oil lamp and studied her face in the mirror. The girl who peered back at her was not the same confident one who knew exactly who she was, what she wanted, and how she planned to achieve it. This girl's eyes reflected traces of self-doubt, uncertainty, sadness, and fear that hadn't been there before.

With a convulsive shiver, Abby turned down the wick to extinguish the lamp and crawled back into bed seeking the body heat that was no longer under the quilts where she'd left it. Another hour ticked by before she was warm again and drifted into slumber.

Watching Paul, Geordie, and Abby interact with such loving enjoyment during breakfast, Corbin was gripped with a spasm of grief for Cullen so strongly it literally choked him. Using it as a legitimate reason to excuse himself, he left the table and took refuge outside, bracing his intense emotions in the frigid air.

Corbin wondered if he would always feel un-whole and incomplete without his twin or, as he sometimes felt with Abby, almost autonomously himself – like the night they'd spent at the cabin. With Cullen, it never occurred to him to be less than satisfied with the duality of his being. No one except Abby had challenged his need to *feel* or to *be* anything distinctly his own self. It was, he acknowledged, a slow, painful, and terrifying conversion, and he wasn't fully convinced it was worth it. Cullen was gone and as perplexing as it was to contemplate, he wasn't sure of the purpose of such an effort either.

It would be folly to pin his hopes of success on Abby for several reasons. She was in Boonsboro temporarily. From what Corbin already knew and had seen with his own eyes, Abby belonged with her family and probably with her brother's best friend Edmund. Although he was well aware of Abby's own forceful will, her family would encourage her in that relationship. She was too finely bred to make a permanent choice of teaching in the backwoods of Maryland. She was destined for a higher purpose and position.

These thoughts only served to depress Corbin further, so he wandered along the streets noting flagrant signs that the war had come through Winchester with a fury. It was dark when they had arrived the night before, and he hadn't noticed the scars on the large oak, maple, and beech trees and boarded windows of the houses now visible in the light of day.

He had turned the corner back onto Braddock Street when he saw Abby on the manse front porch, evidently looking for him. She smiled when she spotted him and sprinted purposefully to his side, taking his arm in an effort to hurry him along.

"Geordie and I are going to find Davy. Would you like to come or stay with Papa?" she whispered, her lips barely moving, like a ventriloquist with a dummy.

At that moment he strongly resented the thought of being her dummy and shook her hand from his arm.

"You go on. I will walk around for a while," he hissed back through clenched teeth.

Abby gave him a quizzical glance and shrugged. And, to avoid any further conversation via ventriloquism, Corbin turned and walked away. He would apologize when and if his mood improved.

Geordie had hitched their father's Amish buggy to Solomon, Paul's ancient steed, and was waiting for her.

"Is Corbin all right? He did not look so well when he left the breakfast table," he asked in concern.

"I really do not know," she admitted, her mouth twisting into a slight frown as she glanced in the direction Corbin had been heading. "He is a reserved fellow. I suppose he just feels strange with us all talking around him like magpies."

"We shall all make a greater effort to help him feel welcomed," Geordie said as he helped Abby into the buggy, "but for now you and I must focus our efforts on finding our prodigal brother, the lost *black sheep*. Maybe between the two of us, we can convince him to come back to the fold."

As close as she was to her brother and as much as she trusted him, Abby knew she had no right to betray Corbin's confidences. She also doubted Geordie could appreciate Corbin's fierce pacifism without strong religious convictions. She shared Corbin's sentiment but was aware she'd barely scratched the surface in her efforts to understand the complexities of her cousin's heart and mind. And, after last night's reverie, she was forced to admit she did not even possess an understanding of her *own* inner convolutions. That distressing confession was enough, along with the lack of sleep, to give her a nagging headache.

The two siblings had driven around town for almost an hour when they stopped at Tanners Tavern and hostelry.

"You stay in the buggy while I go inside to ask about him, Abby. Papa says he has been running with a rough crowd, and we have checked every reputable hostelry in town. That just leaves the *dis*reputable ones."

"I have been in a tavern before, Geordie. Night before last, Corbin and I stayed at one in Ranson on our way here. I want to go in with you," Abby insisted, climbing out of the buggy without assistance.

"Still stubborn as ever, aren't you, little sister?" he scowled with disapproval, though Abby ignored the comment and gave him a sweet smile as she headed for the tavern door.

"No you don't!" Grabbing her by the shoulders, he took the lead. "At least allow me to go in first… if you *please.*"

Despite his misgivings, the establishment was empty of customers and Geordie asked the serving maid, who appeared in the kitchen doorway, if she knew Davy Graham.

"Oh yes, sir. Everyone knows *Davy*. I haven't seen him this morning but he's likely to be in Miss Rosie's room upstairs. It's the first door on the left."

Still appreciatively eyeing the handsome officer, the girl gave him a flirty smile and turned back reluctantly to the kitchen. Most of the soldiers who came and went through the establishment were enlisted men with bad manners. She could tell this one had class, but she was mystified as to his reasons for seeking Davy.

Giving Abby a nudge back toward the entrance, Geordie began a stronger round of dissuasion. Despite his commanding general's moral influence over the men in the 2nd Corps, what Geordie hadn't learned in the military college he had seen in the Army. There was no conclusive evidence of what he suspected he might find upstairs, but he was determined that his sister would not be exposed to it.

"If I have to carry you out to the buggy and tie you up with the reins, you are not going up with me. So, are you going to leave on your feet or over my shoulder?"

"Why are you bullying me, Geordie? I came with you to find Davy, and if he is upstairs, let's go get him."

"We shall discuss my rationale for *bullying* you later," Geordie countered with exasperation and reached for her.

"Don't you dare!" she hissed and backed away. "If you are going to be that unreasonable, I will wait for you right here."

Glaring at her as she planted her bottom on the chair nearest the stairway, Geordie debated his next move. Deciding not to make a scene, he gave her a final warning and ascended the stairs mumbling in frustration that he should have such an obstinate sister.

Geordie's light knock was answered by a pretty young women in a worn silk dressing gown, her hair a mass of untidy dark curls.

"I'm not takin' any customers 'til after I have some breakfast, so if you ain't in a hurry you can wait downstairs."

"No, um… I am looking for my brother Davy Graham. The girl thought he might be up here. I apologize for disturbing you."

His suspicion had been confirmed, but facing the reality gave him a sick feeling in the pit of his stomach.

"That's all right then! Davy's here, but he's asleep. Come on in and I'll wake him up," she insisted with a bright smile and took his arm. "He'll be so glad to see you…. Oh!"

She stopped and stared at Abby who had followed Geordie into the room. "Who are *you*?"

"I am Abby, Davy's sister," she answered calmly, ignoring Geordie's glower of disapprobation and clenched hands that she knew he very much wanted to put around her neck.

"Really? Davy never mentioned a sister. But he talked a *lot* about his big brother." Rosie beamed at Geordie.

"I suppose he forgot about me," Abby suggested with an attempt at humor to cover the awkwardness of Geordie's scandalized expression as she continued to study the other girl.

Abby judged her to be about her own age, though she looked older. Her curly tousled dark hair was tied in a yellow ribbon, and a dimple appeared on her right cheek when she smiled with her expressive full lips. And, though there were dark circles under her large brown eyes, Abby conceded she was pretty.

With a nervous giggle, Rosie plopped on the bed and gave the mound of quilts a shake. "Wake up, Davy darlin'. We got *company!*"

"Tell them to go away," came from the mound as it moved beneath her hands. At the sound of his brother's voice, Geordie's face softened with tenderness, all angst dispelled.

"It's Geordie," he announced loudly, ripping the bedcovers off and exposing Davy's bare body to the chilly room, rousing him in an instant.

"*Geordie!*" Davy gasped, and struggling to balance on his right knee and left stump, gripped him in a firm embrace around the neck. "What are you doing here? *Are you all right?*"

"Gratefully alive, brother. *I have missed you,*" Geordie's voice was husky with emotion. "Get up and get dressed, and I will buy you and your friend some breakfast."

Still dazed with sleep, Davy glanced up to see Abby and quickly covered the lower half of his body. "*Abby…* when did you get home?"

"Hello, Davy. I am still teaching in Maryland but came home for Christmas. We will wait for you downstairs and can visit then."

She paused in the doorway and turned back with a tentative smile. "It is *good* to see you, Davy."

Ten minutes later the four were seated at a table in the taproom, Davy and Rosie polishing off bowls of grits and gravy. Abby sat quietly watching them as Geordie gave Davy a brief account of the recent victory at Fredericksburg.

Their papa was right; Abby would not have recognized Davy, particularly in a crowd. She wasn't the only one in the family the war had altered, though perhaps his modifications were more visible than hers. Besides the missing limb, his light brown hair hung to his shoulders and his full beard reached the nipples on his chest. The shirt and trousers he had thrown on to come down weren't dirty, but very faded and worn, and instead of a boot or shoe he wore a carpet slipper on his one foot. She was glad to see that he was at least clean.

There was an awkward pause as Geordie waited for his brother to give an account of his own activities. When it didn't come, Rosie chimed in, "You should come back tonight to hear Davy sing. He's just *wonderful* and everybody loves to hear you, don't they, Davy?"

"I do not think they will be coming back, Rosie," Davy said dryly, looking directly at his brother as if his words could be interpreted as a challenge.

Geordie shook his head sadly and returned the steady gaze. "No, but we were hoping you would come with *us* to the Christmas Eve service and stay over through tomorrow."

"Papa evicted me, Geordie, ... surely you are aware of that. I do not think my presence will be welcomed at the service either."

"Papa *does* want you there, Davy. It has been over six *long* months since we were all together. Please say you will come," he pleaded.

"I will consider coming *if Rosie* is included in the invitation." He reached over and took Rosie's hand, prompting looks of astonishment from both Abby and the girl.

"Certainly Rosie is welcome. Isn't she, Abby?" Geordie insisted with a quick but emphatic glance in her direction.

"Indeed," Abby hoped her smile wasn't too unnatural. "We would be *pleased* if she would come with you, Davy."

"If it would be no *bother* to anyone, I really *would* like to go, Davy." Giving him an entreating smile, Rosie turned her attention back to Geordie.

"Davy's been readin' to me from the *Pilgrim Progress* and the Bible, and I've been *really* interested."

"All right," Davy's voice as well as his blue eyes retained a hefty load of defiance. "Rosie and I had best stay and work tonight, but will come tomorrow. Tell Papa and Annabel we will come for dinner as long as there are no problems with us *both* being there. I doubt they would approve of our sleeping arrangement anyway."

"I will not argue that point, Davy," Geordie conceded with a wry smile, "but I do encourage you not to *intentionally* vex them. We may not condone your choices, but we all love you very much, and will truly welcome Rosie in our home."

Riding back to the manse, Geordie noted Abby's silence.

"Were you very shocked by Davy's 'sleeping arrangement'? I tried my best to spare you the exposure to that… *unsavory* situation. Whether you appreciate it or not, Abby, I am your big brother and it is my *honor*, as well as my concern that makes me protective of you."

He sighed with a shake of his head. "I should have tied you up like I threatened. Papa will not be very happy with *either* of us."

"Then we will not tell him," she stated matter-of-factly. "I am *not* a little girl, Geordie, and, believe me, *nothing* would ever be shocking to me after what I saw at Sharpsburg and the slave market in Richmond. I am sorry for Davy and that poor girl, though they have clearly contributed to their own deplorable state of affairs."

She heaved a melancholic sigh. "When it comes right down to it, all that *any* of us can do in this *deplorable state of affairs* called 'war' is to try to survive it in whatever way we possibly can. Perhaps that is what Davy and that girl are trying to do."

"That does not sound like you, Abby. We are to live to *'glorify' God and enjoy Him forever'* as we learned in the children's catechism. Have you lost your faith in the Lord's providential plan for your life, His purposes for you? Surely you can see His good providences in providing a home for you with Uncle Seth, and in giving you the opportunity to teach the mountain children."

"No, I have not completely lost my faith but I *am* sorely confused and disturbed about many of 'His providences,' what He *allows*. There are many things that make no sense to me that others, specifically you and Edmund seem to have no problem with.

Doesn't the Bible teach us to respect human life? 'Thou shalt not kill.' If that does not apply anymore, what world am I living in?"

Sensing the larger issue and putting his arm around her, Geordie drew her close. "Sharing another's passions is a blessing, but *true* relationship always rests on the choice to love the other, no matter what the differences may be. And, for me, that includes Davy and *Miss Rosie* as well as you.

"I love you, Abby, no matter what you could *ever* believe or do. And Edmund feels the same. He wanted to come home with me but knew you would *not* if he did. He wanted me to have this time with you and that is unselfish, *generous* love for us both. Edmund is my dearest friend and *truly loves you*."

"I cannot think about Edmund, at least until my own mind is clearer. I have forgotten what it feels like to have peace of mind and spirit. I feel as if I have lost my bearings in a world devoid of reason… only *senseless chaos*. If I could explain it to you and Papa then maybe you could help me, but I *cannot*."

'Do you think I can so effortlessly rise above the brutalities of war, Abby? Do you think I peacefully go to sleep at night without *terrifying dreams* and do not *jump out of my skin* every time someone makes an unexpected noise or movement? Do you think I do not *grieve* for the comrades that have fallen beside me, or wonder about the souls *I have sent into eternity . . . all* those who will never again hold the ones who love them? You *must* know that *I hate the killing too!*

"The *only reason* I can keep my sanity is by *hanging onto* the precious truths of God's word and know He '*holds me by my right hand.*' He *holds my hand with His left* and *with His right hand He defends me,* just like Papa used to do when we went for a walk on the street. Without Edmund and the general there to remind me of it, I would be lost too. Without them and the ever-present Spirit, I could *never survive it all for long. None of us could!*"

Abby studied his face, his dear, beautiful face, his eyes focused on something far away and her own filled with tears for him, for herself.

"Though it grieves me to know of your distress, Geordie, it is also a relief to know that the slaughtering troubles your soul like it does mine . . . that I'm not the only one feeling tormented by it. *How can you still choose to fight*, Geordie? Tell me that."

"Although I deplore the violence, I believe that defending one's home and loved ones is an honorable thing, and I honor God by fulfilling my duty to do so. I wish this war had never started, that Lincoln had never sent an army against us, but there is no inward conflict in my soul to do what I must, Abby. I would tell you if there was . . . my conscience is *clear*."

His quiet confidence fueled Abby's frustration and she cried, "*What if I lost you? What would I do without you, Geordie? This war cannot be right! And what about the evil of slavery? Did Papa tell you I assisted four fugitive slaves with two infants in their escape?*"

The look of pure love he gave her brought fresh tears tracking down her cheeks, and he gently wiped them away with his leather-gloved thumb.

"We are all called to do our part in times like these, Abby. You are doing *your* part and I am doing *mine*. We must leave the outcome and our future in the Lord's omnipotent hands. We must be brave and *rest our souls* in the peace only He can give us."

Filled with too much emotion to speak, Abby slipped her arms around his waist and held him tightly until they reached the manse. She followed him into the crowded carriage house, where he began to remove Solomon's harness, and noticed Corbin tending Mercury and Mars. Her cousin gave her a tentative smile and she, coming to his side, embraced him.

Interpreting Corbin's worried look she gave a slight reassuring nod and returned the same look of concern for him. In response he gave her arm a light squeeze, which made her laugh out loud. Oblivious of Geordie's curious glances, they exchanged another look of acknowledgement and grinned at each other. They understood each other completely without words, just as he had communed with Cullen.

CHAPTER 18

CHRISTMAS 1862

For the past several Sundays, Paul had continued to preach boldly on the legitimacy of Christ's kingdom over all other national and political powers, using texts such as Daniel 7:13-14: *"I saw in the night visions, and behold, one like the Son of man came with the clouds of heaven and came to the Ancient of days, and they brought him near before him. And there was given him dominion, and glory, and the kingdom, that all people, nations, and languages should serve him: his dominion is an everlasting dominion, which shall not pass away, and his kingdom that which shall not be destroyed."*

Again this year, Paul's Christmas Eve's service text was taken from the ninth chapter of the *Gospel of Isaiah*. *"For unto us a child is born, unto us a son is given: ... of the increase of his government and peace there shall be no end, upon the throne of David, and upon his kingdom, to order it, and to establish it with judgment and with justice from henceforth and even forever. The zeal of the Lord of hosts will perform this."*

His New Testament texts included John 14:27: *"Peace I leave with you, my peace I give unto you: not as the world giveth, give I unto you. Let not your heart be troubled, neither let it be afraid."* And he concluded with the Apostle Paul's exhortation to Timothy that he be ready for Christ's manifestation: *"He who is the blessed and only Potentate, the King of kings, and Lord of lords, who alone has immortality . . . to whom be honor and everlasting power. Amen."*

After his closing prayer, the congregation stood to sing.
"To us a Child of hope is born, to us a Son is giv'n,
Him shall the tribes of earth obey, him all the hosts of heav'n.
His name shall be the Prince of Peace, forevermore adored,
The Wonderful, the Counselor, the great and mighty Lord.
His pow'r increasing, still shall spread, his reign no end shall know;

*Justice shall guard his throne above, and peace abound below.
To us a Child of hope is born, to us a Son is giv'n,
The Wonderful, the Counselor, the mighty Lord of heav'n."*

Afterwards, as Paul, Abby, Corbin, Annabel, and he walked home in the cold night air, Geordie lamented, "I do wish Davy and Rosie could have been here for that beautiful service."

He was holding the lantern and his face was lit by the light. "Nevertheless, I *am* grateful they will be coming tomorrow, and I am praying it will be a beginning of reconciliation with the Lord and the church... and with our family."

"What kinna work did ya say that gal Rosie's doin'?" Annabel asked.

When Geordie hesitated, Abby spoke up. "We did not ask, but would assume she is a serving maid there at the tavern."

"Um... you did not hear what she said when she came to the door?" he asked her in a quiet voice.

"No, not entirely. I just heard her say something about not working until she had breakfast."

The group stopped and all eyes turned on Geordie in expectation.

"Rosie is a prostitute," he said quietly. "I hope that does not make any difference to any of you. She is a sinner in need of a Savior, just like Davy and the rest of us."

"Of course it makes no difference," Paul answered without hesitation, having already surmised the truth. "Christ had great compassion for prostitutes, and we shall follow his example. Though it grieves me greatly to know Davy is *participating* in this way, I am not surprised."

"Rosie said Davy was reading to her from the Bible and *The Pilgrim's Progress*. I would say that is a good sign at least," Geordie pointed out.

"Oh, Lawd!" Annabel muttered under her breath as they moved on. Wha's this fam'ly comin' to? Abby comin' wearin' men's *britches*, an' Davy comin' with a *ha'lot* woman! *Lawd, have mercy!"*

"He is indeed merciful, Annabel, and that is the only basis we have for *our salvation*," Paul reminded her gently.

Feeling time with her family slipping away too quickly, Abby stayed up later to talk to her father. Annabel sat in the light of the lamp finishing a new wool dress for her and he rested in his worn chair in front of the fire. Sitting on the hearth in her dressing gown beside him, Abby leaned her head on his knee.

"Things will never be as simple as they used to be, will they, Papa?"

"Life has not been 'simple' since Adam and Eve rebelled against their Creator, although we have a longing to return to that simple, sinless existence that will not be realized until Christ's return."

"*I* know, but what about *now?*" she sighed in frustration. "Are you and Annabel still helping the fugitives?"

"Not as much as we would like to do," Paul answered, looking over at Annabel who nodded without looking up.

"There are quite a few patrols in our area right now and apparently they have caught several slaves on the run. How about you?" Paul asked with an effort to suppress the fear that clenched his heart.

"Corbin and I have not agreed to continue doing what we did last month, but if there is another opportunity, we will do it again. We *must do what we can for them*, Papa. Compared to the whole desperate situation, it seems such a small thing… like a drop of water among thousands dying of thirst, but at least it is *something*. I told Geordie about it, and he seemed to encourage my choice to help. That is more than Edmund did when I told *him*."

Needing to soothe his own spirit as well as Abby's, Paul silently caressed her hair while her thoughts continued to unwind.

"I can understand Edmund's wanting me to be safe at home, just as I would like Geordie and him to get out of the army and come home, but if Geordie can accept that I am doing what I think is right, why can't *Edmund?*"

"It's a rare man who kin unda'stan' a woman, chile. Ya can't 'spect um *all* too. But it don' mean they ain't worth keepin'," Annabel answered. "You go on ta bed now, missy. Ya don' need ta fret s'much. The good Lawd'll work it out in time. Jus' give Him time."

On Christmas morning, no one in the family hurried downstairs in expectation of gifts; each had already been exceedingly blessed with the others' loving presence. It was more than enough, knowing so very many families were bereft of their loved ones, either temporarily by the war or forever by death.

Corbin, watchful of Abby as always, could feel her anguished joy as she gazed from face to dear face around the table during the quiet, simple breakfast meal. He envied the love he saw in her eyes when she looked at them and was equally shamed by it. He would have given his soul to have her look at him with the love she had for Geordie – and the absent Edmund. It wasn't entirely his imagination that when her eyes lingered on Geordie, she was seeing the other whose picture she carried with her always.

Davy and Rosie arrived late morning, he with defensive wariness and she with tentative hopefulness. Their initial discomfort and Abby's inhibitions were soon dispelled by Geordie's gift of infectious joy, which he spread liberally with each smile, word, and touch.

Paul said little as he watched Geordie's magic take hold of the room. At times like these, his grief for Rosemary emerged like an oncoming tsunami and threatened to drown him. The ache in his heart was always with him, even when he wasn't consciously thinking of her, but seeing her reflection, her gestures, her spirit in their children, and especially in this special son, sent him adrift in a flood of joyful agony.

Miraculously, Annabel produced a roast chicken stuffed with giblet cornbread and the meal was hailed as a feast rivaling that of any table. And she flushed with pleasure when there were raves over her apple dumplings for dessert.

Despite Annabel's protests, Rosie insisted on helping her with the cleanup while Abby dismantled the candelabra on the table and lit the lamps in the parlor. Meanwhile, Geordie had stoked the fire into a roaring blaze, the warmth of which was later reflected in the lively game of cribbage between three teams – Geordie and Rosie, Davy and Abby, and Paul and the reserved but surprisingly formidable Corbin.

There was a good bit of good-natured ribbing between the brothers and reminiscing while the evening wound down with cups of hot hard cider, which Annabel had made and stored the winter before under the house. And, as intensely as Paul cherished memories of Christmases past, he treasured this one with nostalgic fervor as never before.

It was dark when Geordie drove Davy and Rosie back to the roadhouse and, before leaving, held his brother in an embrace long enough to make Davy squirm. Then he kissed Rosie's hand and charged her to *"make Davy behave himself."*

As they waved goodbye, Rosie wistfully commented, "You sure got a wonderful family, Davy. They treat me like I'm *worth* somethin'. Why would you ever want to leave 'em?"

"Yes they *are* wonderful... but *I am not*. That is *why* I left them."

"They love you anyhow. If *I* had one like that, *nothin'* could make me leave. I wish they *were* mine," she sighed.

"Take them then! You can *have them* with my blessings!" he shouted in anger with a pain so deep he clutched his chest. "They're all yours! You can have the *damn church too!* It's no good to me either."

Rosie shook her head as he hobbled inside on his crutches. Her practical nature couldn't comprehend the squandering of such desirable legacies.

The following morning as Geordie prepared to leave, Abby clung to him, wetting the front of his uniform frockcoat with her tears. Holding her tightly he whispered, "I love you, Abby girl. You be careful doing what you have to do, and I will be praying for your success."

"I love you more than anyone in the world, Geordie. Please, *please* stay safe. You are the glue that holds this family together... that holds *me* together. *We are depending on you to come back to us,*" she whispered into his chest.

"I promise to take every reasonable precaution, and Edmund and I always look out for each other. But all the same, our lives belong to our Redeemer King. *He* is the one who holds all things together, Abby, not I. I will write you soon."

There were more tears after he left, and Paul did his best to console her. A short while later, Abby kissed her father and Annabel, mounted Mercury, and followed Corbin out of town going north toward Ranson, where they would again be spending the night before a second day of travel back to Boonsboro.

"I do not know why I was so emotional about leaving my family this time," she said apologetically when they stopped to rest the horses. "I am not usually such a crybaby. Thank you for making it possible for me to go home to see them."

"It isn't hard to understand your love for them. I only wish…" he paused with a sigh, "maybe someday I will be able to talk freely to them. There are not many I would want to talk with like I do you, but I think I *would* like very much to share my thoughts with your papa and Geordie."

"You can write them. I am sure they would like that."

"Maybe so, but it isn't the same, is it?"

"No, which is why I have trouble doing it," she admitted with a sigh. "I am already missing them."

"Not like I miss Cullen," he muttered under his breath, pulling himself up into the saddle. As much as he'd enjoyed the evening before, his grief had been aroused and was now as palpable as the frigid air that filled his lungs.

"We had better keep moving," he said louder, tugging his coat more tightly around his body. "It looks as if it might snow."

Guiding Mercury beside him, Abby pursued another line of inquiry. "What did you think of *Rosie?*"

He gave her a searching look before offering his reply. "I liked her all right. She looked me in the eye when most people do not bother but… why does it matter to you what *I* think of her?"

Abby flushed with the unspoken acknowledgement she wouldn't have asked Geordie or her father that question.

"I am just curious." She tried not to sound defensive. "I think she cares a great deal for Davy, though I am not sure what he actually feels for her."

Her pondering wasn't based on Davy's attitude toward the girl but rather on how he could share a bed with someone who brought other men to that same bed – for money. On the surface he gave the impression it didn't bother him, though Abby couldn't conceive of why it wouldn't if Davy *did* care for her. Perhaps he just needed a place to sleep. Those *reputable* hostelries around Winchester weren't free and likely weren't even cheap. Before she could steer her wondering thoughts in a different direction, she wondered what Rosie charged for a visit to her bed.

Abby's concepts of human sexuality included contributions by several sources. Beside the casual exposure to the differences in male and female bodies she gained in growing up with brothers, the first descriptive impressions were horrifying – the assault on Annabel by her Uncle William Spencer.

Then she'd heard talk of sexual matters occasionally arising in the dormitory of Augusta Female Seminary, and Abby's natural curiosity commanded her attention to any details offered. It seemed the opinions were divided between those who believed that *ladies did not enjoy that sort of attention*, and those who insisted their experiences had taught them otherwise.

Her dear papa also made an attempt at providing inexplicit terminology when they returned from Geordie's graduation exercises in Richmond. Paul had pointed out that it was the great Creator who designed male and female with bodies that could join, who brought them together and, since all was pure and pleasurable in that garden paradise, so was the couple's sexual union.

"That is how it should be within the bond of Christian marriage, Abby," he'd said with a wistful expression, and added softly, "That is the way it was between your dear mother and me."

Apparently, it could also be, if not *pure*, then *pleasurable* outside the bonds of marriage according to several classmates. And Abby was led to conclude, Rosie was not sleeping with Davy out of necessity, even if Davy might be.

Also, Abby's own experience when she'd been physically close to Edmund lent support to the likelihood she would enjoy a more intense level of physical intimacy. She very much liked the feel of his arms pressing her against his strong, warm body and his soft mouth confidently claiming her own.

With an abrupt jerk, drawing a curious glance from Corbin, Abby dismissed the thought from her mind. She could never marry Edmund; she would be a disappointment to him, and with annoyance wiped away the tears that welled in her eyes. Still, she reached into the pocket of her buckskin jacket and felt the solid, square shape of the tintype photo. She could not provide a rational reason why she continued to carry it, though most likely it was the fanciful notion that as long as she kept it with her she could keep him safe.

That night as Corbin settled on the floor beside the bed she occupied in a small, cold room above a noisy taproom in Ranson, Abby's thoughts drifted back to the earlier theme. *What had the proprietor thought when she asked for a room to share with her brother?* There was definitely no family resemblance between Corbin and herself, and she definitely didn't look like a "respectable lady" in her trousers, buckskin jacket, and knee-high military boots. *Did the proprietor and patrons assume Corbin and she were up here…?*

His voice startled her from further alarming imaginings.

"Did you ask your papa what he thought might happen when President Lincoln's Proclamation goes into effect?"

"*What?* Oh, yes, I did. He thinks it will be generally ignored but would likely motivate the slave owners to hire more unscrupulous men to catch those who try to leave, thinking they were actually free. He also said he wished he knew if President Lincoln's intent is to nullify the Fugitive Slave Act so slaves could be free by crossing the Mason-Dixon. What do you think?"

"I have no idea. I guess we will find out soon enough. It's only six days until the New Year. I wonder if, by the end of 1863, the war will be over."

"I sincerely hope so! How many more will have to die before there is nobody left to fight it? If women ruled the world, there would be no wars."

"I don't know about that, Abby. Davy told Geordie the women in Winchester hate the Yankees more than the men do. He said women dump their chamber pots on the Union soldiers' heads when they walk down the street. Do you sometimes feel like the whole world has *gone mad?*"

"All the time," she admitted with a yawn, "and often feel like *I* am the one leading the charge. Goodnight, Corbin."

What neither knew at that moment was that Union General Robert Milroy was at the door of Winchester, ready to take up winter quarters.

CHAPTER 19

Ben Graham returned to his company after a four-day pass that ended Christmas Day, thankful to have had the brief time with Fiona and her family in Richmond. As his wife had lain beside him in their bed that morning, wrapped in his arms, she had given him the news of her pregnancy. And, since that moment of wonder, he had been torn between sweet ecstasy and dreadful fear.

He was thirteen when his mother died in labor, and he still carried with him superstitious fears attached to childbearing, not entirely discarded with education and spiritual maturity. When choking terror took hold of him, prayer was the only effective measure in restoring equanimity and peace of soul.

But even this balm of solace was challenged when Ben was called to duty the day after his return. His attendance was required at a court martial of two men from the Richmond Greys who had been caught in the act of desertion. When they were sentenced to execution and his responsibilities brought him into their presence to pray with and for them, he was forced to face his own sense of guilt. He had been allowed leave to go home when they had not.

Jimmy Thigpen was seventeen and the only son of his widowed mother. His home was in Norfolk, and he hadn't been back in almost a year. When he'd joined the Richmond Greys, it was his first time away from home and Ben knew of his struggles with severe bouts of homesickness. Like Ben, he had missed the battle of Antietam when influenza had passed through the ranks, and after the battle at Fredericksburg in which the young man had witnessed the carnage of war for the first time, Jimmy had come to Ben in tears. With bravado belied by the fear in his eyes, Jimmy told him that he was not afraid to die, but how much he wished to see his mother and the ocean again before then.

Dewey Foster was the man who had recently lost his wife in childbirth and was sorely worried about his three young children. Dewey told Ben that his wife had been left to work the small farm outside Beulahville on her own, and he feared she hadn't been able to harvest enough to feed them through the winter. He, like Jimmy, requested leave but had been denied.

Ben performed his duty and stood beside Captain Brown as the order to fire was given, but he closed his eyes, unable to bear the sight. He would write to their families and tell them – *how much they had been loved*. He did not want them to suffer shame as well as the grief, though he knew he couldn't spare them. Nothing on earth could do that. *Would he tell them that he would have done the same if Fiona needed him?* Just the thought of it made his gut clench and his head swim, and he prayed he would not pass out. *Dear God, would this ever be over?*

The executions were the first in the regiment and had been ordered as a deterrent to others in the growing number of deserters in the whole army. It was Ben's strong opinion that the measure might also have the opposite effect.

Knowing that delaying the task wouldn't relieve Jimmy's mother or Dewey's children, or even his own pain, Ben took out paper and pen as soon as he returned to his tent. Staring at the blank page, he recalled that after the victory at Fredericksburg, Edmund told him Jackson's view of desertion: *it was not only a dishonorable dereliction of duty but a grievous crime against those who remained, those who had laid down their lives, and the widows and orphans they had left behind.*

27 December, 1862

Dear Mrs. Thigpen, (Ben began)

At noon today, your dear son Jimmy became another victim in this war of endless tragedies. As his chaplain, I can only offer you the comfort of knowing that he is now at peace and rest with our Lord, no longer to suffer the plague of war that tore him from your arms and is still ravaging our lives and land.

The greatest grief Jimmy suffered during the months of military service was his separation from you and his home. It was a grief that especially bore down on him during the Christmas season till he could bear it no longer. Knowing Jimmy as I was privileged to do, he would never have left his post under any threat of danger from the enemy. It was his knowledge that there would not likely be another encounter until spring that prompted him to take leave when his request had been denied.

Though it may bring you little comfort, I offer you my heartfelt condolences, and pray in all fervency that God's Spirit will do what I cannot. I am enclosing Jimmy's farewell letter to you as I promised him. May God be merciful to us all!

Chaplain Benjamin Baxter Graham, M.Div.
Richmond Greys, 2nd Company

After the second letter had been written, Ben spent the rest of the day in private prayer until he could regain the security of his Lord's benediction to continue his pastoral ministries to the rest of the company.

Edmund returned to Jackson's winter base, after spending Christmas with his family at Vermillion, with a depressed spirit. His grieving mother's need of comfort was insatiable and his own sense of inadequacy distressing. Caroline's husband Gerald Mason seemed to be in a similar state of insufficiency trying to meet Caroline's incessant demands for his undivided attention.

Gerald's father, the State Senator, had procured his only son a government job in Richmond where they resided, but Edmund sensed Gerald envied *him*. This was a perplexing thought until finally concluding that, although Gerald was constantly referring to the importance of his work, he would have preferred to be in the army and relieved of Caroline's unappeasable neediness.

At the moment the enlightenment dawned, Edmund had immediately retreated to the stables and laughed hysterically. It was the only thing he was capable of doing to avert hysterical *crying*. No one in the family had asked about his life as a soldier because they *did not want to know!* So, he had dutifully capitulated, excluding all talk of death, disease, hunger, mutilation, fear – and instead endeavored to be cheerful, interested, and sympathetic to their all-consuming, narrow-scoped experiences and petty grievances.

And, when it was commanded, he offered convincing reassurance that "Of course the war would soon be won. All was well with the Confederacy and victory was just around the corner." That is what they wanted to hear, and he'd done his best to put their minds at rest, though his heart beat with resentment. His own mind could not reject the hard truths the others had the luxury of denying.

Edmund envied Geordie's visit with *his* family and was eager to hear all the news from Winchester, which Geordie generously shared, omitting only, out of loyalty to his brother, Rosie's profession and their sleeping arrangement. But details of the Graham family's joyous reunion only served to depress Edmund further and his own need for familial comfort and loving support increased his longing for them.

He was gratified that Abby had been able to go home but was slightly unsettled by the knowledge Corbin had accompanied her. The story of the adopted twins with disabilities, Abby's discovery of her "calling" on their first visit, and the tragedy of Cullen's death at Sharpsburg had engendered Edmund's sympathies, but he now was plagued by pangs of jealousy.

"I suppose Abby has become very close to Corbin since he lost his brother," he mused, with an effort to sound only casually interested.

The suggestion surprised Geordie and he gave it careful thought. "I observed that she holds him in high regard and trusts him. And, despite his limitations, they communicate with one another amazingly well. But I did not see any indication that she has a *romantic* interest in him, if that is what you are asking.

"I do wonder, now that you have brought it to my mind, if Corbin might have 'feelings' for her. Although he is typically quite reserved, even guarded in his aspect, I had the impression that his constant awareness of her may go beyond protectiveness. But that is only an impression, and I certainly would have hesitated to ask directly even if it had occurred to me to do so.

"But please do not allow yourself to be discouraged, Edmund. We will continue to pray for her and for patient trust in the Lord's flawless timing."

"Do you think she is happy?" Edmund asked for the second time.

"Not entirely, although she loves teaching the children on South Mountain. Her spirit is troubled, and I tried to ease her mind by encouraging her in what she feels called to do. She does not approve of us being in the military, you know, but will acknowledge *we* believe it to be honorable. It pains me to see her wrestle in futility to integrate her strong political and spiritual beliefs with those held by those she loves best… and that most definitely includes *you*.

"But it pains me even more to see Davy wrestle with *himself,* and I know it is also futile because he will not admit his problem is internal, not external. He hinted at how he is still fighting for 'our cause' and he will doubtlessly be caught. Both he *and* Abby are taking risks, but Davy is enjoying it."

Edmund sighed. "I rather think Abby enjoys taking risks too. At least she enjoys watching me suffer with worry for what she is *doing*."

Geordie gave his friend a look of gentle reproof. "I do not believe that for a minute. She only wants you to sincerely accept her passions as legitimate, even if you cannot share them. Can you *honestly* do that, Edmund?"

"*Can I sincerely accept it?* I will *try* but, in all honesty, it would be for all the wrong reasons. Not because I *respect* her choices as she asked me to… but because I need her!" His voice shook with emotion. *"Damn it, Geordie, I accept it because I need her! But what if she gets caught?"*

The New Year arrived quietly in Boonsboro with a fresh layer of snow, prompting Abby to declare it a holiday from school. It was also time to celebrate Corbin's eighteenth birthday.

It was easy to forget his real age for there was little about him that could be considered *boyish,* certainly not his sober intensity or even his appearance; his physical maturation and what shreds of boyishness there had been were erased when Cullen died.

Functionally, Corbin had been a man all his life.

In so many ways he was very different from the other males in Abby's life. Despite the tragedies of war, Geordie, Edmund, Ben, even Davy and Paul had what she would describe as *"joie de vivre"* – an expectation of joy. It seemed to her that whatever pleasure Corbin found came as a surprise, and he experienced it with guardedness, as if suspecting it had come to him by mistake.

Actually, it was one of the things that drew Abby to him and became a personal challenge. Though she had been deeply shaken by her experiences, her own innate joie de vivre found delight in rousing his pleasure whenever an opportunity arose.

For his birthday, Abby made him a picture book of her drawings, depicting him in various situations with a variety of facial expressions, and had added humorous captions of what he, or other illustrated characters, would be thinking. On one page she drew him making wild turkey calls, unaware that behind his back was a flock of infuriated turkeys ready to attack him. She was gratified when he laughed aloud at every page.

The awkwardness of not talking to him at home frustrated Abby, though she was now adept at silent communication. She understood, at least partially, Corbin's strong aversion to serve in the army and fear of conscription if his feigned disability was discovered, but she worried that prolonging his silence was detrimental to his spirit. She sensed, rather than cognized, the depth and turbulence that lay beneath the still waters of his placid, meek mien, and believed that freeing himself of the need to be silent at home would relieve some of his internal tension.

When Abby tried to persuade him to tell Seth he shook his head.

"There are too many people in and out of the surgery every day," he argued. "Pa wouldn't mean to betray me, but he would sooner or later make a slip. I don't want to put that responsibility on him. After the war is over, I will tell him."

While the Douglas household went about their routines and General Lee and his army wintered south of Fredericksburg, General Milroy's presence in Winchester was not appreciated by the great majority of citizenry, including most of Paul's parishioners. As the dominant gender by the absence of fighting men, much of the resistance in Winchester, as Davy had said, came from the women who refused to be intimidated by Milroy and his troops.

The rationale for this wholesale defiance, offered to Paul by Frances Pierce, an elder's wife, was based on the "lack of discipline and adequate home training" of which the Union army was deficient to such an extreme measure that she and the other ladies felt a "sincere obligation to remediate." Predictably, neither side was amenable to remediation, and the negligibly disguised antagonism continued throughout the occupation.

The spiritual awakening inspired by Paul's preaching of allegiance to the *Kingdom of God* was put to the test when the general employed harsh measures to discourage resistance, including the requirement that local citizens take an oath of allegiance to the federal government and billeting soldiers in the homes of those who refused. He also declined to intervene when his soldiers vandalized private property.

Paul was exempt from taking the oath of allegiance since he voluntarily opened the manse doors to six low-ranking officers, taking advantage of the opportunity to evangelize and encourage their attendance in worship services. In fact, he encouraged his flock to do the same, pointing out the benefits of legitimate avoidance of the oath taking.

He also welcomed the opportunity to demonstrate the reality of the true nature of love between Christ the King and his kingdom the Church, and the bonds of fellowship and love between believers that characterize His Church by welcoming Union soldiers to join in worship. *"This is my commandment. That ye love one another, as I have loved you."*

To Paul's grief, the hope of reconciliation with Davy was not realized after Geordie was gone. His one source of consolation was Rosie's presence from time to time at the Sunday morning service.

Rosie consistently made an appearance after the start of the service and chose a seat on the back row in an effort to be inconspicuous, though that was an impossibility. Her identity, occupation, and association with the pastor's youngest son had become common gossip, and the congregants were unified in their skepticism and incredulous disapprobation.

What also became common knowledge was Paul's response to the complaints voiced at a session meeting not long after Rosie's first appearance, which effectively squelched further open challenges and at least drove the gossip underground. He'd begun by taking out his Bible and reading aloud the parable of Jesus recorded in the 18th chapter of St. Luke's gospel – the contrasting prayers of the Pharisee and the publican. And, after closing it and without speaking, his eyes had searched those of each man seated around the table. When he did speak, his voice was gentle but uncompromising.

"Jesus makes it clear that it was the *publican*, who acknowledged his sinfulness and need of mercy, rather than the Pharisee, that returned to his home justified. And as long as I remain your pastor, we will welcome *everyone*... black or white, blue or gray, flagrant sinner or secret sinner... *all* whom the Lord draws to hear His word exposited. It is *His* house, not ours, gentlemen, and we will not dishonor Him by pharisaical discrimination."

Though the girl from the tavern was aware of the censorious attitudes, she bore it without bitterness, and Paul made a special point of speaking to her after the service and before she effected a quick getaway. He repeatedly expressed his concern for her and his desire that she know Jesus and His compassion for sinners, and she seemed genuinely touched by his sincerity. He also voiced concerns for Davy and offered help if it was needed.

Davy not only denied his need of his father's help, he continued his behind-the-scenes acts of hostility toward the Yankees with gleeful rashness. It provided a sense of purpose and pride, even self-respect, in a perverse fashion – the self-respect that had been severed from his soul by the scalpel that amputated half his lower extremity. Furtive, subversive revenge on the enemy became the quest for redemption and reparation, and his own singular contribution to the war effort.

His activities troubled Rosie, but she wasn't convinced she would stop him even if she had the power to do so, which she didn't. She couldn't deny him his sense of triumph, but every night he was gone, she expected him to be shot or jailed by morning, and she was almost amazed to find him in her bed when she woke.

While the armies took their break from action, Abby continued to teach the children of South Mountain and took pleasure in their progress. She also took an interest in their domestic welfare, bringing medicine for their croup and constipation, compliments of Seth who continued to suffer with arthritis, forcing him to cut back on house calls. Abby was especially committed in her efforts to meet the physical needs of the Negro community, drawing Naomi's ire upon her head by raiding the scantily stocked pantry for items to bring them.

Predictably, and in spite of the winter weather, two more runaway slaves had heard about the enclave and taken refuge there. But their desire was not just for refuge, it was for freedom.

On the way up to the settlement the third Saturday in January, Abby informed Corbin, "I am going to tell them today that you can now hear, and it will not do you any good to talk me out of it. You need to start *sometime* and *somewhere* to communicate like the whole human being you are, and *these people deserve all of you, Corbin Logan Douglas!*"

"How are you planning to explain this *miracle?*" he asked warily.

"You will see. Just go along with it."

When they arrived, Abby called a meeting of the community, and when they were assembled, she lifted up her eyes and hands in a gesture of praise.

"Friends, we have the most *wonderful* news to share with you today... *Corbin can now hear and speak!* Dr. Seth discovered a treatment for him, and the good Lord has been pleased to grant Corbin the *gift of sound!*"

There was a general gasp of joyful surprise and a chorus of

"hallelujahs!" and "Thank you, Jesus!" before she continued.

"We are all celebrating this wonderful cure but there is something we must ask of you. If everyone knows he has been cured, then he will be required to fight in the war. But Corbin and I have been called by the Lord to serve in a *special* way. We have been called not to *fight* but to lead those who are *enslaved* to *freedom*. You must all keep Corbin's secret so that we can continue our work!"

Corbin found himself surrounded by a crowd of smiling dark faces all talking to him at once and gave Abby a subtle roll of the eyes. When the excitement died down and order was restored in the small shack that served as schoolroom, she gestured with her head encouraging Corbin to discuss the business of freedom trail while she began her lessons.

"That was relatively painless, was it not?" Abby asked later with a flash of unabashed smugness on the downward trail.

"I must admit, you are an accomplished storyteller. You had even *me* convinced," he grinned. "It feels very strange to have folks actually talk to me... besides you, but I *liked* it."

"Good. I know we did not discuss taking these new arrivals to Mr. Grable, but it was obvious when we came last week we were both thinking about it. I'm not forcing you into it, am I?"

Corbin shook his head, and by his intense expression, Abby knew he was in deep thought. They rode in silence for several more minutes before he spoke.

"Jerome says the slave catchers are everywhere, just like your pa predicted. Our friends are keeping a close watch for them here on the mountain but so far none have been spotted this high up. It's going to get more dangerous, Abby, and you have to be aware of that before we start out again."

"I *have* been thinking about that. I know Naomi has freedom papers; I think it is called 'manumission.' Do you know if Old Tom or any of the other freed ones have them as well? Do you think they might be willing to loan their papers to Jerome and... what is the other one's name?"

"Simon. But to answer your question, I have never seen their papers or know if they actually have them. If you remember what Old Tom told Pa… they left home after his father was lynched and that was a long time ago."

"I will figure it out. Anything we can think of to minimize the risks will be worthwhile. And as much as I dread going again in the cold, it is the best time to attempt it. No one in their right mind would choose a route on the ridge of this mountain in the dead of winter if they did not have to. I wish we had more horses, or even mules."

"We know it's the passes that most likely will be patrolled. But we also know the trail better than we did the first time, and we know where there is a cabin with a hidey-hole. These are our advantages, and we'll make the most of them."

"Whatever you say, General," Abby quipped with a jaunty salute.

"I thought *you* were going to be the *general*," he responded with a snort.

CHAPTER 20

The first action taken by Abby entailed getting a look at Naomi's manumission papers, and she, with only a show of disinclination, allowed Abby to study the wording. Abby's next step took her back up to the settlement to collect the full names and ages of the two men, and with this information, she created Manumission documents, forging the signature of her deceased Uncle William Spencer of Camden Hall as the slaveholder granting the release. She relished the irony of using the name of the one who had perpetrated the rape of Annabel to gain freedom to others.

Abby was pleased with the result of her work, but, nevertheless, she petitioned the Lord in prayer that the documents would not have to be produced. The scheme was so easily fabricated, it was almost frightening. Both Abby and Corbin realized that if they were caught, the penalties for the fraud would result in a much more serious consequence than merely aiding fugitive slaves.

Seth's coinciding concerns prompted his insistence that they take both of his horses for travel, arguing that his patients would just have to come to the surgery for treatment. Hesitantly, but gratefully, Abby accepted the offer. If they were pursued, having a mount for each would provide a better chance of escape.

The final stage of preparation required more careful fabrication, a cover story which Corbin again entrusted to Abby's fertile imagination. Her limited but sobering experiences thus far had taught her to stay close to the truth, and it made sense to stick with her profession as roving teacher to the children on the isolated homesteads scattered in the mountains. She would take some of her books and supplies in case props were called for.

A plausible explanation for Corbin posed no difficulty either – he was her deaf brother along to provide assistance and protection.

And they would use the name she'd given Mr. Reinhart – *McGuffey*, in honor of the author of the readers she used. It was doubtful anyone would raise questions regarding the coincidence.

After careful consideration, Abby's story would entail a need for an Amish buggy, in good condition, and her two friends, Jerome and Simon were taking her to Fountain Dale, Pennsylvania where their relative, a wainwright, had one for sale. The two "freedmen" planned to stay with their relatives and Abby and her brother would be returning to South Mountain with the buggy, satisfied it would be much more practical for her travels than horseback in inclement weather.

When Abby practiced reciting the story to Corbin, his immediate reaction was reasonable doubt but admitted he couldn't devise a better one. By the time they ascended the mountain with the counterfeit manumission documents that she had folded over several times and stained with dirt, their supplies, and the two additional horses, he acknowledged the story had merits. In fact, he wished it *were* true; Seth's curricle had seen better days and he had admired the practicality of Paul's conveyance at Christmas.

It was a clear day with only six to ten inches of snow on the mountain that crunched under the horses' feet as they broke through the icy layer. But the wind was biting, especially in the higher elevations, where the chances of meeting anyone were significantly lower and where they needed to stay. Jerome and Simon were novice horsemen but highly motivated to stay in the saddle, and Merlin and Molly were content to follow Corbin on Mars.

The remnants of Cullen's wardrobe now clothed the rookie riders, but their shoes were their own and had to be tied on their feet with leather strings. As Abby rode behind them, her critical eye questioned the inadvisability of not trying harder to round up some shoes that were in better shape. It was much too late to upgrade now, but her brain was already making plans for "next time."

When they stopped for a short lunch break of baked sweet potatoes donated by Mrs. Mathis, Abby and Corbin encouraged their companions to tell their stories.

"Iz from a 'baccy plantation 'roun Ma'shall" Jerome began. "We wuz makin' it aw rat' til dey sole my woman an' chilin ta somewheas in Geo'gia. I tole um *'Don' do dat ta me! Ya ain't got no rat ta do dat! Dey is mine!'*

"I gots sa mad when dey watten lissen dat I tole da boss I gonna *kill um!* Well, he don' like dat, an' start beaten da debil outa me! I wuz sa bad off, I couldna see nuffen outa ma eye fo' a good while an' couldna do nuffen else neithe'. All dat time I'm a think' 'bout runnin'. At firse I be thinkin' 'bout goin 'ta Geo'gia afta ma woman, but den I figa I bes' not 'cause I knows dey git me. So den I figa I'd go fin' da *North Sta'* an' be free. Den I'd figa out how ta git um back."

One of his eyes seemed to have sustained permanent damage. Jerome admitted his vision was now poor in that eye, and that it seemed to have affected his balance as well.

Simon told them he also had suffered abusive treatment but was motivated to escape from his master in Middleburg, Virginia, by the knowledge that President Lincoln had set slaves free.

"Dat man is da President an' if he say I be *free*, den I *is free!* An' me 'n Jerome gonna join de President's ahmy and fights wif da Yankees!"

Abby had serious doubts about Jerome's eligibility, and the look she exchanged with Corbin told her he was thinking the same.

Dodging slave catchers along the way, some with vicious dogs, the two men had providentially been ferried across the Potomac by the same night boatman who called himself *Charon*, somewhere between Harpers Ferry and Brunswick. He was the one who told them about the enclave of free Negros up on South Mountain. They were half-frozen and nearly starved by the time they found it.

Abby asked if they had heard the Greek mythological story of Charon and all three male companions shook their head. After she told them he was the boatman who ferried dead souls across the River Styx to the shores of Hades, Simon nodded at Abby in sudden enlightenment.

"Dat man say he wuz takin' *dead* folks ta da lan' o' da *livin'!* He be doin' back'ards fom dat story. I ain't sho' wha' he mean by it…

but it make mo' sense ni."

The travelers made better time than on their first trip and began descending into the Harbaugh Valley before sunset. But, before the troop could breathe a sigh of relief, they were approached by two armed horsemen who barred the trail in front of them.

"Where are you and those niggers going?" one of the men demanded, addressing Corbin.

"What makes it your business, sir?" Abby bravely queried back, guiding Mercury forward beside Mars.

Ignoring Abby, the man continued to stare menacingly at Corbin who met his glare with the same hard look.

"He is deaf. If you expect an answer to your question, then answer mine," Abby persisted. "Are you the *law?*"

Finally looking directly at her he sneered. "Not official, but I'm makin' every nigger 'roun' here my business. They better have proof they ain't somebody's niggers or I'll take them rat now… and there's nothin' you and the dummy can *do about it.*"

After a moment's consideration, which definitely validated his claim, Abby turned to the Negros with a nod.

"Show them, and then they had *better* leave us alone."

Dutifully, but visibly trembling, Jerome and Simon produced the forged documents which Abby handed to the slave catcher. The aging of the documents was as bogus as the documents themselves and Abby held her breath, as did the other three, as the man scrutinized them.

Grudgingly, the papers were returned to Abby's outstretched hand, but the man's attitude remained darkly suspicious. He addressed them all with a look of disgust.

"I don't like the looks of ya. Now get out a here!"

With the exhalation of her breath, Abby's indignation returned. "I do not like the looks of you either, mister. I hate bullies, especially *slave-catching bullies!*"

They rode on in silence for several minutes until heartbeats returned to a more normal rhythm.

"*Damn*, Abby!" Corbin whispered between clenched teeth. "*Why didn't you just give them the 'story'?*"

Resisting the mounting hysteria with difficulty, she barely managed an answer without giggling.

"You heard me.... *I did not like his looks.*" She too wondered what had possessed her; brazenness could lead to disaster.

For precautions sake Corbin led them to a crop of woods where they waited until dark, making certain they weren't followed. Only then did they warily proceed to the Grable farm, where they spent the night in the loft of the barn. At dawn John Grable woke them and supplied Abby and Corbin with a bundle of rations for their return journey.

Upon their arrival the night before, Abby asked Mr. Grable about the slave catchers they had encountered.

"Thee *met* him then? Vergil Brent is no one thee should annoy, Friend Abby. He is a brute, who would kill every black brother he sees except those he can return to their masters for reward money. And he would not hesitate to hurt anyone who would help them. Thee should *stay out of his way!*"

Abby assured him she intended to do so.

At Corbin's insistence they found the distillers' cabin again but, at Abby's urging, did not stay long. There were no signs anyone had been there since November, but in preparation for a possible need, he brought more fire logs inside to dry out. It seemed that winter did not deter the brave and desperate souls seeking freedom, and he and Abby should be ready to aid them.

But plans to offer escort services to fleeing slaves had to be postponed during the next month because of an outbreak of influenza on the west side of South Mountain. Seth began to see his first cases the last week of January and instructed his household as well as his patients to take precautions to avoid exposure as well as exposing others.

The Smith children were the first of Abby's students to present symptoms – high fever, severe sore throat, wheezing and coughing, and fatigue. And they were also the first family to bury one–their eighteen-month-old son Rudy. Three weeks later, when most of the other children were recovering, five-year-old Becky Delany took a turn for the worse and was dead by the following morning.

The adults also suffered from the ailment to one degree or another, and Jane Robin's mother, Sylvia, died within days of contact. Also, there were several adults whose recoveries were complicated by pneumonia.

But hardest hit of all were the Negros, and Abby suffered greatly from guilt that she was likely the source of exposure. The first Saturday in February she had no symptoms, but by Sunday afternoon, she was in bed with a high fever. And, although she recovered within a week, several of the Negros did not, including Gideon's mama Ruby.

In total, every one of the Negros was affected and there were seven deaths. The two children in that number were six-year-old Josie and two-year-old Willy Joe. It was mid-March by the time the virus had run its course.

The four fugitive slaves who made their way to the settlement during the epidemic were urged not to stay, and no one could say whether or not they made it over the Mason-Dixon. The thoughts of these poor souls haunted Abby, adding to her sense of guilt and making her more determined that none would ever be lost again.

CHAPTER 21

On March 20th, Abby and Corbin led five more Negros north along the ridge of South Mountain, three women; Nancy, Lizzie, and Mary; and Mary's two children with forged manumission documents and clothed in garments collected by Mrs. Mathis. Nancy and Lizzie rode astride Merlin, Mary rode Molly with one of the children, and Corbin held the other child whose name was Lester in front of him in the lead. Abby astride Mercury, along with their supplies, took the rear.

Over a foot of snow covered the ground in some low places, and heavy clouds above threatened more. Abby observed Corbin looking up frequently with silent concern. He'd attempted to convince Abby to wait another day or two, but she would not hear of it. Reluctantly agreeing, he insisted that they shelter for the night at the cabin rather than making it to Sabillasville in one day.

The young boy, whose head bumped against his chest as they progressed through the woods and rocks occasionally looked up at Corbin and grinned, and he smiled back. The child's missing front teeth indicated he must be about six or seven, Corbin guessed, the same age he and his brother had been when they found refuge with Seth and Corrine. His thoughts drifted to Cullen, and a stab of pain struck his chest, many times sharper than the thudding of the child's head.

Restively he turned his thoughts away and realized with surprise that he enjoyed the feel of the small body against his own. He was unused to thinking about his future, but he suddenly recognized in himself a desire to have a child, a family he could call his own.

It was a painful reverie. He loved Abby, had loved her since the moment he saw her face as she announced her *calling* to be a teacher. But at the same time that he acknowledged his love for her, he knew she would never be his. She was too fine, her destiny too far beyond his small plot of rock and soil. Moreover, she deserved a *whole* man, not one who still doubted his own soundness of identity.

With resolution, Corbin made a silent vow. While Abby was with him, he would take care of her and never speak of love. He would cherish the time with her and give her his blessing when it was time for her to leave. But he wondered if he would ever love another woman without comparing her to Abby. It was hard to imagine that he could.

As they neared the trail through the northern pass over the mountain, his thoughts were interrupted by the sound of distant voices, and he reined Mars with a hushing noise. It was impossible to determine where the sounds were coming from, and though he waited several more minutes, he couldn't be sure. They were at least a mile from the cabin, and the shadows of the afternoon were growing. Guiding Mars close beside Abby, he lifted Lester and placed him in front of her.

"Can you find the cabin?" he whispered.

"I think so," she nodded, her heart thumping at a fast rate. "What are you going to do?"

"I'm going to try to disguise our tracks. They would lead right to us if I don't do something. You had better not start a fire until I know it's safe. I do not know who is out there, but I much prefer them not knowing where we are."

She nodded again and led the way as the others followed close behind with nervous glances in every direction. Abby zigzagged through the trees, doubling back in an effort to confuse a pursuer, and they reached the cabin unhindered. Instructing the others to go in first, she led the horses inside behind them before going back out to drag a large branch and obscure the prints in the snow. At least, she reasoned, she'd disguised the distinctive details of the group's membership.

A half-mile away, Corbin crept close enough to recognize the slave catcher Virgil Brent and his cohort arguing whether to continue their hunt in the impending snowstorm or to retire to Sabillasville for the night. The unnamed associate was taking a berating for choosing the later.

"Just go on back then, ya worthless son-of-a-bitch. If it gets bad, I'll stay at the cabin," Brent roared at his departing deputy and Corbin froze in terror.

Following at a distance, Corbin's first thought was to distract Brent and was about to call out when a shot was fired, hitting his left shoulder just below the collarbone. Burning pain raced down his arm and, fighting to stay in the saddle as Mars shied, he almost dropped the rifle.

Summoning his shattered mental fragments into focus, Corbin shook off the impending symptoms of shock and the instinctive urge to flee. He had no other choice but to stop Brent, even if it came down to killing him or getting killed trying.

But darkness was descending rapidly, and he feared getting lost or, worse still, fainting from loss of blood. He listened intently but could hear nothing except the pounding of adrenalin in his ears. Brent was an experienced tracker and it wouldn't take him long to pick up Abby's tracks. Rather than confronting the man first, Corbin determined to reach the cabin ahead of him – if he could make it.

Abby began to worry when Corbin hadn't turned up and the group was growing even colder with the dropping temperature and no fire to warm them. Opening the door in hopes of hearing Mar's hoof beats or neighs, she thought sure she did. It was beginning to snow and she stepped outside to have a look around.

She definitely heard him now and breathed a sigh of relief, but it wasn't Corbin she saw in the fading light, and gasped . . . .

"Well, well," said an oddly familiar and chilling voice. "If it ain't the *nigger lover* with the dummy. Was that *him* I shot at?"

"You did what?" she forced out through her constricting throat. Her mind suddenly blanked and no plan formulated.

"What are ya doing here, sister," he demanded coming closer. "Are ya by yourself?"

His voice held a hopeful note that raised her anxiety to an even higher level as she tried desperately to think. *What had happened to Corbin?*

Brent dismounted and pushed past her to peer inside the door. He couldn't see in the darkness but heard the sounds of a child's fearful whimper. Abby heard it too, and she shoved the man with all her strength into the doorframe.

"Get the *hell out of here,* you bastard, or I will . . . ."

"You'll *what?*" he jeered, painfully gripping her arm. "Ya talk like a lady, but have the language of a *sailor.* And ya dress like one of those *perverts* that likes other women, *all diked out like that.* What ya *really* need is a *man* inside those knickers with ya, sweetheart!"

He pushed her through the doorway, and stumbling backwards, she fell under the horses' feet. Before entering, Brent fished matches from the pocket of his coat and struck one on the doorpost. Picking up a stick of dry kindling at the right of the doorway, he lit it and waited for the flame to illumine the interior of the cabin.

Abby had crawled under the horses and was shielding the terrified huddled group beside the hearth when his eyes adjusted to the light, and comprehension blazed in his narrowed gaze. Brent's chuckle sent icy chills up Abby's spine.

"Well, well . . . . What have we here? *What have you brought Papa,* sweetheart?"

"You touch them and *I will kill you…* with *my bare hands,* if I have to," she dared him, knowing her threats were absurdly empty.

In her panic she had forgotten the pistol in her saddlebag, still on Mercury's flank. The only chance she had depended on getting her hands on it. Deeming her to be no threat, he'd left his rifle on his horse.

"I will make you a bargain… I have some *money.* You can have it if you leave us alone. These are *freed* Negros and we can prove it, so they are not worth your trouble anyway," she bluffed, the blood pounding through her veins, sending oxygen to brain cells, and warming her limbs for action.

"*Where's* the money?" he asked suspiciously.

"I will get it," she said edging closer to the horses. "I hid it with the other supplies."

"I don't trust you a mite. You get back over there, and I'll do the lookin'."

He pulled the saddlebags off Mercury and, motioning the group toward the back of the cabin and away from the hearth, set the bundle of kindling Abby had laid ablaze with the remains of his torch. Keeping one eye on Abby, he bent to inspect the bags and immediately came across the revolver.

"You *damn sneaky pervert!* You don't have no money, *do ya?"* he roared in anger, and noting the gun wasn't loaded, threw it, hitting her hard in the chest.

Abby was ready to despair when she heard Corbin's voice from the doorway, *"Mine* is loaded, Mr. Brent and though I despise violence I *will* shoot you."

Corbin did indeed hold the rifle in Brent's direction, but his voice was unnaturally weak, and he swayed slightly on his feet. The small hole in his coat and the dark bloodstain on his left shoulder were discernable even in the dim light. He held the rifle to his right shoulder with his right hand on the trigger, and Abby was well aware of this disadvantage.

His adversary quickly assessed the situation and replied with another snigger, "Ha! *He* ain't deaf and dumb. *You,* missy," he winked at Abby with a wag of his finger, "are the biggest liar I have *ever* seen! Don't you know liars go to hell? You was lyin' about these niggers too, I bet."

Brent then turned his attention back to Corbin leaning against the doorframe and calculated his chances. The look in Corbin's eyes told him not to try anything foolish but all he had to do was wait.

"You ain't lookin' too good, fella," he said with mock concern, "maybe you oughta sit down and lemme have a look at that shoulder. You're gonna fall down if ya don't."

Corbin knew this to be a fact and could feel his remaining strength slipping away like the last grains of sand in an hourglass.

"Abby, can you give me a hand?"

It happened so quickly it was over in a few furious seconds, but Abby lived it in slow motion. As she started toward Corbin, Brent seized her arm and swung her at Corbin, knocking the rifle from his hand and upsetting his precarious balance.

As soon as he let her go, Abby fell, but her hand landed on a split log, and when Brent lunged at Corbin, she sprang forward and landed a hard blow squarely on the back of his head with an arm-jarring whack. When he hit the floor, she struck his head over and over till drops of blood and brain matter splattered her and everything else within four feet, including Corbin.

Abby felt nothing and saw nothing but the face of the Shockoe slave breaker as she emptied her impotent rage with each pounding blow of the wooden weapon.

"Abby . . . Stop. Abby . . . he is dead." She barely heard the soft voice, but she obeyed.

Her breath was coming in gasps from the exertion and her heart pounded like an anvil against her ribs. She stared at her trembling, bloody hands frozen around the club for a long time before she could pry them loose, and the sound of the wood hitting the floor seemed louder than the trumpet on the Last Day.

The Negros watched in horrified silence as Abby crawled to Corbin now struggling into a sitting position with his back against the doorframe. Laying a gory hand on his injured shoulder, she began to shiver violently, and he reached up to gently cradle her cheek.

Still without speaking, Nancy and Lizzie went through Brent's pockets, and after wrapping the pulverized head in a bandana, pulled the body out of the cabin. Abby gave them a grateful nod and, once the trembling stopped, wiped her hands and face with the snow Lizzie was carrying in by the armful while they began cleaning up the carnage.

The frozen liquid's efficacy to purge was sorely inadequate, but Abby retrieved her medical kit, and while the women continued to scrub and the children kept the fire burning, applied alcohol and bandages to Corbin's shoulder. The bullet had gone straight through and Corbin, in a moment of coherency, told her that was a good thing.

When he was either asleep or unconscious, Abby took off the

disgusting coat she was wearing, wrapped herself in a blanket and went outside for fresh air, scrupulously averting her gaze from the inert shape on the ground to the left of the door. Suddenly overcome with nausea, she stumbled to a large tree and vomited with violent heaves.

It was snowing hard, but she didn't care. The smell of blood and smoke inside had awakened again the memories of Antietam Creek and she thought she had rather freeze than go back in. As her thoughts began to gather, Abby heard whinnying sounds and turned her attention to Mars, removing the saddle and covering him with the blanket. There was no room inside for another large animal, but she tethered him as close as she dared to the stone chimney hoping he might feel some of the warmth.

The bracing cold air also seemed to steel her nerves, and locating Brent's horse, she looked through the saddlebags for anything useful. She took his rifle, a tin of beans, a bedroll and blanket, and a logbook back into the cabin where the bedding and blanket were gratefully received. After looking through the logbook in which he had accounted for each slave caught and rewards received, she burned it in the fire.

On their last trip, Abby had found glass jars near the site of a dismantled still and, now she filled two of them with clean snow for drinking. Finally, she once again scrubbed her face and hands in the wet snow washing as thoroughly as she could in an act of futile ablution. With a last deep breath of the frigid air, she resigned herself to go back inside, prompted only by worry for Corbin.

When Abby reentered, Nancy exchanged Abby's coat, now relatively cleaned, for the jars of snow and placed them beside the fire. Once melted, she gave one to Lizzie to pass among the children. The other she handed first to Abby to drink, then Corbin, before she and Lizzie together towed him on one of the blankets away from the door and closer to the fire.

Abby picked up the rifle, and sinking to the floor close to Corbin, sat cross-legged with her back against the wall.

"Thank you," Abby whispered to the women, who solemnly nodded and lay down with the others already snuggled together on the other side of the hearth. She could already hear the phlegmy breathing of the sleeping children.

All the activity had been accomplished in silence with the exception of only the barest whispers. It was a silence that shrieked and bawled of endangerment and horror, but they were together and alive, and that remained the basis of their hope and consolation.

After a fitful night, Abby woke to find Corbin awake and gazing at her. "Are you all right?" she asked anxiously putting a hand to his forehead. "Do you have a fever?"

He shook his head. "It is *you* I am concerned about, Abby."

With her hand still resting on his hot forehead, she assured him in a quiet tone, "Do not worry, just tell me what to do with . . . him. We cannot just leave him here. We don't have a shovel, or I could bury him."

"I have been thinking about that, and if we can get him on the horse, it would be best to throw him off a rock ledge and hope anyone who finds him will think he fell."

He was speaking in a whisper and his breath was more shallow than normal, seriously worrying her. She knew he was feverish though he had denied it. Rolling over and getting up, Abby added the last of the dry firewood to the dying embers.

"You lie here and try not to start bleeding again while I go into Sabillasville and ask Mr. Grable to bring his wagon as close as he can, and I will bring our friends to him. Then I will dispose of . . . Mr. Brent and we can go home."

Mercifully, Abby had no further trouble delivering the fugitives after the women helped her to sling Brent's body over his horse's back, and with a good bit of effort, the body eventually came to rest at the bottom of Buzzard Knob. She sincerely hoped the buzzards would enjoy their meal and leave nothing behind except clean, unidentifiable bones.

Also attributed to the Lord's mercy were Mr. Grable's more thorough cleaning and bandaging of Corbin's wound, and his return to his father's house for further competent medical care and recovery. They arrived close to midnight and Abby was so exhausted from physically bolstering his stability in the saddle she could barely stand. Then she slept until the evening of the following day.

Seth speculated but asked only rudimentary questions, wisely choosing not to press for further details. "Who shot him?"

"A slave catcher."

"Where is the man now?"

"He is dead . . . a fatal accident."

" Are the Negros safe?"

"We got them safely to another."

"Is it safe enough to go again?"

And she shrugged her shoulders; she did not know the answer.

While Corbin recovered, Abby writhed with the effort to suppress all recent memories and avoid introspection. Though she frequently felt Corbin's intense gaze on her, probing the wound in her soul, she had to trust he would do nothing to rip it open, as she would never aggravate the injury to his shoulder. The difference was that his was healing and hers was not.

Abby would not speak of it, but Corbin and Seth heard it in her sighs when she was awake and her moans in the night when dreams would not be kept in abeyance. They were afforded no entry to the locked vault of those memories, and though Corbin knew the dreadful source, he had no remedy to offer the consolation she needed. But, despite his painful wound and his father's dissuasion, Corbin spent each night in impotent vigilance on the floor outside her bedroom door – his own self-imposed acts of contrition for the silent guilt he bore.

Corbin was fully aware of her dark memories but not the questions that haunted Abby without respite. She was willing to risk her own life helping a slave escape but *how could she presume to know the best way to accomplish it? How could she do it without risking the safety of others? What presumptuous insanity, what arrogant pride was driving her? Why did she assume such a weighty obligation rather than be satisfied with her role as a teacher?*

These were some of the questions Abby could not allow herself to contemplate yet. The ground under her feet, which had gradually become substantial again in the six months since Antietam, had begun to erode, and she fought against the current tugging her toward mental and emotional dissolution. If she were to survive, she mustn't think about what she had done – never.

Intuitively she knew that in order to keep her fragile sanity and maintain an adequate level of function she must again rely on what had been learned, by utter necessity and not conscious determination, on the banks of Antietam Creek – Abby dissociated her mind and emotions from the traumatic experience.

As the war went on with no end in sight, the need for Seth's services had not diminished, but his patients' ability to pay had. There was no other source of income for the household, and for the first time, Abby experienced the guilt of a non-contributor. Reluctantly, Seth encouraged Naomi to find supplemental income anywhere she could when he was unable to pay her. And it occurred to all three of them that without Dorothy Mathis's assistance they would likely go hungry.

Dorothy had been coming more frequently to the Douglas home during the winter, bringing supper and helping Seth in the surgery. Her quiet efficiency had a soothing effect on all three in the household, and though occupied with mental wrestling matches, Abby recognized and appreciated the result of her efforts, and thanked her.

A week after the return from the cabin, Abby was helping Dorothy clean up the kitchen garden before planting. Dorothy's expertise with plants included medicinal herbs, and she had expressed interest in teaching Seth in the use of them as medical supplies dwindled. In addition to the proofs she had already produced, Seth's interest extended beyond the garden.

As she worked and directed Abby, Dorothy appeared to enjoy sharing her knowledge and love of herbs.

"Our Indian friends taught us a great deal about the medicinal properties of many native plants such as this thyme, gentian, echinacea, gravel root, ginger root, horseradish, evening primrose, and Joe Pye and pink weeds," she pointed to each and explained their uses.

"And, of course, the English and German settlers added their own knowledge and used plants, such as this foxglove, feverfew, lamb's ear, milkweed, St. John's wort, and peppermint to treat a wide variety of symptoms. And this yarrow, used in wound healing, dates back to ancient Greece.

"These are medicinal herbs that I am putting in here, but I have some lavender and bee balm in my garden that I like for their fragrance and oil. When warmer weather comes, I will plant some of the bee balm in this one to repel the insects. If you like, I will make you some lavender sachets when it blooms. The fragrance has a soothing effect that may help you sleep."

"I would appreciate that," Abby said meekly.

"I admit to being enormously gratified that your sensible Uncle Seth appreciates the value of these herbal blessings. It would be a tragic waste to ignore them, particularly in this difficult time of war. When this garden gets established, he will have all the help God's earth can supply."

Abby agreed and directed her mental faculties to remembering everything she'd been told, heartily welcoming the distraction from her troubles though they were never far from her mind.

After a time, Dorothy's peaceful humming gave Abby the courage to ask, "Mrs. Mathis, when I wear trousers, do I look like, um . . . an *unnatural lover* of women?"

To her credit Dorothy did not appear taken aback.

"Of course not, dear. You look like a practical and modest young lady who knows how to ride a horse. It may not be the way others would choose to ride, but I wager they wished they had your pluck."

Dorothy was gratified to see Abby's facial muscles relax into a natural smile, although the dark haunted look in her eyes remained.

"You are a beautiful woman, Abby, all the more beautiful because you are so oblivious to it."

While Abby struggled with her memories, the Army of Northern Virginia strove to survive on limited supplies. The bureaucrats in Richmond, it was widely rumored among the camps, were more concerned about their own survival than they were about the army defending them.

In desperation General Lee sent General James Longstreet and his corps to southern Virginia and into North Carolina to bring back provisions, but even with these additional stores, the army began preparing to meet the Army of the Potomac without adequate nutrition and necessities. Influenza and scurvy broke out, debilitating many before the warmth of spring promised to provide fresh produce.

As Edmund and Geordie surveyed the pitiable condition of the volunteer soldiers in their brigade, they marveled at their dedication. Although there had been those who deserted during the harsh winter, most men had stayed despite the lack of resources and the knowledge they were significantly outnumbered. The young captains concluded that these men stayed for the same reason they did, because of respect and trust in their commanders. That and their dependence on God's mercies were the source of their army's successes and they knew it.

CHAPTER 22

MAY 1863

On the night of May 1st, in the Confederate encampment outside Chancellorsville, Captain George Graham, of Commander General Robert E. Lee's 2nd Corps in the Army of Northern Virginia, sat in his tent and, by the light of the lantern, wrote a letter to his sister. He had already given the mail currier one he'd written to Papa, along with Edmund's addressed to his mother.

It was a ritual exercised by warriors on the eve of battle all through history called *"the death letter,"* although Geordie preferred the term "last words." Edmund and he adhered to the practice, though the substance of the letters varied according to the occasion.

Tonight, Abby was the one on his mind, and Geordie found the words difficult to compose in a way she might receive them well. He'd often thought about their conversation at Christmas, and now it was time to say more. Her image came into his mind and he smiled; she was so lovely and so intensely uncompromising. And the latter descriptive adjective was where the difficulty lay.

Tomorrow, the Stonewall Brigade would join the entire 2nd Virginia under Lieutenant General Thomas Jackson in an audacious flanking maneuver to attack Union troops from behind their line. Jackson was the only officer General Lee trusted with such a daring plan since every man under his command, including several of the older generals whom Jackson had offended, would not hesitate to follow *Stonewall* anywhere at any time.

Edmund entered as Geordie finished his letter.

"Hopefully, there will be an opportunity to post this tomorrow to Abby," he said, tucking the envelope in his leather satchel. "Let us have our prayers together and hit the cot. We will have an early start tomorrow."

"Did you know that Ben and his regiment of Richmond Greys have also been assigned to the 2nd Virginia? I told him where we were, and he said he would come by tonight if he could manage it."

"Ben is here? It will be so very good to see him."

Geordie got up and left the tent in anticipation. The scantiness of supplies had necessitated the separation of the corps and the brothers hadn't seen each other since the battle at Fredericksburg in December.

Ten minutes later the brothers embraced and spent the next hour sharing news and words of encouragement. Before he left, Ben prayed with both Geordie and Edmund and promised to look for them again when the battle was over.

The following morning, the troops of the 2nd Corps gathered and Geordie and Edmund, assigned as adjutants to Major General A.P. Hill, rode beside him as they followed Brigadier Generals Rodes and Colston leading their brigades on the twelve-mile march south on Wellford Furnace Road then north on Brocks Road. A detachment of Georgia infantry guarded the rear as J.E.B. Stuart and his cavalry kept General Sickles distracted from their movements.

As they rode side by side, Geordie noted the tense countenance and posture of his friend and asked in a low voice, "What are some of your favorite childhood memories, Edmund?"

Glancing back, Edmund smiled at this obvious attempt at distraction and gave the matter serious thought.

"For some reason, I do not remember a great deal," he mused, keeping his voice to a whisper in deference of their orders. "But I can definitely remember the first time my father gave me a pony."

His smile widened and he continued to elaborate as his memory awakened. "I think I was six and, though I had been put on the back of the horse since I was able to walk, I had never had one of my own. He was a black Shetland and I named him Scalloway… that's a village on the west of the Shetland Mainland. I thought it had a wild *ruffian* sort of sound that appealed to me. In those days I dreamt of being a *pirate*."

Edmund's smile turned wistful and his soft voice reflected the same. "I had not thought of old Scalloway in a very long time. Thank you for asking and bringing it to my mind, Geordie. Now, tell me one of *your* favorite memories."

"Actually, I was thinking of a particular one when I brought it up." Leaning back in the saddle, he looked up at the clouds. "It was a beautiful summer day, like this one, and Papa had rented a buck wagon to take us up into the mountains for the day. I remember this scene so vividly I could paint it.

"Abby was just a baby, and after we had eaten lunch, she fell asleep while mama was nursing her. Her eyes were closed, and a dribble of milk ran down her cheek. Harry was under a tree contentedly reading, and Papa asked Ben, Davie, and me if we would like him to teach us to fish, and of course we did.

"He had two poles and told Davy and me to share the shorter one. So, we dug up worms, and Papa showed us how to stick the hook through." He paused before admitting sheepishly, "I was a tad squeamish, but Davy stuck it right on.

"He took his turn first and the hook was not in the stream longer than two minutes before the pole almost jerked out of his hands. He was only three, and we would have lost the whole thing for sure if Papa had not been quick enough to grab the pole and hold on.

"We were jumping up and down with excitement, and Papa let Davy take the pole while he and I hauled the fish in by the line. It was a good-sized trout and Ben dropped his pole and tried to help us too. All four of us were laughing and whooping so hard both mama and Harry came to watch. But somehow the fish got the hook out of his mouth or broke the line and got away. You should have heard the sighs of disappointment and poor Davy was wailing.

"I promised him that we would come back and get that fish when we got bigger," he paused with a wistful sigh. "We have not made it yet, but as soon as this war is over I will keep that promise. Davy does not need two whole legs to fish, and I *will* take him."

Lost in their own reveries, they continued on in silence.

When they reached Orange Turnpike, General Jackson ordered Rodes and Colston to spread their troops in a mile-long line and quietly approached General Howard's XI Corps. It was after 5:00 in the afternoon when Jackson gave the order to attack, terrorizing the surprised Yankee troops with the blood-curdling Rebel yell and pouring into their camp.

The plan was so successfully executed they were able to scatter the Union corps all the way into Chancellorsville. Hill's division followed up in a sweep that drove Hooker's army east toward the Rappahannock River with only Sickle's hold on Hazel Grove separating the two parts of Lee's army.

But darkness was falling rapidly, frustrating Jackson's plan to trap the fleeing Union army against the river. Unwilling to give up, he ordered Rodes and Colston to continue to *"press on!"*

When General Hill, with Edmund and Geordie by his side, attempted to point out the risks of continuing in the dark on unfamiliar ground, Jackson, convinced Hill could still catch the enemy before they had time to cross the river at the United States Mine Ford, wouldn't hear of it.

"We are going to *crush* them this time, General Hill," Jackson insisted. "We have *got them* and it is time to *end this once and for all! You must cut them off at the ford!"*

"Yes, sir," Hill saluted.

After an intense but inconclusive skirmish, darkness forced Hill to make a decision he knew would displease his commanding officer.

"Damn! We cannot even see what we're shooting at! Captains, spread the word to withdraw, and then we must report back to General Jackson."

With their regiment directed safely behind their line, Captains Claiborne and Graham were following Hill in the dark in search of Jackson when a volley of shots was heard close by. Knowing they were within their own line, the alarmed officers urged their mounts toward the sound.

As they came nearer, Hill yelled orders to *cease fire* and, through the darkness, discerned the party who had been fired upon by the pickets guarding the road, several kneeling beside a prostrate form on the ground.

"*What's happening here?*" Hill demanded, dismounting and rushing forward, closely followed by his adjutants. "*Who is this?*"

"*Dear God, it's the general,*" choked Edmund, looking over Hill's shoulder as the officer knelt beside the fallen man held in the arms of Captain Smith.

Jackson was still conscious, though dark stains were spreading, and Hill, glancing up at Graham, ordered, "*Get a litter!*"

It took Geordie only seconds to remount and head toward the field hospital, yelling "*Litter... I need a litter! Where is an ambulance?*"

"*Here is a litter, sir,*" someone ran forward and handed it up to him as Geordie reined in his horse to grab it, "but I believe the ambulances have gone back to the hospital."

"*Get one out here, quickly!*" Geordie shouted as he turned and raced back to the scene of the tragedy. He refused to allow his thoughts to contemplate the worst of outcomes and prayed for the sparing of the general's life.

It had been only five minutes when Geordie returned with the litter, but Federal cannons had begun firing into the Confederate positions by the time Jackson was hastily laid on it, delaying the effort to get him to safety and medical attention. Immediately when there was a lull in the bombardment, four men took hold of the litter corners and ran for the camp – Geordie on the left back corner, Edmund on the right. At that moment, the thought of requesting Hill's permission to go with the rescue detail did not occur to either, although it could have resulted in serious charges.

When another roar of cannons burst in flashes of blinding light and debris, one of the litter-bearers fell, dropping Jackson on the road. Instantly, Captain Smith protectively shielded him with his own body as the others flattened on the ground until the shelling stopped.

With adrenalin continuing to pound through his system, Edmund stumbled onto his feet again and ran with the other bearers through the darkness before realizing it was not Geordie who held the opposite rear corner of the litter. Glancing around without seeing him, Edmund handed over his quarter load to Lieutenant Douglas and turned back to the sight of the last explosion.

The clouds drifted away from the moon's full face, and he found Geordie lying face down where he had fallen, his back ripped open by the shattered shell. Still fueled by the rush of adrenalin, Edmund picked up his friend and, balancing his body across his shoulders, dashed after the men bearing Jackson.

"It will be all right, Geordie, you and the general are going to be just fine. I have got you, Geordie.... I will take care of you...." Edmund panted over and over in ragged gasps, his mind refusing to acknowledge the extent of the injury his eyes had seen.

They were loading the wounded Jackson on the ambulance when Edmund gained the attention of a medical corpsman who produced another litter onto which Edmund gently laid his load. His ears were still ringing from the blast and he heard the corpsman's voice as from far away.

"I am sorry, sir. We cannot help this one."

"*Of course you can!* You *must!*" Edmund shouted frantically, gripping the man's arm. "*He is badly hurt and should be attended right away! He just needs to* . . . ."

"It is *no use*, sir. He is not *breathing*." Pulling free, he callously dropped Geordie's body into the wagon bed, leaving the litter for viable casualties. "We must get General Jackson to Doc McGuire."

Edmund continued to stare after the ambulance wagon, the sound of his heart beating wildly in his ears while his brain registered only one thought . . . *"NO, he is NOT dead! NOT DEAD! This is all just a horrible dream!" Jackson . . . Geordie . . . surely it was all a hideous dream.*

The numbing shock persisted as Edmund ran back to intercept General Hill who was dictating messages to the currier. Suddenly, there was another explosion, and Edmund's arm was abruptly seized. Gripping Hill's elbow, Edmund attempted to support him, but both legs had apparently been hit, and the man with the highest rank who had just assumed command sank to the ground.

"Captain Claiborne," Hill ordered with a wince, "find General Stuart and bring him back here. Tell him he must now take command of the Corps."

"Yes, General," Edmund mechanically saluted the grounded officer, and dashed for his horse. As he mounted, Edmund heard Hill's irritated bark to the currier.

"Never mind writing it down now, Adams. Just get your ass over to General Lee and explain what's happened to General Jackson and to me. General Stuart will need his approval to take over. *Somebody get me a litter, damn it!*"

Early the next morning, Sunday, May 3rd, Edmund rode out with General Colston and fought like a tin soldier, without thought or emotion, simply following and passing on commands. Frequently he joined the shouts of other men, *"Do it for Jackson! Remember Jackson"* – always moving forward into the line of fire and smoke.

By the end of the day, exhaustion and lack of sustenance caught up with the 2nd Corps, and they stumbled back to camp where word was spreading that the shots that hit Jackson had been fired by a division of the 18th North Carolina Infantry, believing the riders to be enemy cavalry.

Edmund received this news with a fresh wave of shock and sickening grief and, without conscious thought, searched the camp for Ben. He found him in the field hospital ministering to the wounded and dying.

"Where is he, Ben?"

Ben looked into the smoke and dirt-stained face of Geordie's dearest friend and comrade. There were dark circles under Edmund's deep blue eyes, eloquent with misery and unshed tears.

"I have been granted permission to take him to Lexington tomorrow if I can find a spare wagon to get us to the depot. I sent a telegram to Papa asking him to meet me there. He knows Lexington is where Geordie wants . . . *wanted* to be buried. Do you think it is possible to get leave to go with me?"

Edmund closed his eyes and shook his head. The battle wasn't over – but it was for Geordie. *It was all right then,* he thought. *Geordie would get a proper burial with his family at the gravesite.* The mental images of the mass graves of Manassas, blown open by mortar and trampled underfoot sent a shudder through him.

"I . . . I *wish* . . . but I *cannot* . . . ." Edmund stopped and could not speak in fear his battered spirit would shatter under the full weight of the loss. His eyes were still closed, and he swayed slightly, prompting Ben to put his arm around Edmund's waist and grip his belt to prevent his collapse.

"I will take care of Geordie, Edmund," promised Ben gently. "Right now you need some food and rest. Come on now, I will go with you."

The following morning, as Lee's Generals Early, Anderson, and McLaws continued to pound General Sedgwick's position and J. E. B. Stuart and Jackson's 2nd Corps harassed General Hooker in retreat, Ben accompanied the body of his brother on the train, arriving at last to Lexington by wagon on Tuesday morning, May 5th.

Ben caught sight of his father waiting for him on the platform of the supply depot. He was alone, and Ben was stricken by how the sufferings of war and grief had aged him since last seeing him at Geordie's graduation two years before.

But he didn't approach Paul until the Confederate flag-covered coffin was safely unloaded and another wagon secured to take it to the Presbyterian Church cemetery. Ben then turned around to find Paul standing behind him.

"Papa, *I am so sorry* . . ." was all he could say before his father's arms were wrapped around his neck and they were weeping together.

"It is all right, my boy. Our *'farewells'* will not be forever," Paul assured him softly through his tears. "We cannot bring him back, but we will one day go to him. '*Blessed be the name of the Lord.*'"

Paul had to wait another day to catch a coach headed for Staunton. Ben left the day after the funeral to rejoin his regiment after another painful parting at the depot. Mr. John Baker, with whom Paul had corresponded, had met with them at the church and offered comfort. Also, Superintendent Smith had been very kind, providing a bugler for the small graveside service and overnight accommodations for them as well.

Paul himself had spoken words over the grave of his son and

lifted a prayer of thanks to God for calling Geordie to Himself in electing grace.

"Gracious Father, thou hast answered thy Son's prayer before His agony that those thou gave to Him would be with Him where He is. And thou hast also graciously answered this father's prayer for his son, George Spencer. I rejoice that Geordie is now in thy presence, Lord, and I pray that in further mercy Thou would grant us, his family, thy Spirit of comfort, for without it we may dishonor thee in our sorrow. If his death gives thee greater glory than his life, I cannot refuse to give thee thy due. In His misery and torment for my miserable soul, thy Son would not even accept the myrrhed cup; how then can I refuse the cup overflowing with the mercies His agony bought for me?

Father, may our religion shine through our grief so we may continue the work thou hast assigned us, until the day when thou shall call us home. I lift this prayer in the Name of our Redeemer and King. Amen."

As the last words were spoken, the clouds of heaven burst in a shower of rain as if the angels' tears could wash away the bloodied earth and make the valley fertile again. Paul had wistfully willed it to be true. He thought of the words of Isaiah, *"For it is a day of trouble, and the treading down, and of perplexity by the Lord God of hosts in the valley of vision, breaking down the walls and crying to the mountains...."*

However, it was words of triumph and hope that were drawn from his mouth that were heard throughout the quiet cemetery as he shouted, *"Thy dead men shall live together, with my dead body shall they arise. Awake and sing, ye that dwell in dust: for thy dew is as the dew of herbs, and the earth shall cast out the dead!"*

In that moment it occurred to him that the loss of Rosemary had only been the beginning of the arduous lessons of grief he was obliged to learn. Since her death, he'd learned it could be an effective sifter of all things superficial and insubstantial, and the remains were the kernels of wisdom and truth that could be ground into wholesome sustenance. *What were the lessons he would be required to assimilate with the loss of Geordie? Was it to be reminded of his own sinful, rebellious nature?*

Paul was not easily deceived by the lure of self-righteous justification and outward piety, and he could readily admit, like the apostle Paul, that he was "the chief of sinners." But perhaps *grief* was the most effectual means of training a naturally proud and rebellious spirit, that a thorough consciousness of its own poverty, impotence, and barrenness was the very whip that drove it to Christ. Perhaps only grief could teach him to say, "*O Lord, blessed trouble that compels me to his mercy seat, for underneath are his everlasting arms!*"

A huge knot of apprehension settled in Paul's stomach as he considered the question: *How many losses would it take to achieve such a level of sanctification? How many children would he be required to surrender before learning the hard lessons of grief – that only through suffering was he to learn humble submission, that trials were to be endured with forbearance, not resented?*

Now as he sat staring into the landscape soaked continually with streams of blood and tears, he sighed, *"How long, oh Lord, how long wilt thou permit this tragedy? Thou hast brought us to our knees… must we wait until the time when 'every knee shall bow'? If it be so, then come, Lord, come quickly!"*

It had been presumptuous of him to believe he could be prepared to lose Geordie. Such a thing was impossible for a father, even with a strong theological and practical knowledge and faith in a God of providence. The human spirit, even the only sinless Son of Man, could not be spared the sorrow of death that struck all flesh and bone since the sin of Adam.

As a pastor, it had never been easy, nor would it ever be, to offer words of consolation to grieving parents. Paul never offered them lightly or stridently with the expectation that the recipients would or should be effectively relieved of the travails of bereavement. There was a significant difference between *unwavering faith in the goodness of God* and *soul-deadening denial of the reality of living with the effects of the fall.*

Yes, King David had washed and taken food after learning his child was dead because of the strength of his conviction that he would one day join his son. However, Paul hadn't before, and certainly could not now, interpret David's actions or his words to mean that his grief was purged along with his confessed sins. Rather, in the midst of his sorrow, David understood and met the challenge to exercise his faith in accepting and enduring the consequences of both personal and universal guilt.

It is a sign of true covenantal relationship when the Father shepherds his children through sanctifying flames of affliction, including the *"valley of the shadow of death."* He had promised through Isaiah, *"When thou passest through the waters I will be with thee; and through the rivers, they shall not overflow thee: when thou walkest through the fire, thou shalt not be burned; neither shall the flame kindle upon thee. For I am the LORD thy God, the Holy One of Israel, thy Savior."*

Paul knew and clung to these truths while the pain choked and twisted his craw. Losing Geordie felt as if he had lost Rosemary all over again.

Complicating his own implacable bereavement, Paul's greater concerns were for his two younger children and Edmund. Ben had delivered a brief note to him from Edmund, expressing his sorrow and regret he could not come with Ben to bury Geordie. He had ended it with a plea for Paul's prayers on his behalf.

"Pray for me. We are still in battle now, but I fear the time soon coming when I am faced with the reality of his absence."

When the telegram had arrived from Ben in Chancellorsville, Paul immediately sent a message to Abby asking her to come straight away and then went to the tavern looking for Davy. The news had stunned Davy, and his first reaction had been one of disbelief.

"*He* cannot be dead, Papa. If God would allow this to happen to *Geordie, then I curse Him! I curse Him!*"

Then Davy had gone into a rage, smashing everything within reach until Jerome Tanner hurled him out into the street. Rosie had been patiently sympathetic and promised Paul she'd take care of him. By then, Davy was lying in the road sobbing.

All Paul could do was intercede for him with the Lord – *"Forgive him, Father, and then grant him a true spirit of repentance and willingly come home to Thee. He needs thy comfort now more than ever."*

It seemed his daughter also responded in raging despair at the news, and the response by telegram was from Seth. "ABBY

DISTRESSED AND WILL NOT BE COMING AT THIS TIME," it read. Paul didn't have to read between the lines to know the loss of Geordie would affect her, deeply and intensely, but he prayed it would not affect her irrevocably.

What had he expected? Paul asked himself as the wheels of the coach bounced and jarred him against the window and into the elderly women sitting next to him. He knew his children loved him, but as Abby had said, Geordie was the *glue* that held the family together. He was his mother's child, born with an inherent ability to draw others to him with his love, his extravagant love. What a blessing he had been to them and – oh, how he would be missed!

All his years of learnt restraint and practiced discipline proved ineffectual in tuning out the screams and cries sounding from Abby's room. It was all Corbin could do not to cover his ears and betray his long-guarded secret to the household and surgery patients waiting to be tended as Seth and he stared at each other in helpless agitation at the bottom of the staircase.

Dear God, how was she going to survive this? Less than six weeks ago –Virgil Brent! Corbin shuddered at the memories he himself could not dispel and swallowed the bile rising in his throat. The horrors at Antietam Creek, witnessing Cullen's death, and now the loss of her beloved brother – it was more than anyone could take with their mortal soul unscathed. And there was nothing he or anyone could do to spare her the grievous repercussion. *Oh dear God, please help her!*

It had been almost 3:00 on the afternoon after Geordie's death when Abby had returned from the mountain, and Seth had taken her into his office, giving her the telegram. It had come just before noon addressed to Seth, and after reading it, he'd handed it to Corbin in aggrieved silence.

With a deep sigh, Seth turned back to his patients and explained that he would only see the most critical as there had been a death in the family. Corbin watched the heads nod and bow. Everyone was familiar with such news.

There was another new grave in the cemetery two blocks south of the Presbyterian Church. Another hero of the Confederacy, another son of Virginia was laid to rest ten days after Geordie Graham was interred. Lieutenant General Thomas Jonathan Jackson, CSA returned home to Lexington on the 15th day of May 1863. And there were thousands of mourners who gathered, rather than the two who'd wept by Geordie's graveside.

Among the former cadets who came to pay their respects that day was Captain Edmund Jefferson Claiborne, still a proud but grief-stricken officer in the Stonewall Brigade, who had been under Jackson's command since he led the cadets from Lexington to Richmond two years earlier. Tears blurred his vision when the horse-drawn caisson passed, and Edmund gave his final salute to the man who had taught him to be a soldier.

Edmund had also been among the many members of the brigade outside the house near the Chandler mansion at Guiney's Station last Sunday afternoon when Sandie Pendleton came out to deliver the devastating news.

"The General has died."

And they all sobbed shamelessly and inconsolably, *like sheep without a shepherd* was the image that came to Edmund's mind. But it was the deafening rebel yell that spontaneously rose from the throng of mourners that gave vocal, cathartic expression of their unbroken spirit as well as their devastating grief.

Soon Edmund and the others would be returning to their regiments, but he had an important call to make before leaving Lexington. The stone had yet to be placed so he asked the caretaker and was told where to look; it was easy to find. Under the heavy weight of sorrow, he sank to his knees in the freshly turned earth.

"Geordie, it is Edmund," he began in a whisper. "What am I *going to do*, Geordie? What is going to happen to the *rest of us?* There is no other general who can take his place… *or yours.* I have to know now… *what has it all been for?* Has it been *worth the price that has already been paid?* And for *God's sake,* Geordie… *who can give me the answers?*

"I have the letter you wrote to Abby and I promise to give it to her, not trust it to the currier. What will *she* do without you? I cannot even imagine how much she is suffering, and there is *nothing* I can do to comfort her, *but I will try… I swear it, Geordie!"*

With a deep shuddering sigh Edmond looked up at the sky.

"I thought it might help if I could only talk to you. That coming here might ease this terrible pain squeezing the breath out of me. But you are not here now, *are* you, Geordie?"

On his way back to Fredericksburg, Edmund stopped at Vermillion. He'd ridden from Chancellorsville on horseback, on Caesar, one of Vermillion's own stock, but as he gazed down from the hilltop to his place of birth, nothing seemed the same. It wasn't just the state of disrepair of the imposing façade, the fenced pastures dispossessed of thoroughbred horses, or the fallow tobacco fields. It was as if he was seeing it for the first time, and he felt an alien there.

The greening topography of the land itself was the only truly familiar feature, and this he still claimed as his own. But the rest would never be again, and he felt no grief for its loss. The hallowed ground of Virginia was all he had left to fight for, all that was his own to preserve and defend. It was Virginia he loved, not Vermillion. It was for Virginia that so much of his brothers' blood had already been sacrificed and would continue to be offered.

How much blood is still owed on the price of ransom, Lord? Take my own if you require it too.

BLEST BE THE TIES: A TRILOGY

♦♦♦

Book Two

A TIME of WAR,
and A TIME of PEACE

L.M. Hopson

** Available Now **

CHAPTER 1

Almost two weeks after General "Stonewall" Jackson was laid to rest in Lexington, Virginia, Paul Graham, pastor of the 1st Presbyterian Church in Winchester, stood in the small post station clutching a letter written in his son Geordie's hand. Less than a month before, Paul had buried him in the same cemetery in which Jackson and many other bright lights of the Confederacy would be interred until the Lord's return to earth.

Paul should have remembered it would come, as one always arrived days after a major battle, but in the throes of heartbreak, he had forgotten to look for it. He subconsciously assumed that, like the sight of his beloved son, it would never come again.

Trembling now, he tucked the letter into his coat pocket, headed for the shade of the trees in the park across from the courthouse, and sat down on a stone bench. His breath was coming in gasps of pain when he opened the envelope and read Geordie's final words to him.

Dear Papa,

This shall only be a short note due to our preparations today and my intent is to write Abby before evening prayers and I retire. We shall be rising early to meet General Hooker's army sometime tomorrow.

It is a great comfort to know of your constant prayers for Edmund and me, and we will meet the enemy with the confidence of those with a clear conscience and the knowledge that our Lord directs our path. I confess that at times I am disturbed in my sleep with terrible visions and images, but last night I slept in stillness of peace that could only come by the blessing of the Prince of Peace.

In my dream I saw a place like the one described by Isaiah in chapter 65 ... the creation of the new heavens and earth filled with joyful people, where 'the voice of weeping shall be no more heard... nor the voice of crying.'

Everywhere I have been and everything I have seen since the war began has produced sounds of crying and a flow of tears, my own adding to the overflowing flood.

It was such a remarkable experience to catch a glimpse of the future in my dream – to be reminded of the eternal, rather than the present, with renewing hope. It is this reality I shall cling to tomorrow and the days of war ahead.

I love you, dear Papa!
Your son, Geordie

Overcome with heartbroken grief and thankful praise, Paul covered his face with his hands and wept.

Made in the USA
Columbia, SC
11 June 2022